THE
SILENT PLACES

Also by JAMES PATRICK HUNT

The Assailant
Goodbye Sister Disco
The Betrayers
Before They Make You Run
Maitland Under Siege
Maitland
Maitland's Reply

THE
SILENT PLACES

JAMES PATRICK HUNT

 MINOTAUR BOOKS ♨ NEW YORK

THE SILENT PLACES. Copyright © 2010 by James Patrick Hunt. All rights reserved. Printed in the United States of America. For information, address St. Martin's Press, 175 Fifth Avenue, New York, N.Y. 10010.

www.minotaurbooks.com

Library of Congress Cataloging-in-Publication Data

Hunt, James Patrick, 1964–
    The silent places / James Patrick Hunt.—1st ed.
        p. cm.
    ISBN 978-0-312-54579-6
    1. Police—Missouri—Saint Louis—Fiction.   2. Fugitives from justice—Missouri—Saint Louis—Fiction.   3. Legislators—United States—Fiction.   4. Saint Louis (Mo.)—Fiction.   5. Stalking—Fiction.   I. Title.
    PS3608.U577S55 2010
    813'.6—dc22

                                                                                        2009047492

First Edition: June 2010

10   9   8   7   6   5   4   3   2   1

For my parents

ACKNOWLEDGMENTS

The author wishes to extend his gratitude to his editor, Matt Martz. Also to Lieutenant Darrell Hatfield, Oklahoma City PD (Ret.), and Lieutenant Mike Denton, Owasso PD.

*There is delight in the hardy
life of the open, in long rides
rifle in hand, in the thrill of
the fight with dangerous game.
Apart from this, yet mingled
with it, is the strong attraction
of the silent places. . . .*

— THEODORE ROOSEVELT

*One enemy is never enough.
Two is far too many.*

— COL. DAVID HACKWORTH

THE
SILENT PLACES

PROLOGUE

On the third day of his hunting trip, Hastings found the scrape of the whitetail buck. It was in a field near a patch of hardwood forest in the Ozark Mountains. Three hours' drive from St. Louis and about an hour to Branson, if Branson was to your liking.

The scrape on the ground was the buck's mark, an attempt to draw out the does during the mating season, the rut. The whitetail buck would paw the ground or thrash saplings or overhanging branches with his antlers, leaving his scent from the glands on the top of his head. Letting the does know he was in town. Hastings had hunted most of his life and he knew that the buck would return and check his scrapes regularly for females attracted by the scent and the possibility of a match.

But the whitetails are smart. They possess an amazing ability to elude the hunter. They can smell the hunter hundreds of yards away, if the hunter's dumb enough or inexperienced enough to be upwind. They know how to hide and they know their range better than any man. Contrary to popular belief, they do not run blindly in panic when sensing the hunter. They may travel just a few steps and stand perfectly still in grassy or bushy cover, their coats blending in, while the hunter walks right by, unaware. They're sneaky, the whitetails, especially the bucks.

Hastings knew the odds of bagging one were slim. It usually took fifty hours to spot a buck, and that was for an experienced hunter.

Hastings had seen plenty of signs of deer: tracks and droppings, the day and night trails, et cetera. But the scrape told him there was a buck around.

He moved away from the scrape. He walked slowly and quietly and avoided unnecessary motion, such as swinging his arms or turning his head—movements animals associate with humans.

He sort of smelled like an animal, too. For a deer can detect a freshly soaped man a mile away. Hastings had not gone so far as to use a masking scent like fox urine, but he had not bathed since arriving at the cabin three days earlier.

It was a good day to hunt. Overnight, there had been a light rain, which softened the ground, decreasing the possibility of crackling twigs or leaves underfoot. It was late November, and Hastings had feared that there would be a frost overnight and that would make the ground crusty and loud and the deer would hear him coming. The wind can carry sound as well as scent. But there had been no frost and the ground was soft.

Early morning now and the sky was gray and cloudy.

Hastings walked and scanned and soon he came to a field of tall crops stretching out for a hundred or so yards before coming to an end at a forest. The crops were brown and gray, similar to the color of a whitetail buck at this time of year. Hastings surveyed the field with his binoculars. Panned left to right, saw something near the left periphery, and stopped.

And there it was.

Oh, he was a handsome fella. Probably around 180 pounds, his antlers having maybe five points a side, which made him an older buck. His white tail was not erect, which meant he did not feel threatened. And that meant he probably was not aware of the hunter nearby.

Hastings estimated the distance between them to be about eighty yards. A humane shot would be one that killed the deer very quickly, if not instantly. The bullet would have to hit the deer's heart or lungs or central nervous system.

Hastings was armed with a bolt-action rifle. He believed that nothing quite matched the accuracy of a bolt-action rifle. His was a Winchester model 52. It had been built in 1977, the line having then been discontinued in 1979. He had found it at an estate sale twelve years earlier and paid seven hundred dollars for it, which was a bargain. He could sell it for three times that now, but he wouldn't.

Now he stood and watched the animal. He wanted to see if the buck would remain where he was long enough for Hastings to stalk him. He could probably shoot him now, but at this distance and with the crops in the way, the odds of a clean kill shot were slim. Besides, almost anyone could point a gun and shoot it. The expert could creep within a few feet without being detected. Hastings remained still and tried to determine if the animal was nervous or about to move.

The animal seemed unaware and not apprehensive. Hastings looked around to plot a course. He would need to remain downwind of the animal and out of sight. The crops in the field were about shoulder-high. If he crouched or went to the ground, he could get closer.

Hastings started forward, and that was when the clouds parted, just, and the sun came through and reflected off the scope of his rifle.

A glint of light. That was all it took.

The buck lifted his head and turned and saw him. A moment passed between them, Hastings remaining dead still, in the hope that he would not be noticed, but it didn't work and the buck took off.

Hastings ran after him, going at an angle as the deer cut right across, not going for the cover of the woods, but elsewhere, and Hastings thought it was dumb, running like this after an animal that could move at thirty to forty miles an hour, but he ran anyway, keeping his rifle at his side, and then the buck went down an incline and disappeared from sight, and Hastings almost laughed at his own foolishness, but he kept going, as much out of curiosity as anything.

Hastings ran and jogged and then he reached the edge of the field and looked down the hill.

The buck was in a small lake, swimming across.

The whitetail deer is a strong swimmer. Some have been observed crossing lakes a mile wide. This buck was strong, moving through the water steadily. Hastings had no doubt he would make it to the other side. Walk out, shake the water off, and trot off to find himself a seasoning doe. After the loving, maybe tell her about the dumbass hunter who'd given himself away.

Hastings looked about. There was no tree to lean against. He could sit down, steady the rifle on his knee. Or he could lie on his stomach, shift his leg forward to steady himself, and get the shot that way. Either position would work. The deer's movement was restrained and the kill shot would be assured.

But Hastings sighed and lowered the weapon. He knew he couldn't do it. Not with the animal in the water, moving through it strong and sure. Not like this.

Hastings took another look at the brownish gray beast swimming away. Three days of cold and loneliness, work and rank smell for nothing.

"Maybe next year," Hastings said. As if the buck could hear him.

ONE

They pulled Reese out of his cell at 2:12 A.M. Three prison guards, one of them holding a riot gun on him, another gripping a nightstick, the third one with his hands on his hips, showing the others he wasn't afraid of the prisoner.

John Reese was fifty years old. He had been in prison for twelve years now and he had never taken a swing at a guard. He was a slim man, almost of slight build, and not overly tall. But there was a coiled-up air to him. His eyes were alert and penetrating. He had kept his body strong, his wind up. Once, in the yard, an inmate had made the mistake of presuming Reese could be dominated. Reese casually snapped the man's pinkie like a twig, kicked his leg out, then drove the palm of his hand into the man's nose, smashing it to pulp. Reese was left alone after that.

In prison, time is an enemy—a thing to be feared and respected. You do the time, but you cannot let the time do you, even when you're facing a life sentence.

Reese allowed himself to look at the lead guard's watch.

Two-twelve, coming up on 2:13. The middle of the night. The time when Soviets liked to grab enemies of the state. The dreaded knock on the door in the middle of the night. Take them when they're cold and tired and their defenses are down.

Reese thought, What more can they do to me?

He said, "What do you want?"

The lead guard said, "Warden wants to see you."

Bullshit, Reese thought.

But he kept it to himself. Odds were, the guards themselves had not been told the whole story. He could ask them how much they knew, but he didn't want to give them the satisfaction of looking vulnerable, yet alone scared.

Soon he was out of his orange jumpsuit and back in civilian clothes they had brought him. Loose-fitting dungarees and a gray sweatshirt and a cheap windbreaker. Kmart clothes. Maybe wanting him to feel comfortable, maybe wanting him not to look like he'd broken out of prison. Looking like shit, but what the hell. He was out.

He was in the cell twenty-three hours a day as it was, behind a double steel door and with no window. Put in solitary so he couldn't tell anyone what he was doing there. Sealed in a coffin, only breathing. If it were an hour or so less of coffin time, he would not complain. Again, he thought, What more can they do to me?

About two hours later, he began to have an idea.

He sat between two very large men in the backseat of a Chevy Suburban. The windows were tinted. Reese had looked in the backseat to see if there was anyone there. There wasn't. If they had put him in the front seat, it would have made him nervous. A setup, possibly, for an old gangland-style execution. Get the speed up to about seventy, the tired man relaxes and leans back in his seat. Then someone behind would put the barrel of a .22 to the back of his head and put two bullets in it. The Israeli commando way, though they usually didn't put their victims in cars.

The prison guards had turned him over to these guys. There were two men in front, one of them with a shaved head. None of the men were wearing a suit. They weren't feds. These were mercenaries, probably ex-military. Special Forces. Reese knew the type.

Reese's hands were bound in front of him. They had used plastic twists rather than handcuffs. That was at least something.

The guy in the passenger seat in front was tall and well muscled and had cheekbones that suggested Cherokee ancestry. His name was Clu Rogers. At one point during the drive, he turned and gave Reese a long look, snorted, and smiled, as if to say Reese didn't impress him much.

Reese gave him nothing back then. He looked out the window at the darkness and stars. They were in wide open country, and he wished he could enjoy being out of prison.

Still looking out there, Reese said, "Who you fellas working for?"

The man on his right turned and looked him over, surprised that Reese was finally saying something. But he didn't say anything, and neither did anyone else.

Reese said, "CIA?"

Silence.

Reese said, "I would say Company. But nobody really says that anymore. It was going out of style when I was in the spook business. And that was a long time ago."

More silence.

"I guess things have changed since I've been in," Reese said. He looked at the man on his left and then at the man on his right. "Sure looks like they've lowered their standards."

One of the men sighed, and then the man on Reese's left lifted his arm to give Reese a sharp elbow in the ribs. Reese doubled over, gasping. It hurt plenty, but he had tensed himself, halfway expecting it. They weren't as professional as he had feared.

The one in the front seat turned again to look at him.

Clu said, "Why make it hard on yourself?"

Reese managed to say, "Bored, I guess." He took a couple of breaths. Then said, "Are you the one in charge of this mission?"

"Yeah."

The Suburban slowed to take a turn off the small highway onto a dirt road. Soon they were in a wooded area, trees walling them in on both sides.

Reese said, "What's the nature of this mission, soldier?"

"Old man," Clu said, "I'm going to give you some advice, and you don't even have to pay me for it. Just sit there and keep your mouth shut. Cause if you don't, the next words out of your mouth are going to be 'Ow, ow, ow.'"

"I told you," Reese said, "I'm bored. Where you from?"

Another elbow from the man on his left. This one was harder.

Clu stared at him, shaking his head. Some people don't listen.

Reese exhaled and said, "Texas? No, you don't sound like a Texan. Oklahoma, I'll bet. Somewhere around Muskogee."

"Very good," Clu said.

"I'm good with voices, dialects. It's something you pick up when you travel around a lot. You know how you can tell if a guy's from Pittsburgh? He calls his mother 'Mum.' Like the English. It's true, really. Now an Okie from Muskogee, he's got his own special twang. But when you get down to, say, Durant, they start sounding more like Texans. Though they're both Okies. Both from the same state. Funny, isn't it?"

Reese saw the man's cold smile in the darkness.

"*You're* funny," Clu said.

"I have moments," Reese said.

Reese looked out the windows again. The headlights illuminated the dirt path in front of them, pushing through, leaving darkness behind.

Reese said, "Where do you think you'll do it?"

After a moment, Clu said, "Do what?"

"Oh, come on," Reese said. "You know."

Clu said, "I know you're a traitor to your country and a smart-mouthed piece a shit to boot. In my opinion, they should have done it a long time ago." Clu shrugged, showing he could be philosophical about someone else's death. He said, "What difference does it make anyway? They had you in solitary. This won't be much worse."

"Maybe not for you."

"You were condemned already, old man. We're just carrying out the proper sentence, that's all."

Reese smiled. He said, "Boy, you're really looking forward to this, aren't you?"

"I am now."

For a while nobody said anything. The forest passed by.

Reese made a point of sighing. Then he said, "Well, a man should enjoy his work. You going to tell me who you're working for?"

"On the point of death," Clu said. "Yours."

"At least I'll have that," Reese said. "So, do you miss Muskogee?"

"Not a bit."

"Can't say I blame you," Reese said, "You ever hear that song 'You're the Reason God Made Oklahoma'?"

"No."

"It's a country song."

Clu turned around and looked out the windshield. He was sick of this man's silly bullshit. The man had probably lost his marbles in the joint. It happened to guys in solitary. Clu said, "I don't listen to country music."

"You don't know what you're missing," Reese said, and threw his elbow into the man's face on his left. The sharp force of it burst the man's nose, making a distinct crunching noise. Before the man could scream out in pain, Reese had reached past him to the door handle. He heard someone yell as the door popped open and he saw a blur as the man in the front started to pull a weapon, but Reese grabbed the lapels of the jacket of the man next to him and pulled him with him, using him as a shield. Gravity took them out of the opening and Reese flipped the big man over so that he landed on top of him when they hit the ground. Then they rolled together for a few turns and Reese broke free of him. The Suburban skidded to a halt and Reese got to his feet and ran, slipping into the darkness of the woods. Moments passed before shots were fired into the trees.

Approximately forty miles away, two men waited at an abandoned train depot.

The train depot was small and old and wooden, its clapboard sides faded and worn by more than a century of sun and elements. There were a couple of wrinkled chamber of commerce posters on the walls, a halfhearted attempt at boosting local tourism. Wooden benches and stone floor and not much else. There was another bench outside on a wooden platform bordering the tracks.

The younger of the two men sat on the bench outside. He pulled his coat around him because it was cold. He did not understand the other man's attraction to this old dump. It was as good a rendezvous as any other because it was isolated and private, but *goddamn,* couldn't they have picked a place that had some heat?

The man he answered to was standing near the track with his hands in his coat pockets. His name was Dexter Troy. He was forty years old. A tall man, wide in the shoulders and narrow of waist.

Dexter Troy panned the area, west to east. He rested his eyes on the east, imagining a Union Pacific steam train coming into the station. Part of him wished they were bringing John Reese on such a train. Bound by chains, guarded by Pinkerton detectives. They would take him off the train and put him in a cell and take him out to the gallows in the morning. Hanging would be a better death for a traitor. Let the public see what happens to such a man. Better that than doing it in secret, burying him in the woods.

Like a lot of veterans of Special Operations Command (SOCOM), Troy had heard about John Reese. Reese was a veteran of the army and the CIA and the Cold War. A man from another time, another era. Younger men, men like Clu, would find Reese a curious, perhaps even pathetic, figure. They would find it difficult to believe that he had once controlled fortunes. When it slips away, Troy thought, it really slips away.

Troy's cell phone rang and he answered it.

"Yeah."

"Dex," a voice said. It was Clu, the team leader of this mission, second in command. From his tone, Troy knew he had bad news. He did.

Clu said, "He escaped."

Troy closed his eyes, opened them. "Explain."

"He jumped out of the car while it was moving. Pulled Cody out with him."

"Cody?"

"He's got a concussion and his arm is broken. But he's alive."

From his place on the bench, the young man watched and listened as Dexter Troy sighed.

Troy said, "And what about the quarry?" He was hoping that he, too, had died in the fall.

Clu said, "He ran into the woods. We're still looking."

"Well, keep looking, you idiot. It'll be daylight soon." Troy said. "Have you reported this to anyone?"

"Negative."

"Good. I'll contact you later."

Dexter Troy clicked off the phone. Resumed his stare on the eastern sky.

The younger man walked up to him and said, "What have we got?"

"A manhunt," Troy said.

Reese continued south. He moved, but he had stopped running, because he knew after a time that it was not necessary and that it would be bad if he just ran himself to exhaustion. Running was panic. He moved at what he considered a quick walk.

He had gone through survival school at Fort Benning thirty years before. They had trained him then to survive in different environments and to learn about where you were going. How to find food and water, how to travel through different kinds of terrain, how to doctor yourself. They had instructed him specifically that rest could be more valuable than speed.

He had jumped from a vehicle that had been moving at a higher speed than he would have liked. He had tucked and he had rolled and he had used a man as a cushion, but his feet had hit the ground and then he'd tumbled and flown without control. He had maintained consciousness and, probably through sheer luck, not broken any bones. But when he put some distance between himself and his pursuers, he felt the pain from his head to his fingertips and he knew his legs and hips would be bruised purple and yellow by morning. Along with the bruises to his ribs.

But he was alive and he was free. But now men were coming after him, and if they were mercenaries, they might have night-vision goggles and high-powered rifles that could take you down at eight hundred yards. Yeah, rest was more valuable than speed. Particularly after you'd had to jump from a moving vehicle. But men were coming after him. And if they were as well financed as they looked, they might get a helicopter, using searchlights and body-heat sensors. He had to keep moving.

God, it was cold, though. He had only the clothes they had given him and a windbreaker, which had torn at the sleeve when he hit the ground. No gloves, no thermal underclothing, no hat. The instructors at Fort Benning had told him and the others at Ranger School that cold lowers your efficiency, decreases your ability to think. Moreover, it could mess up your perspective. Too much cold and all your thoughts would begin to focus on getting warm. Everything else would be secondary.

He should stop and build a fire. Like the man in that Jack London story. To build a fire. And live. Except that the fire and life would not be extinguished by snow falling off a branch, but by a sharpshooter crouching in the brush.

Reese looked east. He estimated he had about an hour and a half of night left. The sun would rise and he would be exposed to daylight. Visibility was more of a threat to him than cold. When the sun rose, he would have to find a place to hide and rest. That would be the proper thing to do. The thing he had been trained to do. But instinct told him to get as much distance as possible.

Forty minutes passed, and he saw lights in the distance. Then he heard the faint sounds of traffic. A truck's exhaust. Music. Who would have thought he'd ever be glad to hear such a thing?

Another thirty minutes brought him to a truck stop. Before the sun came up, he was in the back of a semitrailer, sharing hay and shit with around thirty head of cattle. He placed himself in a corner and covered himself with hay. He was asleep when the truck moved back on the highway.

TWO

The day after the mistrial, Howard Rhodes was called to Capt. Karen Brady's office. Hastings went with him. Lt. George Hastings was Rhodes's supervisor and had been so for two years. Rhodes was in his early thirties, tall and handsome. He had a bit of a regal bearing and he was faintly aware of it. He was the only black detective on Hastings's squad.

When they arrived at the captain's office, Karen Brady widened her eyes in surprise. She had not expected Hastings to come with Rhodes. In her mind, the issue did not concern Hastings, and she had hoped to be able to deal with Rhodes alone.

Hastings said, "Karen," acknowledging her with a politeness and respect that was due her rank, if not her person, but letting her know at the same time he was there.

George Hastings had always had a tenuous relationship with Karen Brady. He believed he had nothing personal against her. He did not consider her a bad person. But he knew she had never been more than a mediocre detective. She was not good with people, whether they were from the street or cops.

Now she said, "Close the door." Using an order tone, probably trying to get something back on Hastings now.

Hastings closed it, and that was when he noticed that Deputy Chief Fenton Murray was also with them. Well, well, well. The morning was full of surprises.

The deputy chief and the detectives greeted one another. Karen motioned for the detectives to take seats. They did, and then they were on opposite sides of the captain's desk, the brass facing members of the homicide squad.

Hastings did not exactly trust Fenton Murray. To begin with, Murray had never worked as a detective. His entire career had been either in patrol or administration. Homicide detectives have a reputation for being snobbish and elitist, and that reputation is, to a large extent, deserved. But detective or no, Murray was no dummy. Murray was also an African-American. He was wily and cunning, as most men are who have the ambition to be chief. People who had worked with him years earlier had said he was a good, conscientious police officer, but they knew he wanted to be at the top. Or near it. He was an able, intelligent man and he not achieved his rank by luck or circumstance. But for all that, Murray was quietly threatened by homicide detectives who believed they might be smarter than he was, and he was not above the occasional power play to keep them in place.

Now Murray said, "So what happened yesterday?"

Rhodes looked briefly at Hastings. Hastings nodded and then Rhodes told them about it.

Rhodes said, "I got into the courtroom and took the stand. They swore me in and the prosecutor, Ms. Delaney, conducted her direct examination. She went through the intro—my rank, how many years I've been a detective, and all that. Then she asked me about the night of the Ochoa murder. We went through it slowly and then at one point she asked me about the search of the Medeiros residence—"

"Medeiros?" Murray said.

"Yes, sir. Eloise Medeiros. That's the name of Cavazos's girlfriend."

"Okay. Continue."

"And I said, at some point, I testified that we knew she had been associated with the Furia gang. La Furia. And then I told her how we knew about Cavazos's role in that. And that was when the defense attorney objected."

Murray said, "Why?"

"Well," Rhodes said, "at first I thought it was a hearsay objection. I had been told about Cavazos's prior threat from a friend of mine at narcotics. In fact, I was sort of ready for that. But that wasn't what it was. It wasn't a hearsay objection. The defense attorney objected and approached the bench."

"Where were you when this happened?"

"I was still on the stand. They didn't excuse me."

"So you could hear what they were saying?"

"Yes, sir. They were whispering so the jury wouldn't hear them. But I could hear."

"And what did you hear?"

Hastings said to the deputy chief, "You know what he heard."

Murray raised a hand to Hastings, shushing him and keeping his attention focused on Rhodes. "What did you hear?"

Rhodes said, "I heard the defense lawyer say we had violated the order in limine, you know, the pretrial order, that the judge had previously granted. We weren't supposed to bring up Cavazos's gang association or his previous threat to Ochoa—he was the murder victim—over dealer's territory."

Captain Brady said, "Then why did you?"

Rhodes said, "I didn't know about the judge's order."

Murray said, "The prosecutor didn't tell you?"

"No, sir. No one told me."

Murray shook his head, and that gesture alone almost made Hastings lose his temper. It was unspoken, but it was a clear sign that he did not believe what Rhodes had said. Murray said, "That's not what she says."

Then Hastings spoke.

He said, "How do you know? Did you speak to her about it?"

Deputy Chief Murray finally acknowledged Hastings. His expression was angry. Murray said, "I spoke with someone about it."

"Who?"

Murray gave him a look that told him he'd better watch his step.

Hastings said, "Was it Jaffe?"

Herb Jaffe was the district attorney.

Hastings said, "Or was it the chief?"

Murray said, "That's not important."

"Well, it certainly is," Hastings said. "The issue here is whether or not Detective Rhodes was advised about the order in limine before testifying. He says he wasn't. You tell me the prosecutor says he was. Well, I've discussed this with Detective Rhodes and he's told me he was not advised."

"And you believe him."

"I do."

"Lieutenant, I can appreciate your loyalty to your man," Murray said, "but what I'm dealing with—"

"I know what you're dealing with. A district attorney who's angry and embarrassed and looking for a scapegoat. If there's a question about who's telling the truth here and who's trying to cover up their own mistake, I think it's just as likely it was Ms. Delaney as it was Rhodes."

"So what, then?" Murray said. "Marla Delaney's lying?"

Hastings said, "I'm not trying to call anybody a liar. I'm just suggesting that—"

"That Marla Delaney is lying about this. There's no way around it, Lieutenant. Say it or don't."

"It's possible she's mistaken," Hastings said. "Why don't we put it that way, if it'll make Mr. Jaffe happy? All I know is, Howard is not lying."

Captain Brady and the deputy chief gave Hastings their serious looks. Feeling comfortable and strong with their authority.

Hastings said, "Look, in an administrative investigation, you have the authority to request that Howard take a polygraph examination. He's willing to do that. And prove to you that he's telling the truth."

Murray smiled and seemed to suppress a chuckle, like it was a juvenile idea. He said, "That's not going to fix this. What are we supposed to do if he passes? Ask Marla Delaney to take a polygraph?"

"That shouldn't be necessary."

Rhodes said, "Sir, I don't mind taking a polygraph. Whether or not she does."

Murray gave Rhodes a sharp glance. Now he felt Rhodes was

beginning to work with Hastings, boxing him in. His irritation showed, and when he spoke again, he went on the offense.

Murray said, "I must say I find your attitudes very…disappointing. The defendant, Gregorio Cavazos, was a vicious gang leader and murderer. A very bad man and a serious menace to this community. The city of St. Louis would have done well to get him off the streets and into prison. Yesterday, the district attorney's office was very close to securing a conviction against Cavazos for murder in the first degree. And then Detective Rhodes got on the stand and blew it clean out of the water. The defendant's motion for mistrial was granted, and now Cavazos walks. He's a free man. And you two come in here concerned about blemishes on a career. I expected better."

"So did we," Hastings said.

The deputy chief caught Hastings's meaning. He lowered his voice to a warning tone and said, "Excuse me?"

Hastings said, "Sir, we're sorry that Cavazos was freed. But it is not the detective's fault. He was not advised of the order in limine. Ms. Delaney probably just forgot to do it. You know how overworked the prosecutors are. But that doesn't mean we should stand by and let one of my people take the rap for it."

"Do you have any idea how angry Herb Jaffe is?" Murray said. "The dismissal has been on the news. This is very, very embarrassing to him and to his office. He wants action."

A moment passed and Hastings said, "You mean he wants this man fired?"

Karen Brady and the deputy chief exchanged looks.

Murray said, "That's not going to happen. But we do need to do something."

Hastings said, "You mean you're actually considering formal discipline?"

Murray didn't answer him. Neither did Captain Brady.

"Are you serious?" Hastings said.

"George—" Murray said.

"Now wait a minute," Hastings said. "The district attorney's office screws up, and instead of admitting it, they're going to blame it on a cop. A black cop. And you're allowing this?"

Murray said, his voice almost a shout, "What the hell does his being black have to do with anything?"

Hastings said, "It *shouldn't* have anything to do with it."

"Sir—" Rhodes said, suddenly very uncomfortable.

Murray continued staring at Hastings. He was as angry as Hastings had ever seen him.

"Are you implying, Lieutenant, that Herb Jaffe is a racist?" Murray said. "Are you suggesting that *I* would be complicit in such a thing?"

"I'm suggesting, sir, respectfully, that certain people at the district attorney's office *may* be cynical enough to believe that a prosecutor should be believed over a ... detective who doesn't have the kind of clout others in the department do."

Captain Brady looked down at her desk. Rhodes looked at Hastings. Hastings looked back at Murray. Murray glared at Hastings.

"Lieutenant," Murray said, "I'm going to give you a chance to retract that."

An awful silence filled the room. Moments ticked by.

Then Hastings said, "I'll retract it, sir. If you will agree not to issue any discipline to Detective Rhodes."

The deputy chief tightened, and for a moment both Rhodes and Karen Brady wondered if he was going to rush Hastings. But he didn't.

The deputy chief said, "This meeting is adjourned. Get out, both of you."

THREE

He rubbed the wrist bindings on a sharp rail in the cattle truck. He was patient and thorough, and eventually the friction got them off.

The cattle truck got him to Chicago. He took this as a good sign. It was a big city, easy to hide in, easy to steal from. He had thought about stealing a car at the truck stop. It would have been warmer and more comfortable than the back of a truck. But he knew the theft would be reported and he would probably have been caught. North Dakota was too wide and open—not enough cover. It was better to hide among crowds.

In Chicago, Reese made his way to Marshall Field's and bumped into a man coming off the elevator. Reese said he was sorry and the man said that was okay and Reese moved off. The man was not aware that his wallet had been taken until he tried to pay for dinner later that evening. By then, Reese had bought a change of clothes and a decent meal.

The meal, he had at an old German restaurant on State Street he had always liked. He ordered the veal and fried potatoes. Accompanied with two bottles of Bass ale. Twelve years since he had enjoyed a good meal, and it was so good, it was almost worth waiting for. Reese knew something about war and combat and he knew that men in battle reminisced more about good food than they did women.

Afterward, he caught sight of himself in a bathroom mirror and stopped and looked at his reflection. It took him aback. A man looking back at him: thin, with short blond hair, graying at the temples. Himself, but someone else. Or maybe he had been someone else before and now he was himself again. Wearing corduroy pants that fit, a crew-neck sweater, and an oxford shirt beneath. A white-collar fellow, an urban professional. To most, an entirely nonthreatening figure. He could be a college professor or a doctor. Was this him? Had a good meal and decent clothes given him a rebirth?

No, it hadn't.

Reese left the restaurant and walked north. It was a cold, blue-sky Chicago day. The air clean and crisp, the architecture a welcome sight. Reese enjoyed the walk, letting the day and the sights unfold for him. What a pleasure it was to walk outside of a prison's dog run, a street stretching out long and far, no wall at the end of it. A few blocks of walking and he was no longer cold. He continued for another mile and a half and then he was in a residential area. Tall marbled condominiums and apartment buildings. He saw a city truck pull an old Chevy van out—sideways—from a parking space so it could be towed away. He enjoyed the sight and sound of the friction of the tires dragging across the pavement. Near the tow truck, a woman walking her poodle smiled at him and said, "It's been there for weeks." Letting him know the owner of the van had it coming. Reese smiled back, showing friendly agreement. The woman was looking at his clothes and his appearance as if he were a neighbor.

Reese walked another block before turning a corner. There he saw a car he knew he could steal and that he liked. A late 1990s Mercedes-Benz S-Class.

He switched the license plates with those of another Illinois vehicle at a rest stop outside of the city. Then he drove to a small town called Madison, Indiana.

The small white-brick house sat on a cliff overlooking the Ohio River. Reese had left a key to the house under the large brown stone near the front porch. He found the key and let himself in the house. Everything was as it had been. He had not been there for thirteen years. He found his tools in the garage, next to the boat and a Pontiac Bonneville he had left there. He took the tools and returned to the utility room in the house. He pulled the washing machine away from the wall. Then he visualized a sort of square in the wall. Using a hammer and chisel, he knocked out a patch of wall. He pulled the broken bits of wall loose and then out.

Then he illuminated the dark compartment with a flashlight. In the hole, there was a bag containing $114,000 in cash. There was also a passport and other documentation identifying him as Paul Bryan. There was another set of documents for his wife. He left them there.

His hair was darker in the Paul Bryan photos. And he would be over a decade older now than when the photo had been taken. But this could be updated easily enough.

The battery in the Pontiac was dead, so Reese drove into town to buy another one. After replacing the battery, he backed the Pontiac out of the garage and put the Mercedes back in its place. The Pontiac was registered to Paul Bryan.

Reese had dinner at the local Golden Corral. He decided it wasn't as bad as prison food, but it wasn't much better, either. After eating about half the entrée, he had a piece of apple pie and a cup of coffee. He enjoyed that part of the meal.

After that, he drove to a movie theater. He thought he would enjoy seeing a movie after all this time. But he only managed to sit through half of it. It seemed like it had been written for teenagers and he didn't understand why all the people in the theater were laughing. He also found that he missed being outside. He left the theater and went for another walk.

And as he walked, he thought again of time. Units of time. How he used to battle those units. Him on one side, time on the other. He had been thinking about time during the movie, wondering how much longer the movie was going to last. Maybe that was why he had left.

That night, he walked along a country road. Between cornfields and under starshine. He walked and he thought. And he planned.

The next morning, he drove the Pontiac to the local convenience store and picked up a copy of *Auto Trader*. Then he drove to a local diner and paged through it while he ate. He circled three cars, all of them being offered by private sellers.

The first seller was a housewife, whose husband was at work when Reese showed up. She was lonely and unattractive. She was also curious about him, asking him questions about his family and where he came from. Reese, the ex-spy, handled it well enough. But he made an early decision not to do business with her or her husband.

The second seller was an elderly, retired couple wanting to unload their Lincoln Continental. They lived in a house next to a massive RV. In the driveway next to the Lincoln was a small SUV that could be hooked up to the RV. The couple seemed decent enough and didn't seem overly curious about him. But the old man wore a blue cap bearing the insignia of the USS *Enterprise*. Reese asked if he had been in the navy. The old man said he had. A retired master chief with thirty years in. It was enough to spook Reese. He'd never met a dumb master chief. The old man might be very good at remembering him, remembering things about him. Reese told the old man he'd give the Lincoln some thought and get in touch with him.

The third seller was a lady in her early thirties with two kids. She was offering her ex-husband's car, a 2004 Mercury Marauder. She said she had full title and handed him the keys and told him he could take a test drive. Then she went back in her house, holding a cell phone to her ear. She'd hardly given Reese a glance.

Reese drove the car around the block. He liked it.

He returned to the woman's house and asked her to show him the title. There were no liens. She owned it outright. Reese asked her how much she wanted. She said the Blue Book value was eighteen, but she would take sixteen five. Reese said, "Okay." And he counted out that sum in hundreds, laying it on her kitchen table. Then he asked her if she could deliver it to him at the Madison Safeway that afternoon. She said she could.

That evening, Reese made room in his garage for the Mercury. He backed the Mercury into the garage. Then he spent the next few hours creating a false bottom in the trunk. He examined his work when he was finished.

To the inexperienced eye, it would appear normal. A trained drug dog would be able to sniff narcotics if they were placed in the secret compartment. But Reese had not made the compartment to store narcotics.

Reese left the car alone, telling himself he would check the spot welds the next day.

He went into the house and made a pot of coffee. He drank the coffee with sandwiches he had bought at a deli. While he ate, he read the Indianapolis newspaper. He read all the stories about the war in Iraq and Afghanistan. At times, he shook his head, wondering when the clowns had taken over.

Reese had been an agent for the CIA when the CIA was run by the current president's father. Like most people in the intelligence community, Reese thought the father had some sense. The father was not an ideologue. Like Eisenhower, Bush senior would look at all the options presented to him and carefully consider the possible consequences of each. Then he would choose the alternative that offered the maximum chance of success with the minimum chance of disaster. This was standard intelligence procedure. It wasn't especially pretty and it required a certain dispassionate worldview. But it was realistic and, more importantly, it worked. There was nuance back then, as there always should be in intelligence work. But Bush the Younger proudly proclaimed he didn't do nuance.

Reese finished his dinner and put the dishes in the sink. Then he set about dyeing his hair.

He finished the job around ten o'clock. He rearranged his now-dark hair, cutting bits here and there. Then he put on some clear eyeglasses. The same man he was before, with the same build. The same, but different. The change was effective. He looked like Paul Bryan now.

FOUR

Ronnie Wulf, the chief of detectives, had asked Hastings if he would have a cup of coffee with him, and Hastings would later tell himself he should have seen it coming then. Hastings had butted heads with Wulf on a serial-killer investigation once. But whatever tension had been between them was resolved at the end when Wulf took measures to protect Hastings from the chief of police, who had not been happy with the way things went down. They were not close friends, but Hastings thought Ronnie Wulf was basically all right.

Now they sat in the small snacking area in the basement of the police department.

"George," Wulf said, "the chief wants you and your team to take an assignment."

Hastings said, "Regarding homicide?"

"No. Not exactly."

Hastings said nothing. Waited for the man to add something.

Ronnie Wulf said, "Senator Preston. Alan Preston. You know who that is, don't you?"

"Of course."

Senator Alan Preston, Republican-Missouri. He had been elected to the U.S. Senate eight years earlier. He had had only token opposition in his reelection campaign. Hastings had voted for him the first time, against him the second time.

Wulf said, "Years ago, before he was a senator, he was an assistant U.S. attorney in Washington. He prosecuted an ex–CIA agent for selling arms to Syria. The agent, this ex-agent, his name was John Reese. A very bad guy. Betrayed his country, probably had agents killed. Agents who were working for the United States. Preston tried the case against him and got him sentenced to prison for life. At sentencing, the judge told Reese that if he could have, he would have sentenced him to death."

Hastings said, "For murder?"

"No. Apparently, they never actually charged him with murder. What they got him on was the arms-selling thing. Treason."

"So he got a life sentence?"

"Yeah. But, two days ago, he escaped. From a maximum-security federal holding center in North Dakota."

"How?"

"I wasn't told. I don't know if the chief was, either. He assaulted a private security guard, put him in the hospital. No one's seen him since. The guy's some sort of Rambo or something. He was an army Ranger, then a CIA agent, and then an ex–CIA agent, if that makes any sense to you."

"How did he escape?"

"I asked that, too, and was told I didn't need to know."

"Okay. What's it got to do with us?"

"Well, apparently, sometime before his trial, this Reese told someone in jail that he was going to have Preston killed."

"How long ago was that?"

"Twelve, thirteen years ago."

"And the senator thinks he's going to come after him now?"

"The senator's concerned. I'll put it that way. He's got a wife and a daughter. The daughter's a college student."

Hastings didn't like where this was tracking. He said, "But there's no homicide now. What does this have to do with me or the guys on my squad?"

"The chief wants you to guard the senator. You and your guys. Sort of a stakeout."

Hastings sighed. "But that's not detective work. We're homicide."

"I know you're homicide. George, this is not shit duty."

"Baby-sitting a senator who may or may not have a vengeful convict after him? Sounds like shit duty to me."

"Maybe so. But this is coming from the chief."

Hastings studied Ronnie Wulf for a moment. Then he said, "The chief or the deputy chief?"

"Goddammit, George, this is not punishment."

"Ronnie, I've known you for years. Be straight with me."

"I am."

"Are you going to tell me this has nothing to do with Howard Rhodes or what I said to Deputy Chief Murray?"

"No, I'm not going to tell you that." Wulf leaned closer. "No, I won't tell you that. And now I'm speaking for myself: George, you cannot talk to the deputy chief that way and not expect any recrimination. Christ, *I* don't get away with speaking to Murray that way."

"Well, what would you have done? The DA fucked up and *lied* about it and they were trying to lay it off on Rhodes. Christ, they were trying to get him fired. I couldn't sit back and watch that. I couldn't believe Murray was going to go along with it."

"Well . . ." Wulf was not going to say what he thought about that. He eventually said, "I understand that. And to an extent, I admire you for it. But you accused them of being racists."

"I did not do that."

"Yes, you did, George. You said they were picking on Howard because he's black."

"I didn't mean it like that," Hastings said. Though he more or less had, and he knew it. He said, "And I . . . sort of backed down on it."

"Yeah, well you also sort of refused to retract it. Right?"

"Sort of."

"Yeah, sort of. But let's be honest, George. You got pissed off and you just didn't want to back down to Fenton."

"That's not—"

"Yeah it is."

"Well, what do you think I should have done?"

"Never mind what I think. It doesn't matter what I think. Look, George, you say something like that in a city like this, you better be able to back it up. *Especially* if you're saying it to Murray. He's sensitive about that shit. There are black cops at the PD who already think Fenton's a sellout. *You don't say that to him.*"

"I was talking about the DA's office, not Murray."

"But that's not how he sees it." Wulf said, "At the beginning of this, it was just about Howard and the district attorney's office. Now it's about you and Murray. Do you see what you've done? He drew a line and you crossed it. You insulted him. Now, George, you did. In your oh-so-subtle way, you called him a chickenshit. Don't tell me you didn't."

"They were going to discipline Howard."

"Be that as it may, George, you fucked up. You want to get your twenty in and draw your pension, you don't pick fights with the brass. That's the way it is."

"You on their side?"

"Don't say that shit to me. I don't need it. Listen to me. Fenton Murray is not the shitbird you may think he is. He's got flaws, like anyone else, but overall he's a good cop and a good man. In my opinion, which is between us, I think you both bear some responsibility for this mess."

"No one's pulling him off his shift, though."

"No, they're not. And that's just the way it's going to be. This is a solution, okay? That works for everyone."

"'Solution'? You mean this was your idea?"

Wulf said nothing.

Hastings said, "So this is the compromise you've mediated? Me and my guys have to baby-sit a senator and his family?"

"George, you're only looking at the downside of this. You're not getting demoted. Howard's not getting demoted. No one is getting any formal discipline placed in his file. You have been given an assignment that will last for, at most, ten days. Just while the senator is in town for a few days. By the time it's done, everyone will have cooled off. Trust me on this."

"It's shit duty."

Wulf's expression hardened, his patience exhausted.

"Okay, maybe it is," Wulf said. "But tell me, Lieutenant, when did you become exempt from that? When did you reach the point that you get to pick and choose what assignments you work? 'Cause let me tell you, I don't have that luxury, and I'm your fucking supervisor."

Hastings started to answer, but Wulf raised his hand and said, "Whatever talent you possess as a homicide detective does not exempt you from regular police work. That includes working traffic, internal affairs, and, yes, stakeouts. If you think you get to pass all that shit by because it's beneath you, you better resign now and open up your own goddamn detective agency."

Wulf stood up. Hastings remained seated.

Wulf said, "You are to report to Captain Anthony in administration at oh eight hundred hours tomorrow morning and proceed under his supervision. That's an order."

FIVE

Professor David Chang taught Calculus I and II, Differential Equations, and Advanced Engineering Mathematics at a small private university in eastern Ohio. The university and town were tucked away in the mountains, about an hour's drive from Zanesville. He was a slight man, about five seven, with thick dark hair and a sort of fluid, easy manner. He was also a spiffy dresser, well groomed, and stylish.

His Differential Equations class was often discussed in somber tones by the engineering students. "You got Chang for Diff-E-Q? Good luck, man. It separates the men from the boys." Smart guys were known to have failed his class. A common ritual for his most recent engineering students was to be handed back their first graded exams. About two-thirds of the class would receive Fs. A pall of anxiety and gloom would descend over the classroom and invariably one of the students would meekly raise a hand and ask, "Uh, do you grade on a curve?"

Chang's answer was always the same: "That's not my style."

Now he took a question from one of the students regarding the use of the del operator. With his usual patience, Chang went through the problem on the board again. The bell rung and Chang dismissed the class.

Chang dropped by his office for only a few minutes. He did not want to be there too long, lest one of his students come by for help. He checked his messages and his schedule. He had one week to prepare the fourth exam for the semester. Then there would be the final exam in mid-December.

He left the engineering building and started the walk to his car. He had unlocked the car door when a man called out his name.

"David."

Professor Chang turned and looked at the dark-haired man standing a few feet from him. It took him a moment to place the colonel. But only a moment.

"John," Chang said.

Chang moved toward John Reese, extending his hand for the greeting.

"John. My God, how are you?"

"I've been better. David. I'm calling you David now."

"It's my Christian name," Chang said. "My wife converted, too. Years ago. She's a Eucharistic minister now at the church."

His name before had been Yu Kam-Chai. He was born in Beijing. He had a sister who was a prostitute and had eventually become enslaved by one of the triads. She angered one of the mid-level bosses and he beat her to death with a teakwood club. Yu Kam-Chai wanted to avenge her death, but his sister's killer was a *shan-chu*, a protected enforcer of the 14K Triad. Kam-Chai was willing to give his life to avenge his sister, but he was not willing to surrender the lives of his own wife and children, who would be killed along with him. An American agent, posing as a businessman, approached him and offered to help. The American agent said he would kill the *shan-chu* in exchange for information about the 14K's narcotics trade and its relationship with Taiwan. The American told Kam-Chai his name was Lessert, but Kam-Chai would later learn that it was Reese. A sniper's bullet took care of the *shan-chu.* A year later, things got hot for Kam-Chai and Reese smuggled him and his family out of the country and set them up in the States. Yu Kam-Chai became David Chang.

Now Chang paused. "John, are you all right?"

Reese said, "I need your help."

Reese felt uncomfortable in their living room.

He had always liked Chang's wife, who had taken on the name Mary since coming to the States. And he was glad to see her now. It had been fourteen years since he had brought them here. Mary Chang was still slim and attractive. She called him John and insisted he have some tea.

Reese said that would be nice. Then he told her he was sorry for imposing. She told him to shut up and then left him alone with her husband.

Reese said, "The children."

Chang said, "Ben is an engineer in San Francisco. Julie is a senior at NYU."

"A senior in college?"

"Yes. She's been accepted to medical school."

"My God. I remember when she was practically a toddler."

"It goes fast," Chang said.

"It does and it doesn't," Reese said, thinking, Depending where you are. "I'm sorry to do this."

"Don't insult us," Chang said. "You are our guest. And we are indebted to you."

"You are not indebted to me. When I helped you, it was for my benefit. I always acted in my own interests. Or my country's. Your welfare was secondary."

"You sound like a man trying to persuade himself." Chang shrugged. "Whatever your purpose was, I and my family are indebted. You are familiar with the expression 'No good deed goes unpunished.' Perhaps by coming here, you lift a burden from me."

Reese said, "I don't understand."

"You don't need to."

"I'm a fugitive. Probably wanted for assault and battery."

"Assault?"

Reese told him about the incident in North Dakota.

Chang frowned and said, "But why? You were locked up. Why did they take you out?"

"They couldn't kill me while I was in prison. Beyond that, I don't know. I don't know why they wanted to kill me. They already had, in a way."

A moment passed and Chang said, "John. What about your wife?"

"She died. Five years ago."

"I'm sorry," Chang said.

Reese shook his head, did not make eye contact with his friend. He feared what would happen if he did.

SIX

Hastings called the members of his homicide investigation team into his office and gave them the news. The men on his squad at that time were Sgt. Joe Klosterman, Detective Tim Murphy, and Detective Howard Rhodes.

Klosterman said, "So Wulf screwed us, then."

"He didn't screw us," Hastings said. "He's forced into a place he doesn't want to be."

"Sounds like he's still siding with them," Klosterman said.

"All right," Hastings said. "That's enough. I don't want to hear any more criticism directed at Wulf."

They were all quiet for a moment. Then Rhodes said he was sorry.

Murph said, "What are you sorry for? You didn't do anything wrong."

Rhodes said, "Well, now you're all being punished because of me."

"It's not because of you," Hastings said. "It's because of me."

"Oh, the hell with it," Klosterman said, "Who cares? It's done. Are we going to have to work hoot shifts?"

"We might," Hastings said. "I'll know more tomorrow after I meet with Captain Anthony. Okay. That's all for now. Go get your backlog in order. Joe, hang around here for a minute, will you?"

Murph and Rhodes left the office. The door was closed, leaving Hastings and Klosterman alone.

Sgt. Joe Klosterman was probably Hastings's closest friend. Klosterman was younger than Hastings. A big man with a mustache. Put him in coat and tails and have him dance gracefully to "I'm in Heaven," he'd still look like a cop. He liked to tell jokes, liked performing. He had been married for nineteen years and was still head over heels in love with his wife, Anne. The father of five children, he refrained from swearing and using vulgarity in front of Anne and the kids. He and his family attended Catholic Mass regularly and were active members of their parish. At work, he employed the cop's typical vocabulary, which included frequent use of the words *turd*, *douche*, *fucker*, and *motherfucker*.

Now, Klosterman looked at Hastings and Hastings looked back at him and made a sort of "Forgive me" gesture. It made Klosterman laugh, and Hastings laughed with him.

"Sorry, man," Hastings said. "I fucked up."

Klosterman said, " 'You don't have the balls to back your own. Racist *fuckers*.' " Using a nerdy white-guy voice to imitate Hastings. It sounded a little like Paul Lynde. Or Richard Simmons.

"Sorry," said Hastings.

" 'As far as I'm concerned, you can all just go *ffff*uck yourselves,' " Klosterman said, still using the voice.

"I didn't fucking say that."

Klosterman laughed and shook his head. "Ah, don't worry about it, George," he said. "It's only ten days."

"Okay."

Klosterman said, "Will this clean the slate with the deputy chief?"

"I don't know. Wulf seems to think so. By the way, don't go

around trashing Wulf or Murray on this. I've got enough shit to deal with as it is."

"Okay."

"Anyway, now that I've calmed down, I can kind of see the spot Wulf's in."

"What?"

"Well, he wouldn't tell me, and he probably never will. But I got the feeling the chief and the deputy chief really wanted to hammer me on this, but Ronnie talked them into doing something less severe."

"Well," Klosterman said, "I guess I should be grateful. If you got busted to sergeant, I'd have to be supervised directly by Karen. Or some other dipshit lieutenant. And I don't have your gift for diplomacy."

"Neither do I, apparently."

"You ever work stakeout before? Surveillance?"

"No. You did, didn't you?"

"Yeah. The Henry Commission, six years ago. Back when they were trying to bust the commissioner corruption ring."

"How was it?"

Klosterman shrugged. "A lot of time in a van or an apartment building, listening to phone taps. I was stuck there with Bill Toomey. You remember him?"

"No. Never worked with him."

"He retired two years ago. Get this: retired, moved out to this land he had in Tennessee. *Died* a year after that. Poor fucker. Anyway, Bill was kind of a tough guy. Old school. Six foot four, intimidating as hell. Remember Gene Hackman in that bar scene in *The*

French Connection, taking control of all those guys? I'd seen Bill Toomey do that for real. I told you he was from Tennessee. He started out with the PD at a time when cops regularly said *nigger* on the job and didn't care who heard it. So he had to kind of unlearn that sort of thing later in his career. Anyway, like I said, he was a tough guy. But then I was stuck with him in this van for ten hours a day, kind of getting cabin fever, and, man, he almost drove me crazy. Waxing nostalgic. Talking about his first girlfriend, his childhood experiences, how his mom liked his brothers more than him, how sad he was he never had a son, and on and on. Real gushy, you know. A couple of times, I thought he might start crying on me. Who knew he was such a sensitive man."

"Any confessions about teenage homosexual encounters?"

"No, but I would not have been surprised."

"Well, that's all rather touching."

"Yeah. If we'd had another week of it, we'd've either beat the shit out of each other or gotten married."

"I guess you learn things about each other, cooped up like that."

"Oh, too much, homey. Too fucking much."

Hastings said, "He died a year after retirement?"

"Yeah."

"He didn't..." Hastings made a gun of his finger and pointed it to his head.

"Oh, no. Heart attack. The man liked his salted meats."

SEVEN

After dinner, Chang took Reese to the studio behind the house. The studio had been converted from a garage. In the studio were a desk and a couch. The walls were paneled, and high bookshelves lined two of the walls. On another wall were Chang's degrees from Ohio State University and a banner for the football team. He had become addicted to college football over the years. Chang told Reese there was no phenomenon in the world comparable to American college football. He said it was an excellent way to channel humanity's tribalism and aggression. He told Reese he had missed some great games, being in prison. Reese nodded politely, not knowing if his friend was being humorous or genuine.

Chang asked Reese to take the other end of the heavy oak desk. Together, they moved it to another part of the room. Then Chang lifted the rug where the desk had been and lifted a door that revealed a stairway. Chang went down the stairs and Reese followed him.

This was where Chang kept his weapons.

There were over fifty of them—handguns, rifles, even a couple of machine guns. A good many of them were antique. He had an English breechloader, made by Rowland in 1720. Two pocket pistols, made by Alexander Forsyth and Company, circa 1815. These were kept in the original wood case with the small boxes containing the percussion powder. He had a brass-barreled flintlock holster pistol, favored by pirates in the early 1800s, and a couple of four-barreled Sharps pistols.

Chang opened a drawer and removed a modern-looking Austrian rifle.

"This is what I was telling you about," Chang said.

It had been developed in the 1980s. Built in modular form so that several of its parts could be changed. The barrel could be quickly removed and exchanged for one of any four, each with a different length and function—a submachine gun, a carbine, a rifle, or a light machine gun. It had a built-in optical sight and an attached, inverted-V stand.

Chang handed it to Reese. Reese held it, let it become familiar to him. He said, "Okay. But do you have a Winchester Model Seventy?"

"Ah," Chang said. "The American sniper rifle. I do, in fact."

Chang went to another compartment, where a rifle hung on two pegs. He took it down and handed it to Reese.

The Model 70 Winchester .30-06 Springfield sniper rifle. Attached to the top was the long and slender Unertl scope. The rifle's stock was a beautifully crafted walnut with a semi–Monte Carlo hump. It was accurate at eleven hundred yards and had a range beyond that. It was the rifle used by the Marine snipers in Vietnam.

Chang said, "You need handguns, too, I suppose?"

"Yeah. Three, if you can spare them."

"I have plenty," Chang said.

Chang opened a panel, revealing a case containing several handguns. Chang pointed to a Colt 1911 and said, "I have a silencer for this." He handed the gun to Reese while he got the silencer from another drawer.

Reese held the Colt. He said, "I'd like a Ruger three fifty-seven revolver, if you have one."

"I have one," Chang said. "Have you tried the Smith & Wesson airweight? It's the regular snubnose, but a lot lighter."

"Can you spare one?"

"Yes."

Chang retrieved a black one. He checked the cylinder to make sure it was not loaded. Then he handed it to Reese.

After a moment, Chang said, "I also have another rifle you're familiar with. The Russian-made Mosin-Nagant. It's not as effective as the Winchester, but I remember it working perfectly well on a target in Beijing."

Chang smiled at Reese, but Reese did not smile back. Reese would never admit to Chang that he'd been the sniper sent to kill the *shan-chu* all those years ago. Or that he'd used a Russian rifle to do it.

EIGHT

The shift came to an end and Hastings walked to his car in the parking lot.

His car was a chocolate brown 1987 Jaguar XJ6. It had been seized by the police department pursuant to the RICO Act and given to him as his work and take-home car. It was a fast car with a Corvette engine that gave off a wonderful snort.

In the car, his cell phone rang. He saw that the call was from his daughter and he answered it.

"Yeah."

"Daddy?"

"What's up, pumpkin?"

"I'm at basketball practice. Mom's supposed to pick me up. But I don't see her here."

"Sshh—" Hastings closed off the bad language. "What time was she supposed to pick you up?"

"Six-thirty. It's six-forty now."

"Have you called her?"

"Yeah. No answer."

"Damn it. Is Mrs. McGregor there?"

"Yeah. Do you want me to ask her for a ride?"

"Yeah. . . . No, wait. Let me talk to her."

"Hold on."

Hastings waited and Terry McGregor got on the phone. Terry

was a neighbor of theirs. She had a daughter, Randi, who was Amy's age.

"George?"

"Hi, Terry? I'm in a bind here. Amy's mother was supposed to pick her up and take her home."

"Your home?"

"Well, no. Actually, her mother's home. But, listen, could you take her to my house? Her mother can pick her up there later."

"Sure."

"I'm really sorry to impose."

"George, be quiet. You live around the corner. It's not an imposition."

"Okay. Thanks."

"We'll see you soon."

"See you."

Hastings checked his watch. He had fifteen minutes to get to the restaurant in the Central West End.

He didn't make it.

Carol was waiting at a table alone. He greeted her, kissing her on the cheek.

"Sorry," he said. "I was on the phone with Amy. Her mother was—" He stopped. Carol had told him before she was tired of Eileen stories.

Carol said, "Eileen was late or something?"

"Something," Hastings said. "It's taken care of."

Carol didn't respond to that. She looked down at her menu, a little peeved. Hastings decided that it would pass in time. Then his phone rang again.

"Sorry," he said.

It was Eileen, his ex-wife.

Hastings walked away from the table before answering it. He sensed then what the conversation was going to be, and his sense was exactly correct.

Eileen said, "George, I'm at the school. Where the hell is Amy?"

"She got a ride home with Mrs. McGregor."

"What? Well, that was fucking nice. Why didn't anybody tell me?"

"She tried to call you. You didn't answer your phone."

"I left it in the car. I was at Wild Oats, buying groceries. I was going to make her dinner."

"You still can. Just go by my house and pick her up."

"Shit. I'm supposed to drive all the way to South St. Louis, pick her up, and then drive her to West County?"

"Yes. Eileen, this is your fault."

Eileen said, "It'll be eight o'clock before I can make dinner. Now we'll have to order pizza."

As Eileen answered him, Hastings made the mistake of looking over at Carol. She gave him a look back that was not friendly.

"Then order pizza."

"Who's giving her a ride?"

"Mrs. McGregor. I told you. She's a neighbor of ours."

"Well, can't you call her and have her drive Amy to my house?"

Hastings exhaled. "No," he said.

"Why not?"

"Because I'm not asking her to do that. She's already done enough for us."

"Well, give me her number, then. I'll ask her."

"You're going to ask a total stranger to drive your daughter out to West County so you don't have to drive to South St. Louis to pick her up?"

"Yeah. What's the big deal?"

She doesn't see it, Hastings thought. She really doesn't.

Hastings said, "No."

"No?"

"No."

"You mean you're refusing to give me the number?"

"Yes. I'm refusing to give you the number."

"Fine," Eileen said, "I'll pick her up at your house. God, you're such a child sometimes."

Eileen clicked off and that ended that conversation.

It wasn't much better at the dinner table.

Carol kept her eyes on her menu. The waiter came with their drinks. Carol gave the waiter her order without asking Hastings if he was ready. Hastings wisely ordered an entrée without thinking much about what he actually wanted, and the waiter took their menus and left them alone.

Hastings said, "Sorry."

Carol shook her head, not making eye contact with him.

At other times, Hastings might have elaborated on the apology, given her a fuller explanation. But now he wasn't feeling that generous. Another stupid fight with Eileen, a day of getting bawled out by the brass.

He said, "Carol, give me a break, will you?"

She gave him a sharp look. "You're mad at *me*?"

"I'm not mad. I'd just like to enjoy this dinner and not have to spend half of it trying to get you to forgive me for something that's out of my control. Or have you sit there punishing me with silence."

"It's not out of your control."

"I'm not having that discussion."

"It's not out of your control."

"Look. You knew when we got involved that I'm a divorced father with an irresponsible ex-wife. Eileen does these things, you know, and I have to deal with it. That's the way it is."

"Eileen's not your daughter. Or your little sister."

"She's the mother of my daughter. Because of that, I have to deal with her."

"George, try to see it from my perspective. I wanted to spend the evening with you. A nice dinner, a few drinks, and then we spend the night together. Now that's not much to ask for."

"I was five minutes late. Then I had maybe a five-minute call. That's nothing. These are things people with children have to deal with."

"Oh, I see."

He saw where she was going. He said, "Oh no."

"Because I don't have children, I wouldn't understand."

"I didn't say that."

"You think it."

"I don't think it."

"Yeah you do. You just don't say it."

"Well, do you want children?"

And like that, it was out. The subject they had avoided for almost two years.

"I don't know," she said. "My ex and I, we never—I don't know."

"If you don't, it's okay."

She looked at him for a long time. Then she said, "I'm not—I'm not ready to have this conversation."

Hastings sighed and said, "Look, it's out now. Why don't we talk about it?"

"I'm not ready for that," she said.

"Carol—"

"No, George." She looked at him for a long time, not saying anything. Then she said, "I have to go."

NINE

The waiter was gracious when Hastings canceled Carol's dinner order. Hastings ate his meal alone and left a generous tip. When he was finished, he called Amy on her cell phone to make sure Eileen had indeed picked her up. Eileen had. Amy said she was sorry if she'd caused any trouble and Hastings said not to worry, she hadn't, and he would see her in a couple of days. Then he got off the phone before Amy did something stupid, like ask if he wanted to say anything else to her mother.

George Hastings was not his daughter's biological father. He had adopted her after he married her mother, Eileen. Amy was five at the time. Until the marriage, Hastings had had ambivalent feelings about being a parent. He had grown up in an unhappy home. His mother had been a good woman, though not a very strong one. His father had been a shitpoke. A bully and a jerk, angry and bitter for reasons Hastings never figured out. Hastings had never attempted to "resolve" his anger at his father. But he believed he had come to terms with it. Both his parents were dead now.

With that background, he was surprised to find that he loved being a father. Like being a police officer, it was not something he had planned, but something that had come naturally to him. His paternal relationship with Amy outlasted his marriage to Eileen. Eileen left him for her boss, a lawyer named Ted Samster. But, to her credit, Eileen did not fight Hastings on the custody of Amy. She might have had her own selfish reasons for doing this, of course. But Hastings didn't think so. He knew that she knew how much Amy meant to him. And though Eileen could be thoughtless and inconsiderate, she was not cruel.

A few years had passed since the divorce. The hurt and pain of Eileen's betrayal had since dissipated. Now when he got angry at her, it was usually related to some *recent* selfish act. Sometimes when they argued, Hastings thought they sounded like a brother and sister. At times, he thought of her as a sister. Not in a gross way. But that they were family somehow, for good or for bad. Eileen was inconsiderate, immature, beautiful, and vain. Perhaps she had never really grown up. Hastings was honest enough with himself to admit that he had been drawn by her cool blond beauty. He sometimes wondered how she would have turned out if she had not always been pretty. Would she have developed more as a person? Focused on things less superficial? Not put so much of her identity in being a beautiful girl? But then, Hastings knew this line of thinking was itself vain, because he would probably not have gone after her if she hadn't been beautiful. He'd pursued her, charmed her, fallen in love with her, and then married her. And for a few years, he had convinced himself they were happy. Eileen could make him laugh as few women could. And sometimes she could be very insightful. Once, when he was down over a case, she had cheered him up by telling him that he was going to show them "how this shit works." Because that was who he was. That it was his quiet, arrogant confidence that had first attracted him to her. That it was that same quality, in part, that made him a great detective.

Shortly before she left him, Eileen told Hastings he would be better off without her. She had paraphrased Margaret Mitchell and said that like belonged with like. She said she was better suited to someone superficial and materialistic like Ted Samster. In turn, he, George, would be better suited to someone else.

Now Hastings thought, Yeah, but who?

He had been dating Carol McGuire for almost two years now. She was his first girlfriend and long-term lover since his divorce. She was attractive, smart, and sexy. She was also a good friend. She had helped him get over Eileen and had helped him see things that were wrong in his marriage that he was too close to see on his own.

But time is the enemy of every great love affair. And now time was closing in on them. Or rather, reality was closing in on them.

Joe Klosterman had once told Hastings that the girl you fall in love with and the woman you're married to are two different people. Perhaps he had fallen in love with Carol McGuire. But it was becoming increasingly clear that she could not be his wife. Not because she worried about the dumb television-show issues of being a cop's wife. No, the main problem for Carol was Amy.

It was not that Carol disliked Amy. She didn't. Her relations with Amy had always been friendly. But Carol showed no maternal interest in Amy. Indeed, she seemed not to have much interest in children in general. Hastings did not think this made her a bad person. Not everyone was cut out for parenting. Carol had never said she wasn't. But she had never said she was, either. In any event, every time Hastings tried to picture the three of them living together, it didn't work. And that made him wonder where they were going to go from there.

What was the Woody Allen line? A relationship has to keep

moving forward, like a shark, otherwise it dies. And what we've got here is a dead shark.

Hastings parked the Jag in front of his house. He went inside and turned on the lights and found himself alone.

Maybe the shark was dead. Or maybe he could call Carol tomorrow and see if she wanted to talk about it.

TEN

A. Lloyd Gelmers, lobbyist and former congressman, managed to wrap up his work by six o'clock that evening. He called his wife at home. She answered and he told her he had to go to the Capitol Grille to meet with representatives of an insurance company. He said he probably wouldn't be home till after midnight. He asked how their children were and she told him they were fine and then they said good-bye.

The next call he made was to his mistress. Her name was Lana. She was twenty-three years old, from Arkansas, about fifteen pounds overweight, and she had those sort of oversized, gangly breasts that older men like. She was what A. Lloyd sometimes referred to as "quality skank." A. Lloyd said, "Hello, sunshine," and she said, "Hello, baby," and then he told her he'd be at the apartment in forty-five minutes.

Unbeknownst to the present Mrs. Gelmers, A. Lloyd was co-owner of a group of apartment buildings in Silver Spring, Maryland. There were three of them in a row. Redbrick buildings, each one containing eight apartment units. Tasteful and simple. To the common observer, they might have seemed like the sort of place Mary Richards would live. But they were used to entertain clients of his lobbying firm and the politicians they needed. Usually prostitutes and drugs were involved. In some of the apartments, cameras were installed, though not in the one A. Lloyd used.

Sometimes he would meet Lana there, or another girl. Sometimes he liked to go there alone. The apartment was his refuge from the world, which could even wear a man like him down from time to time.

He climbed the stairs to the second floor, unlocked the apartment door, and let himself in.

"Hey, babe," he called out.

There was no response. And it was not until he walked into the living room and dropped his keys on the coffee table that he saw the man with the gun sitting in the red armchair in front of the tall oak armoire.

Reese said, "Hello, A. Lloyd."

Gelmers stared at the man for a few moments. The hair was no longer blond. Though it wasn't gray, either. Dark—dyed? And then he knew.

"John."

"Sit down," Reese said.

A. Lloyd took a seat on the couch.

"Keep your hands on your knees."

"John," A. Lloyd said, managing a smile. "What are you doing pointing a gun at me? We're old friends."

"No, we're old associates. There's a difference. Aren't you curious about the girl?"

"Oh. Lana. What did you do with her?"

"She's in the bathroom. Tied up, gagged. She'll be fine."

"How did you know I'd come here?"

"Well," Reese said, "some things don't change, I guess. Southern girls, hideaways. You always were predictable."

"Can't say the same for you. How did you get out of prison?"

"I was kind of wondering if you could tell me that. A team of mercenaries came bearing the right paperwork. Top forgeries, or, more likely, they paid some people off. Whatever. If you're in prison that long, you don't care who it is who gets you out so long as they get you out. But these gentleman intended to kill me. Do you know why?"

"Now how would I know?"

"Well, you put me in there. I figured maybe you had a hand in getting me out."

A. Lloyd Gelmers was an experienced politician. Lying came easily to him. He put on a disappointed face and said, "John, you're not well."

"I'm alive," Reese said. "I had a lot of time to think about things. Several years, in fact. My lawyer had a lot of time, too. He requested documents under the Freedom of Information Act. You know, trying to help me on appeal. Didn't do any good, obviously. But he found one piece of paper saying the U.S. attorney's office received the initial tip about my work in Syria from a 'reliable informant.' Now who could that be? Who knew what I was doing in Syria?"

"John—"

"Three people. One of them was Jackson, and he wouldn't have told anyone. The second was Carlyle, and he was dead. So that left you."

"John—"

"The reliable informant was the army intelligence liaison to the Senate. Which, at the time, was you."

"John, you're crazy."

"What did you get for that, A. Lloyd? What did you get for giving me up? Was it a favor from someone in the Senate? Or at the Agency? Or was it just vengeance? Anger at me because I always knew you were a fraud."

"John, you're not yourself. You don't know what you're talking about."

"Oh, cut it out, A. Lloyd. I know. Two and two make four. I always suspected it was you anyway. Now I know."

"Okay," A. Lloyd said, "so what, then? You come here to kill me, John? Another confirmed kill?"

Reese smiled. "I was a soldier," he said. "Perhaps you'd understand if you'd ever been one yourself."

A. Lloyd reddened. "Oh, fuck you, John. Come in here with your macho bullshit. Look at you. You look ridiculous. Hair dyed, pointing a gun with a silencer at me. What if I did turn you in? What are you going to do now? Kill me for it? You'll still be nothing. A broken-down fugitive. You're finished. Killing me isn't going to make things any better for you."

"Maybe not," Reese said. "Then again, maybe I'll feel better. Tell me who broke me out and why."

"How should I know? These guys don't tell me everything."

Reese studied his old colleague.

"What guys?" Reese said.

"What?"

"You said 'These guys.' What guys?"

"I don't know."

"A. Lloyd, just tell me what you know."

"All right," A. Lloyd said. "I'll tell you what I know, on one condition. Let me check on Lana."

"Go ahead," Reese said.

A. Lloyd Gelmers went around the corner and into the bathroom.

Reese remembered the girl looking at him in surprise. Wearing a bathrobe, tied loosely at the waist, nothing on underneath. It was a distraction, briefly, and then he turned her around and walked her to the bathroom. She didn't seem that scared, strangely. More curious than anything. Reese told her he was sorry as he sat her on the toilet seat and wrapped the towel around her mouth and then tied her hands behind her back and secured them to the base of the toilet.

Reese heard Gelmers rumble around in there.

In the bathroom, Gelmers ignored Lana and opened the second drawer in the sink cabinet. In the drawer, there was an old black leather bag, his old shaving kit. He pulled the zipper and opened the bag. Looked inside.

Then he heard Reese's voice from the other room.

"It's not in there," Reese said.

Reese had taken the .357 revolver out of the shaving kit.

"Shit," Gelmers said.

Gelmers left the girl tied up, walked back out to the living room.

Reese said, "Now you want to tell me?"

Gelmers said nothing.

Reese said, "Or do you want permission to go into your bedroom, too? And pull that shotgun out from under your bed."

"Found that, too, huh?"

"Yeah."

Gelmers smiled. "Maybe you can tell me where you put it."

"I don't think so."

"It was worth a try," Gelmers said, and stepped forward, grabbed the corner of the armoire, and tipped it forward. Gravity caught it and Reese saw the heavy, massive thing coming down on top of him. He fell out of the chair and onto the floor just before the armoire crashed down on top of the chair. The chair prevented the armoire from landing on Reese and breaking his back, but he was on his stomach, still with the gun in his hand, and when he crawled out from the space, Gelmers kicked him in the chest, then kicked again, aiming for Reese's head. Reese lifted his hands to shield himself, and Gelmers jumped on him and grabbed the gun, and then they both had their hands on it and one of them pulled the trigger, and a bullet went into a Manet print hanging on the wall, smashing the glass. Gelmers was stronger than Reese had thought. A Tasmanian devil of a man, snarling and twisting, not looking quite human, and they rolled and turned and Reese got on top of him, and now the gun was in Gelmers's hand and Reese punched him in the throat, and finally Gelmers's grip on the gun loosened and Reese pried it away from him, but Gelmers grabbed at it again and Reese shot him in the chest before he knew it.

Gelmers fell back, his head thudding on the carpet. The bullet had pierced his heart.

"Oh shit," Reese said. "A. Lloyd. Why did you have to do that?"

ELEVEN

Capt. Dan Anthony was a tall, strapping man. Handsome and well built. He was vain, aware of his good looks. He had been a motorcycle cop for many years and he still wore boots with his uniform. Hastings had met him a couple of times and had found no reason to dislike him. He had never worked with him, though.

Captain Anthony shook Hastings hand when Hastings came to his office. He asked Hastings to take a seat and then asked if he'd like some coffee. Hastings said no thank you.

Captain Anthony said, "What have you been told so far?"

Hastings said, "Not much. Chief Wulf said that a fugitive named John Reese broke out of prison and that they're afraid he'll come after Senator Preston."

"Yes."

"But I don't know much beyond that. Captain—"

"Call me Dan."

"Dan. I'd like to know, is this threat real? Is there a real possibility that this Reese is going to come after the senator?"

"You want to know if it's a rinky-dink assignment."

"No, not necessarily." Hastings had already decided it was. He said, "I just want to know if there's been something concrete. A note or a phone call saying 'I'm coming after you.'"

"To my knowledge, no. But I've been instructed by Chief Grassino to take this assignment seriously."

"All right," Hastings said. "But if it is serious, why bring metropolitan police officers into it? Isn't protecting United States senators the province of the FBI? Or the Secret Service?"

"Perhaps. But this is . . . a delicate issue. Politically, I mean."

For a moment, neither man said anything. Hastings began thinking that Dan Anthony was no fool. And that he would probably be the new deputy chief of administration.

There were rumors that the department was on the verge of changing its command structure. The position of chief of police would remain intact, but there would be an increase in deputy chiefs and assistant chiefs, each having command of a subdivision. Where there had previously been one deputy chief position, there would now be two. Specifically, deputy chief of operations and deputy chief of administration. Beneath that, there would be five assistant chief positions. Feelings about the proposed restructure were mixed. Some police officers thought a change would be good and would create a more efficient police department. Hastings was skeptical. He believed that having more chiefs would lead to more interdepartmental friction and the creation of too many fiefdoms. As things were now, they had a chief and a deputy chief, and Hastings thought two of them were plenty.

Hastings said, "Can you explain?"

"Yes," Anthony said. "But before I do, I want you to understand that you and your men are expected to handle this with a certain amount of tact and discretion."

"My men are professionals. All of them."

"I'm aware of that. What I mean is, I don't want this assignment discussed outside of your team. I know how cops love to talk shop."

"I understand."

"The thing is," Anthony said, "Senator Preston wants to avoid alerting the FBI to this. He wants to keep this . . . local, so to speak."

"But if there's been a threat on his life—"

"There's not been a recent direct threat. Not one that's been confirmed anyway. It's just that he's frightened. For himself and his family. If he alerts the FBI, the whole thing can become public. And the senator has made it very clear that he doesn't want that."

"But why?"

"Why has he asked to keep this discreet?"

"Not so much that. I mean, why use metropolitan police officers when you've got federal agents at your disposal. Probably better trained for this sort of thing than we are."

Captain Anthony sighed. "Again, this is not for publication. But the chief implied that Preston may run for president. He doesn't want national media attention focused on this."

"Or attention from Washington?"

"Yeah, maybe that, too." Anthony frowned at Hastings. A suggestion, perhaps, not to push it too far.

Hastings thought about asking what sort of federal appointment Chief Grassino hoped to land in an Alan Preston administration, but he didn't.

Instead, Hastings said, "So he's asked the chief for a favor?"

"In a manner of speaking, yes."

Hastings shook his head.

"You disapprove?" Anthony said.

"No, sir, I don't disapprove. I just find it unusual, that's all."

"Perhaps it is unorthodox. I agree. But the senator has asked this of the chief and the chief's given it to me to handle."

"If you don't mind my asking, was it your idea to assign me?"

"No. You were recommended by Wulf."

Wulf, Hastings thought. Was he trying to help or hurt? Probably help. . . . Well, what difference does it make now?

Hastings said, "Do you have a file on John Reese?"

"Yes. But it's not much. They didn't give us the criminal file, only a summary of it. Interesting reading, though, for what it is. He was an army Ranger and then he became one of their top sharpshooters. A sniper. Sometime in the eighties, the CIA recruited him. The record gets murky after that. He may or may not have been in El Salvador, Nicaragua, Central Europe, the Balkans, China, and Russia. Sometime in the nineties, he retired from the CIA and started his own arms business. He got rich. They say he sold weapons all over Africa and Europe and the Middle East."

"Ronnie said he sold arms to the Syrians. That's what they arrested him for."

"Yes, that's right. Thank God he was caught. They set up a sting operation, I think, and caught him in Belgium. Flew him back here in chains to stand trial. Here."

Captain Anthony slid a photograph across the desk to Hastings.

Hastings looked at it and said, "This is dated."

"Yeah. He'd be about fifty now."

Hastings said, "A Cold Warrior."

"Yeah," Anthony said, "but the Cold War is over. And this guy lost his bearings. Those weapons he sold the Syrians could have been used on our allies or our soldiers. For all we know, they were."

Hastings said, "Preston prosecuted him?"

"Yeah. He was an assistant U.S. attorney."

"When did Reese threaten to kill him?"

"Supposedly, in Washington, while he was on trial, he told someone in jail that he knew mercenaries all over the world and that if he wanted, he could have Preston killed."

"He said this while the trial was ongoing?"

"That's what I'm told."

"Was it discussed at trial? I mean, anytime a threat like that is made against one of our witnesses or prosecutors, we always bring it to the court's attention."

"I don't know if it was."

"It would seem like a dumb thing to do. For a spy anyway."

"Well, it was a long time ago," Anthony said. "The guy's a traitor, George. And like most of his kind, he did it for money."

"Okay," Hastings said. "We have no idea where he is now?"

"None."

TWELVE

The speck on the horizon grew as it approached and then there was the sound of a helicopter buzzing. The helicopter came into view. A Bell, new and pretty, painted in the blue and white of the company's trademark, contrasting with the green-and-brown forests of the surrounding Tennessee hills. Painted on the helicopter's side was a silvery hawk, the logo of Ghosthawk, Incorporated.

The helicopter landed on a pad near a large western-style ranch house. The blades began winding down and a fit-looking man in his forties came out of the helicopter. His name was Kyle Anders and he was met on the landing pad by Dexter Troy, his chief of security.

With the noise of the helicopter, their conversation was difficult to hear beyond a few feet. But one standing at a distance would have been able to see the anger on Kyle Anders's face. He stopped and said something in response to Troy. Troy made a sort of shrugging gesture but then motioned to the house, where he could explain it better.

In 1996, Clay Anders, owner and CEO of Anders Drilling, died and left his entire estate to his son, Kyle, who was then thirty-five years old. At the time, Kyle Anders was working for a real estate developer in Florida. After his father died, Kyle resigned from that job and returned to his father's home in Houston, Texas. A year later, Kyle Anders sold Anders Drilling to an oil company for $1.4 billion. A year after that, he founded Ghosthawk, Incorporated.

It began as a straightforward security service. Kyle, a graduate of West Point and a former Delta Force soldier, wanted to provide bodyguards to dignitaries and celebrities. He also wanted to give some of his friends from the army and Delta Force in particular a place to work. Kyle Anders had the good luck to be a billionaire's son. But other soldiers less fortunate often found the transition to civilian life more difficult. Kyle helped them find work suited to their training and skills. He also made sure they were well paid.

Kyle opened offices in New York, Los Angeles, and Washington. But his real base of operations was a seven-thousand-acre spread in the hills of East Tennessee. Sergeant York country. Here, he built a sort of private military university. There were shooting ranges, plenty of woods in which to practice war games and combat, barracks, and classrooms.

In the early stages of Ghosthawk, there were those who did not take Kyle Anders very seriously. Some thought he seemed like a rich kid trying to play soldier. But these skeptics overlooked the fact that he had been a soldier himself. And not just a soldier but a member of the elite Delta Force. He had left the army four years after he graduated West Point and, to the understanding of most, had never seen actual combat. Was he someone to keep an eye on? A madman building his own private army? Or was he just spending his inheritance fulfilling an adolescent fantasy?

In either event, his skeptics started to take him more seriously after 9/11. That was when Ghosthawk began its exponential growth.

Long before American troops left for Iraq, Kyle Anders began working Washington for contracts worth hundreds of millions of dollars. He had competitors in this process—Dyncorp, Blackwater, and, to some degree, even Halliburton. But he got the lion's share of the contracts for security work in Iraq. Within a year of the invasion, he had several hundred security contractors in Iraq and Afghanistan. A year after that, Ghosthawk became a billion-dollar operation.

Unlike his contemporaries in Britain, Kyle Anders did not like the term *mercenary*. To him, the word had negative connotations. Mercenaries were soldiers for hire, working strictly for money, indifferent to the mission or patriotism. Anders told all his employees they were not to even *use* the term *mercenary*. They were "security contractors." And though they were being paid by Ghosthawk, Anders reminded them they were fighting for their country.

The men employed by Anders included retired cops, ex–federal agents, former marines, army Rangers, Delta Force commandos, Special Forces soldiers, and Navy SEALs. There were also a few ex-members of the British Special Air Service (SAS), the French Foreign Legion, and Chilean soldiers who had enforced martial law under Augusto Pinochet. Anders's goal was to build a five-thousand-man army.

The media often sought out Anders for interviews. He rarely granted them. He did not like or trust reporters, even the so-called conservative ones. He believed most of them were defeatists or anti-American. His refusals to be interviewed sometimes led reporters to say things about him that he didn't think were true. One journalist surmised that he was "trying to build the world's most powerful mercenary army." Another charged him with wanting to make Ghosthawk the "fifth column" of the United States armed forces—that is, army, navy, air force, Marine Corps, and Ghosthawk.

They don't understand, Anders thought. He was no more a threat to the United States than UPS was to the U.S. Postal Service. His venture was capitalist, not imperialist. And he believed he would be the last person ever to betray his country.

Now he sat behind his desk in his house at his Tennessee compound and regarded his number two.

Anders said, "I just saw A. Lloyd two days ago."

"I know," Troy said. "But it's been confirmed."

"What happened?"

"According to the police, he went to see his girlfriend at an apartment. Before he got there, a man broke in and tied her up and locked her in the bathroom. Gelmers showed up about a half hour later. They had words. Gelmers went to the bathroom, ostensibly to check on the girl. She said he went back out and she heard a scuffle, then a shot. A muffled shot."

"Which means the killer was probably using a silencer."

"Yeah."

"You think it was Reese?"

"Yes, sir, I do."

Kyle Anders sighed. He didn't like to be called "sir." He requested that Troy call him Kyle. He was funny about things like that. Anders didn't like the word *sir* or the use of military ranks or even harsh language. He had no reservations about having lobbyists like A. Lloyd line up prostitutes for men as gifts of persuasion. Yet he personally disapproved of adultery and what he considered to be the coarsening of American culture.

"Don't call me 'sir,'" Anders said, "please. I think it was Reese, too. I wonder what A. Lloyd told him."

"We can only guess. Kyle, I think this is my fault."

"It's not your fault. It's the fault of the men who let him escape. They obviously underestimated him."

"Do you blame them?" Troy said, "The man is fifty years old. We've got men in their mid-thirties trying to pass our physical-endurance tests and failing. And these are former Green Berets, not rent-a-cops."

"You're talking about physical endurance. But there are more important factors. Like the ability to read a situation. Adaptability. Resourcefulness."

"You're saying you'd take him on here?"

"No. I'm saying we underestimated our quarry. That's why it's more important than ever that he be eliminated."

Troy said, "He doesn't know about you. You weren't on the screen when he went in."

Anders was briefly taken aback. He was always sensitive to any suggestion that he had not been in combat, or a soldier of consequence. After a moment, he decided no offense had been intended and that the remark had been inadvertently directed to his youth.

Anders said, "But he will know about me in time. He'll find out about our ties to Gelmers. And to Preston. So we're presented with a difficult situation. We have to find him before he finds us."

Troy said, "Maybe he won't even try. Maybe he's left the country by now."

"No," Anders said. "He'll go after Preston. And when he does, we'll be waiting for him."

Later that evening, Anders placed a call to one of his contacts in the CIA. Over the past few years, Anders had paid this contact almost $200,000 for his loyalty. After the preliminary affable falsehoods were exchanged, Anders asked the contact about John Reese. The contact told Anders that Reese had no family left. His wife had died of cancer while he was in prison. The contact said that Reese had never made close friends with anyone outside the Agency and very few inside.

Anders said, "I understand he did some E and E work. Smuggled some dissidents into the United States."

The contact said he understood that, too.

"Start with that," Anders said. "I want to hear from you tomorrow. Is that clear?"

The contact said it was.

THIRTEEN

Senator Preston's St. Louis home was in a leafy neighborhood between Ladue and Clayton. The neighborhood subdivision was in a hilly area, surrounded by woods and twisty roads. There was a gate at the entrance to the subdivision.

It was Captain Anthony who introduced Hastings to Senator Preston and his chief of staff, whose name was Martin Keough.

Martin Keough was in his late twenties, thin, dark haired, and small of stature. He was a graduate of Harvard Law School and he did not make eye contact with Hastings when they met.

Senator Preston shook hands and led them into a small office.

There were photos in Preston's office, mostly of him with famous, powerful guys. One of them was of Preston and President Bush. Another one was of Preston and Vernon Jordan, both of them laughing at something Bill Clinton had said. They appeared to be on a golf course somewhere. Preston photographed well.

Also on the office wall was a framed clipping of an op-ed piece from the *New York Times*. The headline read WHY WE CANNOT LET AL QAEDA PREVAIL IN IRAQ, and it was written by Alan Preston, junior senator from the state of Missouri.

Senator Preston took a seat behind his desk and gestured for the police officers to take seats. Martin Keough remained standing.

Dan Anthony told them that Hastings would be leading the team of officers that would be watching the Preston home and local senatorial offices.

Keough gave them a rough outline of the senator's schedule for the next few days. Keough said, "Now, we want you around, but we don't want you too close. Do you understand that?"

Keough had been looking at Captain Anthony when he spoke. But it was Hastings who responded.

"No," Hastings said, "I'm not sure I do."

Keough looked at Hastings, as if noticing his existence for the first time.

"Sorry?" Keough said, his tone patronizing.

Hastings said, "I understand you wanting us to be discreet, but are you requesting that we stay a certain distance away?"

"Yes."

The senator said, "Is there a problem, Lieutenant?"

"No, sir," Hastings said. "I'm just not sure what you want us to do."

Keough said, "Protect the senator. Hasn't that been clear?"

"To a point," Hastings said, "yes. But are you actually expecting, for lack of a better term, an assassination attempt?"

Keough sighed, muttered, "Christ."

Senator Preston said, "'Assassination attempt' is a little strong. But if you're asking if this man may be a danger to me and to my family, the answer is yes."

"Of course," Captain Anthony said, giving Hastings a look of warning.

Hastings ignored the look and said, "I understand that, sort of. But if there's a bona fide threat, why not call in federal officers?"

Keough spoke as if to a child. "What is the problem?"

Senator Preston raised a hand to his aide and said, "Hold on, Martin. Let the lieutenant have his say."

Hastings said, "Thank you. I just want you to understand, Senator, that me and my men, we're homicide detectives. We're not trained for security work. A Secret Service agent is trained to look through crowds and spot a possible assassin. But I'm not trained for that. Nor are my men."

"You're a police officer," Keough said. "Aren't you?"

Hastings kept his attention on the senator. "Of course," Hastings said. "But, with respect, that's not the point."

Senator Preston said, "I know what I'm getting. I've discussed this with your chief. As you've probably been told, it's very important that this thing be handled discreetly. Very discreetly. Lieutenant Hastings, this may surprise you, but, like most politicians, I have enemies in Washington. People who would like to embarrass me. To see me compromised. They would like nothing better than to see me make a fool of myself by requesting federal security I don't need. I don't care to be accused of seeking special privileges or of being paranoid."

Hastings said, "But this John Reese *is* dangerous. The file says the military trained him as a sniper. Given that, I don't think there should be any shame in taking official measures to protect yourself against him. If it were me he was after, I'd call in the Secret Service."

"But it's not you," Keough said. "Is it?"

Preston said, "Your point is perhaps valid. But I've given this some thought. It's my personal belief that John Reese is either dead or has fled the country. If he's alive, he's not going to risk getting caught by coming after me."

Hastings saw that Preston had just contradicted himself. Reese was a threat. Then he wasn't. Hastings said, "You say he won't risk coming after you. Why not?"

"Because he's a loser. John Reese cares about the well-being of John Reese, nothing else. However, my wife isn't as dispassionate about this as I am. She worries about me more than I do myself. Besides me, she worries about our daughter, who's a college student here. So. This is the solution I've come up with. A political solution for a family issue. Can you understand the position I'm in?"

"Yes, sir."

"We'll return to Washington in a few days. And then this task, which you seem to find distasteful, will be over for you."

Hastings mentally sighed to himself but otherwise did not respond.

Captain Anthony said, "We're glad to be of service to you, Senator."

Hastings stomached that and then saw Martin Keough raise his eyes as another person came into the room.

"Hello," the senator said, and Hastings turned around to see a regal blond woman in the doorway. She was in her forties. Slim and narrow at the waist, she was wearing a black-and-white dress with a belt in the middle. Hastings stood up.

"My wife, Sylvia Preston."

She came forward and extended a hand to Hastings, perhaps because he was the one standing closest to her.

Hastings introduced himself and the senator told her that these were the policemen who would be watching him.

Mrs. Preston looked into Hastings's eyes as she said, "Oh?"

Hastings said, "Yes, ma'am."

She said, "And do you think you'll be able to catch this man, Lieutenant?"

"I don't know," Hastings said.

She dropped her hand to her side, as if taken aback by his frankness. She kept her focus on Hastings, openly appraising him, as she said, "Don't you?" Her voice a little dry.

She's being tough, Hastings thought. Maybe she sensed something in him. A toughness to match her own. Or maybe she wanted to make him uncomfortable. Hastings debated answering her.

But Captain Anthony said, "We've got our best people working on it, Mrs. Preston."

Mrs. Preston said, "And I suppose that would include you two."

Anthony gave a sort of uncomfortable laugh.

Hastings said, "If he appears, Mrs. Preston. We don't know that he will."

"I see," Mrs. Preston said. "Well, at least you're honest."

This elicited more nervous laughter, from both Captain Anthony and Martin Keough. Hastings noticed, though, that the senator did not join in.

FOURTEEN

Klosterman said, "He said he's requesting police protection because of his wife?"

"Yeah," Hastings said.

"What do you think?"

"I think he's lying."

Hastings and Klosterman were in Hastings's Jaguar, heading west on the Forest Park Parkway, downtown fading behind them as the car dipped down the incline underneath Grand Boulevard and came up and out on the other side.

Hastings said, "Not about everything. I mean, I met the wife and, yeah, she's concerned. But I don't buy it when Preston says he's not worried. I could see that he *is* worried. So this notion about he's only doing this because his wife wants him to, that's a lot of shit."

"Maybe," Klosterman said, "but he's not going to admit that."

Hastings said, "Did I tell you about why he said he didn't want feds involved?"

"Yeah, you told me."

"That's fishy, too. If it were me and my family, I'd call in every man possible to guard me. I wouldn't care what anyone said."

"No," Klosterman said, "but you're not a politician. And you don't have anything to prove, either."

"What's he got to prove?"

"I don't know. He said something about enemies wanting to embarrass him?"

"Yeah. He said if he had federal agents guarding him, he would be 'compromised,' or some nonsense."

"Didn't Anthony tell you he might run for president?"

"Yeah, that's what Anthony says. I don't know. Maybe he will. If that's the case, he's probably more concerned about his political livelihood than anything else."

"You met the wife?"

"Yeah."

"What about her?"

"She's all right," Hastings said.

Hastings slowed the Jaguar for a light, coming to a stop behind an SUV. He thought of the cool blonde in her upscale dress, wondering if she had been a model when she was younger. Looking directly in his eyes, trying to push him around . . .

"I think she's all right," Hastings said again. "She was the first person in that house who didn't talk to me like I was there to cut the lawn."

Klosterman said, "You remember Bill Malone?"

"Yeah."

"He got on with the Secret Service a few years ago. He guarded that little guy who ran for president."

"Edwards?"

"No, the little guy with that good-looking young wife."

"Kucinich."

"Yeah. Bill said that the old hands talked about the best presidents to guard. Apparently, Ford was a real nice guy. Used to bring coffee to the agents when they had to stand out in the cold. Reagan liked to tan himself at his ranch, using one of those reflector thingies. Nixon was weird but okay. They said Carter was one of the worst."

"How so?"

"You know, looked down his nose at them. Treated them like they didn't exist."

"That right?"

"Yeah. Funny, don't you think? Him being a Democrat and all."

"Why should that be unusual?"

"Well, don't you remember? When Carter ran, he said he was a simple peanut farmer and all that crap. He used to wear those sweaters and he carried his own suitcases into the White House."

"Shit," Hastings said. "That was all show. I put more stock in what the people say who had to work with him."

"You ever think about something like that? Secret Service?"

"God no. I'd die of boredom."

"Yeah, I know what you mean. Bill said it was boring but pretty stressful, too. I mean, a lot of doing nothing, and then when you're in crowds with the president or whoever, you're anxious as hell. Looking out there to see if there's a Hinckley or a Travis Bickle."

"Travis Bickle? That's not a real guy. That's from a movie, isn't it?"

"Is it?"

"Yeah, Joe. Don't you remember? 'You talkin' to me? You talkin' to me?'"

Klosterman pointed a finger at him and said, "Dustin Hoffman."

"Robert De Niro."

"James Caan."

"No. It was De Niro," Hastings said, then realized that Klosterman knew it all along.

Joe Klosterman rolled his shoulders, acting out the rest of the scene. "'I don't see no one else here. Who the fuck you talking to?'"

"Okay," Hastings said, hoping that would shut it down.

But then he was doing Scorsese's lines from the film, saying, "'Have you ever seen what a forty-four Magnum would do to a woman's face? Fucking destroy it. Have you ever seen what a forty-four Magnum would do to a woman's—'"

"Enough," Hastings said.

"Okay," Klosterman said. "Yeah, I guess it would be pretty boring. Better pay, though. Say, do you think Amy Carter still has Secret Service agents protecting her?"

"I have no fucking idea."

Hastings made a left turn onto Kingshighway Boulevard, crossed over I-64, then made a right turn onto Oakland Avenue.

Klosterman said, "Preston's a Republican, isn't he?"

"Yeah. But he seemed a bit Carteresque to me today." Hastings shrugged. Screw it. He hadn't gone into police work to get the Alan Prestons of the world to like him. It was too much work, to begin with.

Klosterman said, "Did you vote for him?"

"I did once," Hastings said. "Not the second time."

"How come?"

"The war in Iraq, mostly. Which he supports, even now. I thought it was a good idea at first. Later I realized I was wrong."

"I told you," Klosterman said. Klosterman had said invading Iraq was a mistake from the beginning.

"Yeah," Hastings said. "You told me."

Hastings pulled the Jag into the parking lot of Imo's Pizza. He got out of the car and dialed Howard Rhodes's number.

"George?" Rhodes said.

"Hi, Howard. Joe and I will be there in about thirty minutes. We're picking up a pizza at Imo's. You guys want anything?"

"Hold on," Rhodes said. "Murph, you want anything from Imo's?"

A moment later, Rhodes said, "Yeah, he wants a medium pepperoni and sausage. He'll take it home with him."

"All right," Hastings said. "Anything happen?"

Rhodes said, "Not a damn thing."

FIFTEEN

They were given access to the house across the street. It wasn't for sale, but it was empty. The house was a three-story English Tudor with arched windows on the top floor. In the backyard, there was a crumbling, empty fish pond and fountain, along with a rusted swing set no one had bothered to remove. The house had been purchased by a man who made a fortune in auto parts. He died in the nineties and left his entire estate, worth around six million dollars, to his adult son, who spent the next few years snorting it away. Now the son owned the house but couldn't afford to furnish it or even have it fixed up so that it could be put on the market. The son, now in his forties, was on probation for possession of controlled substances. Accordingly, he was amenable to Captain Anthony's request to use the house for official police purposes.

From the top floor, the police officers had a good view of Senator Preston's house. There were no furnishings, so they had to bring cots and a couple of lawn chairs. They had a television but no cable. Murph had brought a rectangular boom box he had owned for fifteen years. When the television wasn't on, he liked to listen to classic rock on KSHE 95.

When Hastings and Klosterman came to relieve them, it was apparent that Murph and Rhodes were getting on each other's nerves. Murph was listening to a promo for a radio talk-show, the host saying that Miley Cyrus's dad was a jackoff. Murph laughing at it,

Rhodes saying, "It's not funny. I don't know why you think it's funny."

"Evening, ladies," Klosterman said as they came up the stairs.

Rhodes's shoulders sagged in relief. Grateful he would be getting out of there but depressingly aware he would have to come back in twelve hours.

Murph said, "Got a man here who doesn't like Howard Stern."

"He's not funny," Rhodes said as he set the binoculars on a table and moved across the room to get his jacket and coat.

They were different, the two of them. Howard Rhodes was tall and broad across the shoulders. Handsome, refined, and smooth. Many people at the department, including Hastings, thought he would rise quickly. Unfortunately, many would also credit such a rise to affirmative action, as Rhodes was an African-American. But the people who worked closely with Howard knew he was very capable, hardworking, and conscientious and that he would deserve a promotion in time, irrespective of appearances. Howard Rhodes had been a detective for only a few years, most of them under the supervision of Hastings. Like many homicide detectives, Rhodes was a bit of an elitist. There was an aristocratic air about him. This was natural, not feigned. He was not an overconfident man, but he was confident.

Tim "Murph" Murphy, in contrast, was not physically big. He had the size and build of a bantamweight fighter. He wore knit ties and short-sleeve shirts and tweed jackets. After a heavy lunch, he might weigh 150 pounds. But there was a wild-eyed fearsomeness to Murph, an Irish cop air of menace and intimidation that could, as Klosterman said, make a perp piss down both legs. When Murph and Rhodes did the good cop/bad cop act (which is effective even when the suspect knows it is being done), it was usually Rhodes who played the good cop. It's difficult for a pit bull to act nice.

They were like brothers, in a way—bickering and fighting but confiding and sharing, too. Murph was what some would call a typical South St. Louis "hoosier." An uncultivated yokel. And to all outward appearances, that was indeed what he looked like and, to a degree, took pride in. He was a snob, too, in his way. Yet a career in law enforcement had made him tribal, uncomfortable around people who weren't police officers. The same thing had happened to Rhodes, who could now count on one hand the number of good friends he had who were black.

Murph had once told Hastings he had grown up in a household where the word *nigger* was used frequently by both his parents. When he matured and made his own decisions about life, he said this was not something he could write his parents off for. They were, in his mind, otherwise decent people. He told Hastings that was how people talked in that time and in that place. Certainly, as a child, Murph had never imagined that one of his closest friends would be black. Indeed, after working with Howard for a while, Murph sort of *forgot* that Howard was black. Or rather, he forgot and he didn't forget. The two of them could have the most candid discussions about race one could imagine. Perhaps this was because Murph felt little, if any, of the discomfort or guilt that whites often feel around black people. Or perhaps it was because both Murph and Rhodes thought of themselves as more blue than black or white.

Now Murph gestured to the police-issue Ithaca pump shotgun

propped up in the corner. He said to Hastings, "I'm going to leave that here, if it's all right."

"Yeah," Hastings said. He had the same model shotgun in the trunk of his car.

Hastings handed Murph his pizza.

"Smells great," Murph said. "You want a slice, Howard?"

"No."

Howard Rhodes descended the stairs, Murph calling out "Okay" to him, patronizing him.

Murph said, "He's not enjoying this detail."

"At least he got the day shift," Klosterman said.

Murph said, "Well, there's a game on the NFL network tonight, if you get bored. But then, there's no cable here. Well, enjoy yourself, boys."

Murph went down the stairs. Klosterman picked up the binoculars and moved to the window.

A minute or so later, he said, "Did you say the senator's wife is good-looking?"

"I might have," Hastings said.

"I wonder if she leaves her shades up."

"I hope not," Hastings said. Then he dialed Carol's number on his cell phone. Four rings and then he got her voice mail. Hastings left a message and clicked off the phone. He wondered if she was with someone else. Then he felt ashamed for wondering.

A few minutes later, his cell phone rang. He picked it up but saw a number that was not Carol's.

"Hastings."

"Lieutenant? Martin Keough. The senator's expecting a guest in about fifteen minutes. So don't get all alarmed when you see a car at the gate."

Hastings took a breath, thought, Asshole. "I won't," he said. "Who's the guest?"

"A friend of the senator," Keough said, and hung up.

SIXTEEN

A maid asked if Crittenden would like some tea or a drink. Crittenden said, no but that some ice water would be nice. The servant walked out of the room and Crittenden was left alone in the living room with Senator Preston and Keough.

Crittenden said, "So you're interested in running for president?"

Preston said, "I'm exploring the idea, yes. I wanted to see what you thought."

"Why?"

Preston said, "To be frank, I think you wouldn't sign on with a candidate unless you thought he could win. Am I correct?"

Crittenden smiled. "Perhaps," he said.

Jeff Crittenden was a nationally known political consultant and strategist. In the past ten years, he had built a formidable reputation managing campaigns for Republican candidates. He was considered one of the top three political strategists in the country. Though he lacked the charisma and flamboyance of a James Carville, he was just as effective, perhaps more so. He preferred to remain out of the limelight as much as possible. Indeed, there were times he denied having the influence he actually had. Surely, he would suggest, a mere Texas Tech dropout was incapable of being Machiavellian.

People presumed Jeff Crittenden was a religious man. This was because he encouraged almost all of his candidates to appeal to religious conviction in their campaigns. Even the Democrats were doing that these days. But Crittenden was actually an atheist. This fact, he kept to himself. Despite his lack of faith, he did have a certain admiration for the Old Testament's Joseph, counselor to the pharaohs.

What he wanted to do was create a president.

Crittenden said to Preston, "You don't wish to persuade me?"

"I'm not going to persuade you," Preston said. "You either believe in the viability of my campaign or you don't."

"Suppose I don't?"

"We shake hands and say good-bye. And maybe I'll find another consultant."

"Of course."

Keough said, "There are others."

Preston gave Keough a disapproving look. Then he said to Crittenden, "Yes, there are others. But frankly, I think you're the best. I'd prefer to have you on board. So."

"So what?" Crittenden said.

"So do you think I can win?"

The maid returned with a glass of ice water on a tray. Crittenden took the water, sipped it, and sat back. The maid left the room.

Crittenden said, "I think so."

He left it out there. The men grew uncomfortable with the shortness of the answer and Keough said, "You *think* so? That's it, you think so?"

"I'm an adviser," Crittenden said, "not a seer. There are variables that we can't predict." Crittenden looked at the senator. He said, "You're good-looking, you speak well, and you're even-keeled. You're still married to your first wife. Am I correct?"

"Yes."

"No early marriages we're unaware of?"

"No."

"No girlfriends we're unaware of?"

Crittenden did not like using words like *prostitute* or *mistress*. They seemed dated to him and a little too French.

"No," Preston said. "That's not my style."

Crittenden raised a conciliatory hand. "I don't judge, Senator. But I don't like being surprised, either. You understand that a senator has certain freedoms a president or presidential candidate does not have. The freedom to drink, carouse, lose his temper, perhaps even have reactionary views about race. You declare your candidacy for president, it all vanishes."

"You don't think I've considered that already?"

"You *say* you have. But have you? Have you really? Your wife, your daughter ... they lose their privacy, too. Everything will be inspected, opened up. Everything. Past and present."

"I know that, too."

"And you've discussed it with them? You've discussed this with your wife and daughter?"

"Yes."

"What do they say?"

"They're all for it," Preston said. "I suppose you have some concerns?"

"Pardon?"

"Perhaps you have some concerns yourself," Preston said.

Crittenden shrugged. Despite his soft appearance, he was not easily intimidated.

Preston said, "Perhaps you're worried that you'll devote time and effort and, perhaps most importantly, your reputation to my campaign, only to find out that I'm washed out in New Hampshire."

Crittenden said, "Let's not get ahead of ourselves."

"Well, that's not going to happen," Preston said. "I'm not the self-destructing type."

Keough said, "We've taken some polls—"

"I know," Crittenden said.

There was a momentary silence.

Then Keough said, "You know? How could you know?"

Another gesture. Crittenden said, "The initial numbers are impressive, I agree. But, at this stage, polls are essentially meaningless. Gary Hart polled well. So did same guy named Lamar Alexander."

Keough said, "So you're not interested?"

"I didn't say that," Crittenden said. "Let us say I'm intrigued. If you are indeed serious, would you be amenable to hiring a private detective agency?"

Preston said, "To investigate whom?"

"You."

Another silence.

Keough said, "Are you making this a precondition? Because if you are—"

Preston raised his hand again. "Martin," he said. "You misunderstand our friend here. He is a serious man. And he wants to win." Preston smiled. "We do, too. The answer, Mr. Crittenden, is yes. I would gladly hire a private detective agency to investigate me. I'll even pay for it. I'm confident they would find nothing."

Now, Crittenden was quiet, perhaps impressed for the first time since his arrival.

And Preston pushed into him a little, saying, "Okay?"

Crittenden smiled and said, "Let's discuss this again in a week."

The parting was quick and polite. After Crittenden was gone, Keough said, "What was that about?"

Preston sighed to himself. Maybe he would have to get rid of Martin when he made it to the White House. The man was loyal and aggressive, but sometimes he simply did not think.

Preston said, "Don't you see? The little bastard was testing me. If I'd hesitated the least bit when he brought up the private investigation, he would have decided I wasn't worth working for."

"Oh."

"He'll come on board," Preston said. "I can feel it."

Keough left the house and Preston went upstairs to his bedroom.

Sylvia was there, sitting in a chair reading *The Age of Innocence*. She wore a checkered bathrobe over her nightie.

"Hey," Preston said. "I thought you read that already."

"I have," she said.

Preston retreated to the large walk-in closet and began undressing. He came out a few moments later in his pajamas and went to the bathroom. He was looking in the mirror when he heard her ask him if he'd had a visitor.

"Pardon?"

Sylvia said, "You and Martin were speaking with someone downstairs. Who was it?"

"Oh," he said. "Jeff Crittenden. You remember him, don't you?"

"Yes. We met at the White House correspondents' dinner." Sylvia set the book down and looked over at the bathroom door.

The door was open and she could see her husband's reflection in the mirror.

"He was here?" she asked.

"Yes."

"He flew out here to see you?"

"Yes." Alan Preston began flossing his teeth. He stopped after a moment and said, "Well, he called and asked if he could speak with me personally. I said he could if he wanted."

"What did you speak about?"

"He wants me to run for president."

"He wants you to run?"

"Yeah. He was trying to talk me into it. Said I'd be a great candidate, blah, blah, blah. I told him I'd think about it."

After a moment, Sylvia said, "That's more than you told me."

"What are you talking about?" Alan said. "I told you."

"No, you didn't, Alan. You told me the field was thin and that you were as good as any of the other candidates in contention."

"Same thing."

"It's not the same thing."

"How so?"

"Don't cross-examine me. I'm not a witness at one of your hearings."

"I'm not cross-examining you. I just want to know how what I said before was not an indication that I might run for president."

"That's a convoluted question," Sylvia said. "And kind of a shitty one, too. Alan."

"What?"

"Remember when you first ran for office, when you first ran for

Congress? You came to me and you asked me what I thought. And then you told me all the good things that could come of it and some of the bad things."

"Yeah."

"You said it would be a thing we would do together and that if I didn't want you to do it, you wouldn't do it."

"It's the same thing here."

"No, it isn't. You used to ask. Now you tell."

"Oh, let's not go overboard here. If you don't want me to do it, I won't do it. Nothing's changed."

"Sometimes I fear that it has."

Alan came out of the bathroom. He looked down at his wife and said, "Why do you say things like that? You trying to be dramatic? What have I done to disappoint you? You live well. You've got a good home, a good life."

"I'm not complaining about . . . things. Not material things."

"Okay. *Things* aside, have I ever mistreated you? Have I ever been unfaithful? Abused you?"

"Oh, for God's sake. No. That's not what I'm talking about."

"What *are* you talking about?"

"Don't patronize me, Alan. I don't like that."

"I'm not trying to patronize you. I'm just trying to understand where you're coming from. You're speaking to me as if I've been some sort of lousy husband."

"I never said that."

"Maybe you think it."

"I don't think it, either." She gave her husband a look and said, "I don't, Alan."

Alan said, "It's not like I dragged you into this. When I won the congressional seat, you were ecstatic. You liked being my wife. You liked all of it."

"It was different then."

"How?"

"When you were a congressman, it was ... I don't know, simpler. You took it seriously, but not too seriously. We had parties and we had friends. Washington was fun then. We used to make fun of people. We used to laugh together. That seemed to change when you won the Senate seat."

"Look, I'm still the same person. If I take things more seriously now, it's because the times are more serious. If I meet with someone like Jeff Crittenden, it doesn't mean I don't love you or respect you."

He was looking at her now, offering something vaguely resembling an apology. Or pretending to. He seemed to sense her dissatisfaction with his words and said, "I'm sorry I didn't discuss it with you first. I should have told you he was coming by."

"It's okay," Sylvia said. "I'm sorry I got upset. I think this Reese person has me worried."

"I told you not to worry about that."

"Aren't you worried about it?"

"No."

She looked at him. He tried to mask it, but she knew he wasn't being truthful. He was anxious, and she knew it. She waited for him to change his answer.

But he didn't. Instead, he said, "Sylvia, I've never hidden the fact that I'm ambitious. Not from you."

"No, I suppose you haven't. I just hoped we had reached a place where you didn't want...more."

"I won't take any steps without checking with you first. You know that."

"I know."

"Now can we go to sleep?"

"Yes. I'll be there in a minute."

Alan got in bed and Sylvia walked to the bathroom. She closed the door and looked at herself in the mirror. A middle-aged woman looked back at her, seeming to say, Well, here you are.

Go back and look at your life, she thought, if you've got the courage to do it. Sylvia Rains of Mount Prospect, Illinois. The daughter of the owner of a construction firm. She had grown up in that Chicago suburb in relative wealth. Her dad was what he called "small-town rich." Sylvia was the eldest of five children. People always told her she was smart and pretty. She had a great future. When the time came for her to go to college, her dad said he wanted her to go to a Catholic university so she could meet a nice Catholic boy. She could choose whatever Catholic school she liked and he would pay for it. She chose Villanova. When she finished her undergraduate studies, she enrolled in the law school. After that, she got a job in Washington working for a congressional committee.

She loved Washington. She liked its pace, its insularity, its small-town parochialism. For her, it was a great place for a woman in her twenties. A lot of men asked her out and a few older ones made passes at her. She was always gracious in her rejections. Two years zipped by and she met Alan Preston at a party.

What struck her about him was that he seemed like a gentleman.

He was obviously interested in her, but he didn't hit on her. He was cautious about that sort of thing. She knew then that he was a very focused man. She also suspected, early on, that he wanted to marry her.

She was not put off by this. He was always polite and well mannered and seemingly attentive. They talked about politics because they both enjoyed it. She learned that he was also a Catholic. He was from St. Louis. In time, she also learned that he had come from a rather humble background. He did not tell her this, but she was intuitive enough to figure it out. He did not say much about his parents. Once, she asked him what his father had done for a living. He answered that his father was in sales and said nothing more. She got the feeling that Alan thought his father was a failure.

Alan was a handsome man, but he didn't smile much. In time, Sylvia realized this was because his lower teeth were crooked and ugly and he was embarrassed by them. Sylvia had had crooked teeth, too, but her parents could afford to give her braces when she was a teenager. Before Alan ran for Congress, he had his teeth fixed by one of the best dentists in Washington. He smiled more after that.

Before they married, Sylvia took Alan to her parents' house for a visit. Her little brother would later tell her that Alan reminded him of Eddie Haskell. Sylvia got angry and defensive. Alan had had a hard life, she said. He had come from nothing and he had made himself into something. He had not had the sort of advantages they had had. Say what you want about Alan, but there was no question that he tried and that he worked very hard.

When they returned from her parents, Alan asked her to marry him.

Sylvia said, "Why do you want to marry me?"

"Because I think you're the kindest, most decent woman I've ever known. I admire you, I respect you, and I love you."

It had sounded rehearsed to her, even then. But he had never been the smooth romancing type. And that was partly why he appealed to her.

"You didn't say I was pretty," Sylvia said.

"That goes without saying."

And maybe that wasn't rehearsed. She told him she'd think about it. Three months later, she accepted his proposal.

She loved him, she supposed. He had been good to her, as he said. He listened to her and sometimes sought her input on minor issues. But over the years, she started to wonder if he really engaged with her. Once, at a fund-raiser, she saw him talking with the wife of a man who owned an aerospace company. Alan talked to the woman as if she were the most fascinating, interesting person he had ever met. He did so because he wanted her financial contributions. Sylvia was repelled by it, even though she knew that kissing up to such people was part of the political game. Yet . . . there was something else, too. And eventually she figured out what it was: Alan sometimes acted the same way when he talked to *her*, his own wife. Maybe he also told the aerospace manufacturer's wife she was the kindest, most decent woman he had ever known.

Was it all a performance? She wondered. Did he love her? Or did she simply fit the part he needed her to play? The good-looking, mentally stable, even-keeled wife. Their sex life was not especially active. They made love a couple of times a month, but it was perfunctory. She had never thought that Alan had any latent homosexual tendencies. She believed that sex just wasn't that important to him. He was not a man of strong libido. Indeed, he may even have been asexual. That was why it irritated her when he pointed out he'd never been unfaithful to her. No, she thought, he hadn't. But he was not the sort to be tempted by other women.

Alan was smart and he knew how to argue. He was a man who always thought about what he said before he said it. What he had said tonight was ... *perhaps* correct. But it was a little too clever, maybe even calculated. Had he communicated with her, or had he just said the things that he knew would placate her? Had he worked her? Was there a difference?

At times, she felt sorry for herself and wondered if she should have had been more adventurous before she married. Had an affair with a lifeguard or maybe an airline pilot. But she knew that was silly, because she had never been a wild girl and she had always been vaguely repulsed by slutty women. She had behaved herself because it was what she wanted to do. She had played by the rules of polite society and married a proper, decent citizen, and now she was unhappy and empty. And at the same time, she was angry at herself for indulging in what she believed might be adolescent self-pity.

Her mother had once told her, "You can't expect much from a marriage. You can't expect a husband to give you total happiness. That's not realistic. The steady, stable ones will bore you. The exciting ones will always let you down. They'll drink too much or gamble, or they'll cheat on you. You can't have it all."

Maybe her mother had been right. Maybe she just needed to grow up, not ask so much from life. Her mother liked Alan. She said he was a good man.

Her father, though, had never warmed to him and had always kept him at arm's length. Her father had died the previous year. Sylvia had not gotten the opportunity to ask him what he really thought of Alan. She knew that if she had asked him, it would have been a sort of betrayal of Alan. Yet she had respected her father more than any man she had ever known, and she knew he was no poor judge of character.

Now she was forty-five years old. Her father was gone and her mother was unable to understand how she could feel any discontent. Now she was looking at her life and wondering if she was changing or if she was finally seeing her husband clearly. All this . . . mysterious behavior, this keeping of secrets. Alan considering a run at the White House while some escaped convict was out there making bizarre threats against him. Alan was scared and he was pretending not to be. She was his wife. Why couldn't he just tell her things?

Across the street, Hastings lowered the binoculars.

The lights in the master bedroom had gone off a couple of minutes ago. Hastings had let his view drift to the upstairs window. There, he'd seen the senator's wife walk by.

She'd been dressed, wearing a bathrobe of some sort. Not undressed, but Hastings still felt sleazy. Peeper. Pervert.

Klosterman would say it was her fault for not having drawn the shades. But they didn't have shades over there. They had curtains. And this woman hadn't drawn them shut. Besides, what difference did it make? She hadn't been getting undressed in front of the window. She must have done it elsewhere. It was just by chance he had focused the binocs on the window. He hadn't seen anything.

Except he had. The woman standing in front of the window had been talking to someone he couldn't see. Probably her husband. Hastings couldn't hear what she was saying, but her facial expression had told him she was pissed off.

Like most detectives, Hastings liked to observe people. Generally, it wasn't something he needed binoculars to do. He could see people in restaurants, in lines at movie theaters, at sporting events, church socials, et cetera. On his first date with Carol, he informed her that a man sitting at another table with a woman was gay but pretending to be straight and that the woman was looking for a rich husband. That was an easy one. Hastings had never met either one of them. But he looked at them and read body language, which is almost always more truthful than speech. He was showing off for Carol, doing something any reasonably good, experienced detective could do. Carol had snorted at his lowbrow determination and teased him about it, but she had been impressed in spite of herself. She had liked him back then. She'd thought he was interesting and intriguing and kind. And he'd been new to her.

He no longer was. Now they knew each other pretty well, and it was a problem. She still hadn't returned the call he'd made to her at the beginning of his shift.

Klosterman said, "What's up?"

Hastings said, "It looks like they've gone to bed."

SEVENTEEN

Reese took a seat at the bar.

The bartender, a cute woman in her thirties, said, "We're closed."

Reese held up a twenty-dollar bill, putting it under the small bar lamp so the barmaid could see it.

"Whiskey," Reese said.

"We're closed."

Reese lowered his hand. Raised it again. This time, there were two twenties.

"Whiskey," he said again.

The bartender sighed and said, "All right. Just one. Then I want to get home."

Reese nodded and told her Johnnie Walker Black doubled would be fine.

She brought it to him and Reese noticed that she was very pretty in an earthy way. She took one of the twenty-dollar bills and went to make change.

"No," Reese said. "We made a deal."

"It's okay," she said.

"No, take it."

The bartender gave him a look and said, "I'm not like that. I don't feel comfortable—"

"I don't expect anything," Reese said. "Just a drink."

He was at the bar in his hotel. Earlier, he had fallen asleep in his room with the television on, then awoke from a nightmare.

It had started out nice. In the dream, Sara was not well. But they were together. She was pale and weak, but she was in the passenger seat next to him in his car. They were driving to the top of a mountain in Colorado. The day was cool and sunny but not cold. Reese had opened the sunroof and the wind was blowing across her face. She was so beautiful. Even with her head scarf on and her eyebrows fading. The cancer was spreading and now they knew it would take her life, but they would have this day together. She looked over at him and smiled, and he smiled back. He was happy, so happy, that she had come into his life and given it meaning and purpose. He had grown empty and soulless, a shell, and then he'd met Sara and was reborn. She took his hand and said, "I'm getting better, you know." And John said that, yes, she was.

The road twisted and curved and banked and then they were at the top. Reese intended to open her door for her, but when he got out of the car, she was already out, too, walking over to him, extending her hand. He took her hand and together they walked to the parapet, which would give them a glorious view of the valley below.

He got to the edge and looked over and saw . . . nothing. No yellow and brown and green. Just cold mist and emptiness. He turned to his wife. She was gone.

"Sara," he said.

Nowhere to be seen.

"Sara!"

He turned and looked at empty faces. Other tourists or demons. He asked them, "Where is she? Where's Sara?"

No one answered him.

He cried and screamed. *No! This was supposed to be their day.*

Just one day to have together. She deserved this day. How, how could they take this away from her?

Reese woke up, shouting. Soon he realized he was in a hotel room and not in a prison cell. Then he remembered he was in a no-name place outside of a no-name town in West Virginia. He made it to the bathroom before he began crying.

He feared returning to bed. He considered the hotel room and thought he had never felt more alone in his life. He had escaped prison for this. A room alone. He left the room and went to the bar.

Reese had known a man in the army who had been captured by the Vietcong and imprisoned in Hanoi. He was freed in 1973 with most of the other soldiers and allowed to return home. The man told Reese that every day he could get out of bed and walk out a door that was not locked was a good day.

But Reese knew another soldier who spent four years imprisoned and got out, only to learn that his wife had left him for another man. A soldier whose children considered him a stranger. That man never recovered.

Reese could leave his hotel room and walk to a bar. But he could not escape his loneliness and grief. He had not imagined that he would miss his Sara more once he was out of prison. But he did. He knew it was not logical.

His reticence intrigued the bartender. She was not a beautiful woman, but she was an attractive, approachable one and she was used to being hit on by customers.

She said to him, "In town for the night?"

He looked straight ahead, not at her. "Yes," he said.

"What's your name?"

"Paul."

"What do you do?"

"Business."

"What sort of business?"

He turned and regarded her. His expression was neither rude nor warm.

"Hardware," he said. "I'm sorry, I'm not much of a conversationalist."

"You look tired."

"I'll be finished soon."

"No, that's not what I meant," the girl said. "I mean, stay as long as you like. I'm not going anywhere."

The girl placed her fingertips near his hand. "Maybe you'd like to talk," she said.

"No, not really."

"Maybe something else."

He looked at her again. "No, not really."

"You don't fancy me?"

It did not occur to Reese that he had not been with a woman in over thirteen years. Arrest and then trial about a year later and then a lifetime sentence. Most men, upon getting out, would have gone straight to the nearest brothel. Or their wives.

Reese said, "I'm sorry. I'm married."

"Oh. I didn't know. I mean, you're not wearing a ring."

They had taken the ring away from him. It was still at the federal penitentiary.

Reese's words had the effect of making her more determined. She said, "Are you sure?"

"I'm sure. Thank you."

The bartender walked off and Reese glanced at her backside. She was young and she reminded him of someone he knew. Sharon? Or was it Rita? It was Rita, the preacher's daughter. Rita never said no to anyone.

God, what? Over thirty years ago...

Rita Fay Cutler. Not beautiful, but hot and dirty and willing, with a blouse full of promise...

Berry, Texas. A small oil town about a hundred miles from Dallas. Moderately affluent before the oil bust of 1984. John Reese was one of three hundred or so students at the town's only high school. He had been working construction after school then. Making four dollars an hour, which was good money for a teenager in the seventies. At the age of eighteen, he had saved enough money to buy a Li'l Hustler Datsun pickup, one of the best vehicles he would ever own. He would take Rita Fay out to the lake in it, get it up to about ninety on the back roads as she screamed in delight, "Faster, *faster.*" They would park the truck in a secluded area and make love under blankets nearby. There had been girls before Rita Fay, but they had been quick, uncomfortable affairs. Rita Fay was like a woman, demanding and experienced, giving him explicit direction. John Reese was soon mad for her.

Rita Fay had to hide him from her parents, particularly her father. John Reese was a bastard and, worse, a Catholic. Born out of wedlock, he never knew his father. His mother was a cashier at Otasco. She made extra money cleaning the church on Saturdays. She also made a point of taking her only son to Mass every Sunday. When John Reese was a child, most churches did not extend warm welcomes to unwed mothers. But his mother made sure that John received First Communion, in spite of the pointed fingers and hushed gossip. When he reached adolescence, his mother was no longer in a position to force him to go to church.

Reese's mother told him that Rita Fay Cutler was no good. She would lie to him and twist him around and then get rid of him when he no longer amused her. John said he loved her and that they had talked about getting married.

John Reese thought it would work. After high school, he would work full time for the construction company. He would be able to afford his own place. Rita Fay would attend the local junior college. They would see what their futures would be.

About a month before graduation, he and Rita Fay were at a party. Rita Fay told John that another boy was bothering her. The other boy's name was Carl Sommersby. He was bigger than Reese and was on the football team. He also had friends, three or four of them.

John Reese was a loner. He was not a social outcast and he had never been picked on. But he was not a popular kid, either. If he was considered at all, he was thought to be a no-account, nameless figure who had never distinguished himself. Generally, he was left alone.

But Rita Fay, the preacher's daughter, was the sort of girl who liked boys to compete for her. It made her feel valuable. It gave her a kick, too. She liked kicks. Had John Reese not been a hormonal teenager, had he been older and wiser, he would have told the girl to handle it on her own, smiled, and said good-bye. But eighteen-year-old boys generally don't have that sort of insight.

Still, John Reese was more mature than most kids his age. When Carl Sommersby taunted him and tried to get him to fight, Reese said to Rita Fay, "Let's go."

He would remember later that Rita Fay did not answer, just smiled. So Reese turned his back and started to walk away. That was when the Sommersby kid shoved him in the back.

Things happened quickly then. Reese stumbled but did not lose his footing. He turned around and, with no warning, hit the Sommersby boy in the nose, using the heel of his hand, not his fist. Somehow, Reese knew the heel of his hand would be more effective and that noses break easily and that most men are unnerved by the sight of their own blood. Sommersby bellowed and then made a mad rush for him. That was when Reese kicked him in the knee, using the bigger boy's weight against him. Sommersby screamed and went down.

Bystanders later said they heard two cracks: one for the nose, another for the knee.

What struck the other boys was how efficient and businesslike it had been. Reese did not fight the way a kid did. It was as if something quiet and deadly was just *in* him. A violent warrior in the body of a kid. A sleeping dragon.

The police arrested Reese the next day. He was charged with aggravated assault and battery. In the next few days, John Reese would learn that he no longer had a job at the construction company, that his mother could not afford to hire an attorney, that the Sommersby boy's knee was shattered and he was therefore no longer eligible to receive his college football scholarship. He would also learn that not only were Sommersby and his friends ready to testify against him but Rita Fay Cutler was, too. The district attorney informed Reese and his mother that John would be tried as an adult. He was, after all, eighteen now.

Carl Sommersby's father was a man of some influence in the community. Previously, he had prevented a charity foundation from building a home for mentally disabled adults in his neighborhood. He had a seat on the town commission and he owned the most profitable farm machinery dealership in the county. He was not wealthy by worldwide standards, but he was small-town rich, and that can mean a great deal in local affairs. Mr. Sommersby wanted John Reese to go to prison.

The local judge, an elected official, saw where this was going. He intervened and, with considerable effort, brokered a proposition: John Reese could join the army or he could go to prison for two years.

John Reese chose the army. He returned to Berry, Texas, only once. And that was for his mother's funeral.

EIGHTEEN

Hastings met Carol at the Starbucks in Clayton, at the intersection of Hadley and Wydown.

They exchanged uncomfortable pleasantries. Soon Carol said, "You look tired."

He told her about his latest assignment.

She said, "I'm sorry I didn't return your call last night."

Were you out with another man? Hastings thought. But he knew that would be a cop's question. Paranoid, suspicious. You had to shut it off sometimes.

"It's okay," Hastings said.

"And I'm sorry about the other night, too. I think maybe I over-reacted."

"Oh, I don't think so."

"I've never left a man alone at a restaurant before." She raised her eyebrows. "Such drama."

"I sort of sprung something on you."

"You did. But I could have handled it better."

They both avoided talking about children.

Carol said, "So what's Senator Preston like?"

"I'm supposed to keep the assignment confidential."

"Even from me? I'm not the gossipy type."

"No, you're not," Hastings said. "He's an asshole. His wife seems okay, though."

"Sylvia Preston? I saw her once downtown having lunch. She is very pretty. She has that sort of conventional, plastic blond look that would look good in front of a camera."

Hastings frowned. "I don't think she's actually like that."

"Oh? You like her?"

"No, I just talked with her for a second."

"So you don't think she's just a showpiece."

"I don't know her well enough to say that she is or that she isn't. I'm just saying that there might be more to her than looking good in front of a camera."

Carol shook her head, smiling. It was a small thing, and usually Hastings would take it good-naturedly. But for some reason, he didn't like it now.

Hastings said, "What does that mean?"

"Nothing."

"Well, you meant something."

"I guess I meant that I'm just not surprised."

"About what?"

"That you would defend her. Another pretty blonde."

"Another? . . . Are you referring to Eileen?"

Carol shrugged.

"Christ, Carol. That's a hell of thing to say."

"Oh, George, don't be so sensitive. It's just a comment."

"You just said I was superficial. A woman's a pretty blonde, so I defend her."

"Look, all men are superficial. So don't get uptight about it."

"Well, shit."

"You defended a woman when I suggested that she may be . . . less than substantial."

"So what?"

"Would you have done that if Mrs. Preston had been dumpy and plain?"

"Maybe. Would you have insulted her if she was dumpy and plain?"

"I didn't insult her."

"You did, actually. You said she would look good in front of a camera. Like that's pretty much all there is to her."

"Well, she is a politician's wife. And you yourself said her husband was a shitbird."

"That's not her fault."

"She married him. Birds of a feather."

"Who knows why she married him? Who are we to judge? We're both divorced."

"So what?"

Hastings said, "I just think you're better than this."

"Better than—what do you mean?"

"Better than hacking on some woman just because she's blond and pretty. You don't know her."

"I know you, though. I know your weaknesses."

"For what?"

"You know."

"Oh, that's right. Superficial blond women. Like Eileen, right?"

"Yes. Like Eileen."

"You don't know her, either."

"And you do?"

"I was married to her. I know her better than you."

"You do and you don't, George. Every week it's the same thing.

She does something to piss you off, you get mad at her, she gets mad at you, and then two days later, you're on the phone with her, laughing at some cute thing she says."

"Sometimes she's funny. It doesn't mean—"

"Yeah, it doesn't mean anything. I know. I've heard it before. But she makes you laugh, George."

"Don Rickles makes me laugh, too. I don't want to climb into bed with him."

"You don't understand. When I hear that, it hurts."

"Why? Why should it hurt you? She's funny, yeah. She's always been funny. But she's also a fuckup, and I have no intention of getting back with her. She's not my wife. She's not my lover. You have no reason to be threatened by her. None."

"It's an intimacy. It's another sign of intimacy. You always let her off the hook, George. Always."

"You know, I don't know what you want. Am I supposed to end every conversation with her by saying 'I hate you'?"

"You can let her go."

"Well, now you *are* being dramatic. I did let her go. She's gone. She's Amy's mother. I can't very well ask her to move to another state."

Three more customers came into the coffee shop. The line extended and a girl near the back of it took out her BlackBerry to send a text message.

Hastings said, "Carol, you once asked me if Eileen wanted me to take her back, what I would do. Do you remember that?"

"I asked you that a long time ago."

"And what did I say?"

"You said you wouldn't."

"Did you believe that?"

"Yes."

"Don't you still believe that?"

"I do."

"Then . . . what?"

"I just don't see why you still have to be friendly to her."

"I'm friendly to her because she's my friend. And she's the mother of my daughter. If I've given you a reason to distrust me when it comes to Eileen, I'm sorry. But I really don't think I have."

"I trust you, George. I do. But I don't like you being nice to her. I don't like it when you show warmth to her. I wish I were more adult about this. I wish I could be more understanding about it. But I just . . . don't think I can anymore. There. I've said it."

After a moment, Hastings said, "I don't understand. Are you giving me an ultimatum?"

"No," Carol said. "It's not an ultimatum. It's a realization." She looked at him for what seemed too short a time. Then she said, "I need a few days, George. We've got some problems here and we may not be able to resolve them. I need a few days to think about things. Will you give me that?"

NINETEEN

Hastings climbed into his bed an hour later. He got almost four hours sleep before his cell phone rang. He thought it might be Carol calling to patch things up. But it wasn't.

Eileen said, "Did I wake you?"

"Yes. What is it?"

"Nothing. Do you want to go back to sleep? I can call back later."

"I'm up now." Hastings did little to mask his irritation.

Eileen said, "Okay. I just wanted to call and say I was sorry for being a turd the other night."

"Forget it." Bad behavior, followed by apologies, followed by forgiveness. Carol was right.

"Sorry," Eileen said again.

"Really, forget it."

"I mean I'm sorry I woke you up, too."

Christ, Hastings thought. "It's all right," he said. "I needed to get up anyway." Sometimes it was hard to make anger at Eileen last.

Eileen said, "What are you doing in bed? Are you sick?"

Hastings explained his latest assignment to her.

"Geez," she said. "Did you make someone mad?"

"I sure did."

"What's Senator Preston like?"

"He's a fucking jackass. Is Amy all right?"

"Yeah, she's at school. Where she should be. If you're on this guard duty thing, will you need me to keep her until it's over?"

"I think I will. I should know more today."

"No hurry. I don't mind doing it."

"Thanks, Eileen."

"It's all right. How's your girlfriend?"

"Ahhh . . . I think she kind of broke it off with me."

"Seriously?"

"Yeah, that's how it looks."

"Maybe it's temporary."

"Probably not. She said she needs a few days to think."

"About?"

"What a shithead I am, probably."

Eileen laughed. "Yeah. All that time she wasted with you."

"Well, I don't think it's funny," Hastings said. "Jesus, Eileen."

"Sorry. Are you all right?"

"I will be."

"I'm sorry I laughed. It's just that I saw it coming."

Hastings thought for a moment. Then he said, "Do you and Amy talk about her?"

"No more than you and Amy talk about my husband."

"Okay. Fair enough."

"Let me guess," Eileen said. "Something to do with Amy, right?"

"Eileen, I'm really not comfortable discussing—"

"She didn't want to be a mom. Right?"

"That's none of your—"

"George, it was obvious. I may be a neurotic mess, but I love my kid. And she's my kid."

"Yeah, she's your kid."

"You want to get married again, that's fine. But you're going to have a hard time finding someone who'll take on another woman's daughter."

"Is that right?"

"Don't be mad at me for saying it. It's the truth."

"You taking a little satisfaction from this, Eileen?"

"I wouldn't say satisfied. Happy, relieved? . . . Yeah, kind of."

"Well, that's nice of you."

"Well, I like to think sometimes you still love me. And I guess I was a little jealous."

"You're a rather greedy, vain young lady. Isn't it enough that Ted loves you?"

"Oh, he's a second husband. You always want to keep the love of the first. But seriously, George, it isn't about me."

"Well, that'd be a first. What do you mean?"

"What do you think I mean, you idiot? I'm talking about Amy. You think I want the father of my daughter dating a woman who wants nothing to do with her?"

"I think 'wants nothing to do with her' is a little extreme."

"What, then?"

Hastings said, "I think it's fair to say she wasn't all that enthused about being a stepmom. I don't think it helped that she would have been the stepmom of your daughter."

"So it's my fault?"

"No, it's not your fault."

There was a pause. Then Eileen said, "You sure about that?"

"I'm sure," Hastings said.

"Listen," Eileen said. "Ted may have some defects, I know, but I don't doubt that he likes Amy very much. In fact, he's nuts about her. He cares for her. Something you never gave him credit for. And still don't."

"Well, forgive me for not having warm feelings for the man who stole you from me."

"Oh, don't be mushy. It doesn't suit you. Stole me away—*shit*. You're probably more grateful to him than anything."

Hastings laughed. "Yeah," he said, "sometimes." And Eileen laughed with him.

"George," Eileen said. "Are you all right?"

"I'm okay," he said. "You're right: It is for the best."

"Listen," she said, "enough time's passed between us . . . we don't have to be enemies, you know?"

"I know."

"And you know I love you."

"I know that, too."

"Call me if you need anything."

They said good-bye. Hastings walked into the bathroom, wondering at the absurdity of his life. Getting solace from Eileen, of all people.

TWENTY

The headquarters of Henderson Aerospace were in downtown Atlanta. At 5:00 P.M., the chief of security left his offices at Henderson. He got in his new BMW 760Li and drove out of the building's parking garage at 5:05. The chief of security's name was Richard Sinclair. At the age of sixty-nine, he had a trim, athletic figure. He had once been the executive director of the CIA. Before that, he had been the CIA's inspector general.

At 5:08, Richard Sinclair stopped his BMW behind a bread truck at a red traffic light. That was when his passenger door opened and a man got in the car with him. The man pointed a gun with a silencer on it at him.

The man said, "Mr. Sinclair, my name is John Reese. You may not recognize me, but I think you remember my name."

Sinclair stared at him for a moment, processing it. Then he said, "There's been a mistake."

"No mistake," Reese said. "I want you to make a right at the light. Then you're going to get on the interstate and travel north."

"Wait a minute—"

"Let's go," Reese said.

Later, with the city behind them, Reese glanced at the speedometer. They were going eighty-eight miles per hour.

Reese said, "Slow down."

"What?" Sinclair said.

"You're trying to get pulled over," Reese said. "It's a bad idea. A man like me doesn't have much to live for. I'll kill you before a policeman can save you."

Sinclair let the car decelerate to the limit.

"You won't get away with this," Sinclair said. "You're going to have to be reasonable."

"I'm being reasonable," Reese said.

"You've just abducted a law-abiding citizen," Sinclair said. "How did you get out anyway? Early parole?"

Reese observed Sinclair for a moment. God, the man wasn't the least bit sorry. Confident, in fact.

Reese said, "Don't you know?"

"How would I know? And why would I care?"

"Well, I think you're being honest about not caring," Reese said. "Someone took me out so they could kill me. Then I escaped."

"They should have left you there."

"Yeah, they should've. But they didn't."

Sinclair gave him a side glance, making no attempt to hide his disdain. Reese almost admired him for it.

"So now what's your plan?" Sinclair said. "Kill every one who ever worked at the CIA?"

"I don't have that kind of time."

"You'll get caught."

"Maybe."

"Do you know why?"

"Tell me why."

"Because you're a loser. You always were. They made a mistake letting someone like you in. Uneducated, unrefined. After the Church

Committee, they lowered the standards to let people like you in the Agency. State-school graduates, army rejects...men with no honor. Men with no sense of duty or country."

"Right," Reese said.

"Men like you don't belong in intelligence."

"Hm-hmm," Reese said. "Tell me, Sinclair, did you ever do any field work?"

"In Korea, I—"

"In Korea, you worked in communications. You went from Yale to the CIA, communications to analysis to administration. I know. You think I harbor some sort of working-class grudge against you, you're flattering yourself. The truth is, you don't know me at all."

"Then why kidnap me?"

"Sinclair, you know full well why I'm here. Twelve years ago, in your capacity as inspector general, you signed an affidavit swearing that the CIA did not ask me to perform any contract work after I retired."

For the first time, Sinclair revealed signs of anxiety. His hands tightened on the steering wheel; his mouth became a grimace. Now he remembered.

In a voice less confident than before, Sinclair said, "That was not my idea."

"Whose was it?"

"I don't remember."

"Somebody made the decision," Reese said. "Who?"

"I don't know."

"Come on."

"Oh for God's sake, Reese. You know Agency politics. Nobody

ever decides anything. Everything's done by committee and/or group so that no one has to take responsibility for anything. You want to blame me, but you know—deep down you know—it wasn't my decision."

"My defense, Mr. Sinclair, my sole defense against the criminal charges was that I was acting with the authority from and at the direction of the CIA. Woods knew it and I know others knew it, too. Why did you abandon me?"

"We didn't—"

"You did. You *denied* me. You specifically wrote and signed that affidavit."

"I didn't write it. I just signed it."

Reese, his voice raised now, said, "You *just signed it*? You son of a bitch, do you know what that did to me? Do you understand what that did to me? That was my life you were playing with. I was helping you guys."

"Look, it was too risky. The politics involved. We didn't want another congressional investigative committee. We had no choice. Woods was dead. No one else wanted to stand by you. We didn't know you."

"Woods knew me."

"But Woods was dead. We couldn't be sure you were clean. So we did the—we did the politically sensible thing."

" 'The politically sensible thing.' You *lied,* you piece of shit. And I lost everything."

"Listen to me. Listen to me," Sinclair said, for now he was genuinely fearing for his life. "We didn't think it would go that far. We tried to take it back."

"Bullshit. You bore false witness against me. You who speaks of honor and duty."

"No, we did. We tried to stop it. Clifford, Jim Clifford, the general counsel at the CIA, he told the prosecutor later that the affidavit was flawed. But the prosecutor wouldn't listen. The prosecutor said it was 'essentially accurate' and that was good enough. He said you were a bad man and you needed to be punished."

"He didn't even know me."

"But he believed it. He said it was too late. 'The evidence is the evidence.' That's what he kept saying. 'The evidence is the evidence.'"

"And then he went on to become a senator."

"Yes. Yes, he did. And you can't touch him. He was an ambitious young man and he wanted a conviction. It's what ambitious men do. In and out of the CIA. You can't change it now. It's done."

"Take this next exit," Reese said.

"Reese, don't do this. I can—don't do this."

"You can what? Sign another affidavit saying you lied the first time? Even if you kept such a promise—and I don't think you would—who would believe it? I've had you at gunpoint."

"You can't kill me. Please. Listen to me. I'll testify. I'll give a deposition."

"It's too late for that."

Sinclair opened his mouth to press his case further.

"Stop talking," Reese said.

They rode in silence, save for the times Reese gave him curt directions. Left here, right there. Thirty minutes passed and they were on a narrow country road lined by trees. They were in the

Chattahoochee National Forest. Richard Sinclair tried not to imagine the worst. A freshly dug grave waiting for him in the secluded woods . . .

Reese directed Sinclair to drive down a dirt road. Darkness enveloped them. They drove a few miles, the forest closing in.

Reese said, "Stop here. . . . Turn the ignition off. . . . Now hand me the keys. . . . Now get out this way. *This* way." Reese gestured for Sinclair to follow him out the passenger door.

Once out, Reese made him turn around and place his hands on the roof of the car. Reese went through his pockets and found his cell phone. He put the cell phone in his pocket. Then he grabbed Sinclair by the back of his suit jacket and propelled him down the road, ahead of the car.

"Keep your hands above your head," Reese said. "Keep walking."

Reese kept pace a few steps behind him. Then he stopped after a few feet.

"Keep walking," Reese said.

Sinclair continued walking, his feet sinking slightly in the soft, muddy dirt. He was conscious of the cold, the complete darkness, the helpless feeling of being alone. It was dark, but he did not contemplate running. He tried to avoid thoughts of a bullet hitting him between the shoulder blades.

A long minute passed. And another one started and Sinclair heard the car start. For a moment, he was illuminated by the car's headlights and he saw his own shadow before him. Growing and then ending as the BMW turned around and drove off in the other direction.

After the car was out of sight, Richard Sinclair began to shake—the reaction to a near-death experience. He managed not to cry, but it wasn't easy.

It took Richard Sinclair almost three hours of walking before he saw a house with a light. He knocked on the owner's door and managed to talk himself in. His first telephone call was to his wife. He explained to her briefly that he had been carjacked but that he was all right. His wife asked him if he had telephoned the police. Sinclair said he had not but would take care of it later. He asked her to call their son in Smyrna to come get him.

After finishing that call, Richard Sinclair started thinking. He would have about two hours to decide what he would do.

He had almost wept out there on that dark road. Almost wept like a child. He thought now that it was because he'd been relieved that he had not been shot. The shame he felt did not extend from betrayal, but from having been frightened and, to his mind, humiliated.

His car had been stolen. He would have to report that. But what about Reese? Did the police have to know that it was Reese who'd abducted him? If they knew, they would want to know what it was all about. Who was this man who had kidnapped him? What did he want?

He had never met John Reese before tonight. Reese was a number, an unknown man working overseas. Woods had known him. But to Sinclair and other members of management, Reese had been a nonentity.

He wondered if Reese had believed him. For what he had told

Reese was mostly the truth. They had tried to persuade Preston to withdraw the affidavit. Maybe they hadn't tried hard enough, but they had made some attempt. Okay, so no one had gone around the U.S. attorney's office and informed the judge or Reese's lawyer. But that would have been asking too much. It just hadn't seemed that important. Reese was a nobody. For all they knew, he could have been dirty. Many of the green badgers were. Mercenaries, most of them, just trying to line their own pockets. What did they owe such people? Certainly, Gelmers had said Reese was a crook and a traitor. Selling C4 explosives to the Syrians, for God's sake. Why had no one warned him that Reese had escaped from prison? Why hadn't it been on the news?

The problem for now was, How much should he tell the police? If he told them the whole truth, it could bring scandal to him and his family. He might lose his well-paying job at Henderson Aerospace. He might even be subject to criminal charges for perjury and withholding evidence.

And if he didn't say anything about Reese, what then? If he said a stranger had carjacked him so he could steal a high-dollar vehicle, what then? Would Reese go after Preston? Now Senator Preston. Would keeping silent make him partially responsible for Preston's death?

Sinclair thought about it and decided that it wouldn't. After all, Reese had not killed him. Maybe Reese was just insane. Maybe he just wanted vengeance in small doses. Steal a man's vehicle, frighten him, bring him to the verge of tears. Maybe that was all he had in mind for Preston. And what did he—Sinclair—owe Preston anyway? He barely knew the man.

Besides, Preston was a senator now, and a powerful one at that. He would be well protected. Sinclair asked himself what Preston would do if their positions were reversed. He knew the answer, and it gave him some comfort.

Before his son arrived, Sinclair remembered that his car was equipped with a GPS device. Maybe he could find the car without alerting the police at all. A phone call placed to the national dealership could resolve everything.

That was how he found the car. It was left at a downtown parking garage. He never did call the police or anyone else.

TWENTY-ONE

They had flipped a coin to see who would go in the theater with the senator and his wife. The Senator's daughter was in the university's play. *Holiday,* by Philip Barry. Hastings won the coin toss and took a seat behind the senator and Mrs. Preston. Emily Preston played the lead.

For most of the first act, Hastings was pretty bored. He probably had not seen a play performed since he was in high school. *South Pacific* or *Oklahoma*, one of those. He read the program and saw that the play had been written in the twenties, by the same guy who had written *The Philadelphia Story*. Hastings watched Emily Preston and compared her to Katharine Hepburn. Emily Preston wasn't affecting a British or a Yankee accent, but she was trying to affect something he couldn't quite figure out. She was an attractive young lady, but too masculine-featured in the face. Not as pretty as her mother.

There were parts during the play when people in the audience laughed and Hastings didn't. It made him think of Homer Simpson watching Garrison Keillor on television, Homer crying out, "I don't *get* it." Hastings didn't get Philip Barry. But even he could see that the male lead had been miscast. A young midwestern student trying to channel Cary Grant or Ronald Colman, and it just wasn't working.

He saw Klosterman in the lobby during the intermission.

"How's the play?" Klosterman asked.

Hastings grunted.

"Do you want me to go in for the third act?"

"If you want," Hastings said.

"If you don't mind," Klosterman said. "I'm getting bored out here. Any sign of an assassin?"

"No." Hastings turned his cell phone on, checking for messages.

Klosterman said, "Carol call?"

"No."

"You expecting her to?"

"I don't know."

"I'd forget about it if I were you."

"You're not me."

Klosterman said, "You know, I never dreamed I'd agree with your ex-wife about anything. But I think she's got a point."

"You can't stand Eileen."

"Hey, broken clock's right twice a day."

"I shouldn't have told you what she said."

"No, you shouldn't have. But you did. Georgie, never marry the first woman you date after you divorce."

"I wasn't going to marry her."

"That's the problem. She knew it, too."

"Are you through?"

"No," Klosterman said. He lifted his head as Mrs. Preston walked up to them. "Ma'am," Klosterman said.

She acknowledged him politely, then turned her attention to Hastings.

"The lights are dimming," Sylvia Preston said. "Ready to go back in?"

"Uh," Hastings said, "Sergeant Klosterman's going to take my seat for the third act."

"Are you not enjoying it?"

"Of course I am," Hastings said. "Your daughter's very talented. But he's been on his feet for a while and . . ."

She did not hide her disappointment. "Well, okay," she said.

She walked away. Klosterman glanced at her backside, then turned and gave Hastings a "What have we here?" look.

"Shut up," Hastings said.

"I don't know what it is about you and these high-class types. . . ."

"Go cultivate yourself."

They came out about thirty minutes later. Klosterman was dabbing his moist eyes with a handkerchief.

"Oh, Jesus Christ," Hastings said.

"What?" Klosterman said. "It was a great ending. The fuckup brother raising his glass to toast. You missed it."

"Let's go," Hastings said.

They walked behind the Prestons through a poorly lit parking lot. Hastings saw no tears in the senator's eyes. He remembered that the senator hadn't laughed at all during the play. He'd seemed even more bored than Hastings. Another thing: He didn't look at his wife much. He wondered about Senator Preston. A rich, successful man. Yet when he wasn't involved in some sort of power play, he seemed unhappy much of the time, perhaps even bitter. Like a compulsive gambler away from the blackjack table.

Hastings listened for snatches of conversation between the two.

The senator was saying their daughter needed to go to law school. Something about her being a decent actress, but not a great one.

It did not occur to Hastings that he was invading their privacy. Much of his adult life had been dedicated to observing people, looking for weaknesses. It was not something he could easily turn off. When he thought about it—which was infrequently—he realized he wasn't much interested in turning it off.

Now the senator's car was in sight. They had been brought here by a driver. Now the driver wasn't here.

Hastings touched Klosterman's arm and they moved forward, coming up even with the Prestons.

"Just a minute," Hastings said. "Where's your driver?"

"I don't know," Senator Preston said. "He's supposed to be with the car."

"Stay with them," Hastings said to Klosterman.

Hastings moved to the other side of the parking lot, circling back to a dark sedan he had seen when they'd first entered the lot. A man was sitting behind the wheel of the car. Older, late forties or early fifties. Large-jawed and pale-skinned, hair blond or gray. There was a grass knoll separating the parking lot from Grand Boulevard, and Hastings walked behind the knoll and came back up behind the car, now seeing the man's back. His hair blond . . .

Hastings pulled his service revolver from his holster. He held the gun at his side, the barrel pointed at the ground. Then he walked up to the driver's door and yanked it open.

The man in the car turned, startled.

"Police," Hastings said. "Step out of the car, please."

"Jesus!"

"Out of the car. *Now.*"

The man got out and Hastings pushed him against the car, told him to spread his hands on the roof. Hastings checked him for weapons. He didn't find any.

"What's going on?" the man said. "I have money. Please—"

"Be quiet," Hastings said. He looked into the car for weapons but didn't see any there. "What are you doing here?"

The man said, "I'm waiting for my girlfriend. She works at the library."

"A little old to be dating a student, aren't you?"

"She's not a— Jesus, what is this?"

"You're waiting for your girlfriend. Where is she?"

"I just told you. She works at the library. She's not a student here. God."

Now Hastings looked across the parking lot and saw something that cleared things up. A heavyset girl was approaching the car with a confused, frightened look on her face.

She said, "Harvey? What's going on?"

"Marcia!" the man said. "Call the police. This guy's crazy."

"I am the—"

Then Hastings saw something else: the driver of the senator's car now standing with Klosterman and the Prestons. The driver was holding a cup of coffee and a packaged Pop-Tart.

"I am the police," Hastings said, his voice a little lower now. He stepped back and the girl came forward.

"Sorry," Hastings said.

"What's the matter with you?" the man said, his voice a mixture of fear and anger now.

Hastings apologized again and moved away. A few steps away, he heard the girlfriend call out, "Asshole."

When he got back to the Prestons and Klosterman, the senator was looking at him and shaking his head.

"Nice work," Senator Preston said. "Very impressive."

"Alan," Sylvia said, admonishing him.

"Sorry," Hastings said. He wondered how many times he would have to say it tonight.

Later, they were back at the house, across the street from the senator's home. Hastings was at the window, Klosterman lying on the cot, watching Jay Leno. A commercial came on and Klosterman pressed the mute button on the remote control.

Klosterman said, "You know Lincoln was killed during a play."

"I know," Hastings said.

"Yeah, I guess you do. You still pissed at him?"

"Who? Lincoln?"

"No, not Lincoln. Senator Dickhead, that's who."

"Not really."

"Asshole," Klosterman said. "I'm sorry I didn't say anything to him."

"What could you have said?"

"I could have told him we're here because he requested our protection. We do our jobs and then he gives us shit about it so he can look good in front of his wife. Chickenshit."

Hastings shrugged.

"We shouldn't have to take that," Klosterman said.

"I think we do have to."

"Shit detail," Klosterman said.

"Yep."

Klosterman clicked the mute button. Jay Leno could be heard again. A few moments passed and Klosterman said, "Oh hell. How many times can he have Howie Mandel on?"

"Change the channel," Hastings said.

"This is the only channel we can get. You got anything to read?"

"No."

"I've got some paperbacks in the trunk of the car."

"I'll get them," Hastings said.

"You mind?"

"No. I need some air anyway."

Cops, like soldiers, like to read paperbacks. They are in professions with a lot of downtime. Often books were read and discarded in the department's locker room, to be picked up by anyone else with an interest. Klosterman kept a few paperbacks in the trunk of his car.

Hastings walked out to the car, opened the trunk, and observed the scattered collection. It included *Fatal Vision,* Vincent Bugliosi's book on the O. J. Simpson trial, a couple of Fletch novels, and something called *The Chicago Way.* Hastings took two of the nonfiction books and two novels out and shut the trunk.

Stepping back from the car, he saw motion, someone coming out of the house.

It was the woman. Saying something to someone. Hastings heard a jingling of dog tags and then saw the little dog. An off-white Westie.

The dog smelled him and started to growl.

"Hi," Hastings said.

Sylvia Preston squinted in the dark. "Oh, hi. Lieutenant?"

"Yes."

The senator's wife told the little dog to behave. Hastings set the books on the trunk of the car. Then he walked over to her.

Hastings ignored the little dog, knowing that doing so would relax the dog and him. The dog understood and ran off to find a place to do his business.

Hastings said, "I didn't know you had a dog."

"Yes," Mrs. Preston said. "His name is Fred. He's my daughter's dog, actually. We got him when she was fifteen. But . . . I'm the one who's ended up having to take care of him. You know how kids are."

"Yeah."

"I'm sorry. I just presumed you have children. Do you?"

"Yes. A daughter. She's thirteen."

"Here in town?"

Hastings hesitated for a moment, wondering where else his daughter would be. He said, "Yes. Her mother and I are divorced. We share custody."

"Oh. Well . . . that's good."

"Yeah, it is. She's a great kid."

They were quiet for a moment, standing about ten feet apart. The pretty lady waiting in the dark while a little dog ran around in the yard. The policeman feeling awkward. Like many cops, Hastings was class-conscious. He was about to excuse himself, when she spoke.

"About this evening," the woman said. "I'm sorry."

"For what?"

"My husband," she said. "He was rude. He's not usually like that."

Hastings assumed that he very likely *was* usually like that. He said, "It's okay. I embarrassed him."

"He's on edge, I think. He says he's not afraid of this . . . this man. But he is. I am, too."

"I'm sure everything will be fine."

"Are you?" she said. She gave him a steady look, not hiding it. Then she said, "Why did you—why did you question that man, then?"

"Well," Hastings said. "We came back and your driver was gone. And then I saw the man in the parking lot and he fit, roughly, the description of John Reese. I guess I'm a little on edge myself."

"I've never seen anything like that."

"You've never seen a cop make a mistake?"

"No." She smiled. "No. I've never seen a police officer take charge like that. You were very cool. Even when you—" She laughed.

"Even when I realized I'd screwed up?"

"Yes," she said, laughing some more. "I'm sorry. Seriously, you handled it very well. Better than I would have."

"Yeah, well," Hastings said, "it's the, uh, training. I've got to get back in."

"Okay."

He started to walk away, feeling a little off balance. A few feet away, he heard her speak to him again.

"Lieutenant?"

Hastings turned and said, "Yes, ma'am."

She gestured with her head to the back of the unmarked police car.

"Aren't you going to take those books up with you?"

"Oh."

She smiled at him again. "I presume only one of you will be reading while the other keeps an eye on us."

"You've a very discerning woman, Mrs Preston."

"Sometimes," she said.

TWENTY-TWO

David Chang picked out three movies—*Caddyshack, Chinatown,* and *As Good as It Gets.* His wife, who was at home, wanted to see the last one. She was a Jack Nicholson fan, even though she said Nicholson didn't seem to be taking his acting too seriously since he'd played the Joker. Chang paid for the DVDs and walked out to his car.

His Nissan Altima was parked next to a Lincoln Continental. He walked between the cars, when the door to the Lincoln opened and smacked into his car. Chang stopped and stared at the man who got out of the car.

"How clumsy of me," the man said.

Chang heard something behind him. He started to turn around, but then he was grabbed from behind, an arm encircling his neck. He felt the wet cloth against his nose and mouth. Chloroform . . .

Dexter Troy rode in the van with two other men. They had Chang in the van, his hands tied behind his back, a thick piece of duct tape across his mouth. Clu and another man followed them in the Lincoln Continental. They drove to an isolated area in the woods. They stopped the vehicles and pulled Chang out. Then they walked. Two men in front of Chang, three behind. Two of the men held short machine guns with thick noise suppressors that were shaped like oil cans. Another of the men carried a folding chair.

They walked almost a mile. Then they reached a clearing. The man with the chair unfolded it and set it on the ground. Two of the other men placed Chang in it. They untied his hands from behind his back and taped them to the arms of the chair. When that was done, Clu Rogers stepped in front of Chang and tore the duct tape from his mouth.

Clu said, "That hurt you, professor?"

Chang looked up at Clu. He said nothing to him.

Clu moved away and Dexter Troy took his place.

Troy said, "A few questions, Mr. Chang. Answer them correctly and you go free. If you don't, we'll torture you and then we'll kill you."

"Torture me," Chang said, as though the notion made him merely curious. He looked at the men forming a semicircle around him. "I thought terrorists usually wore masks."

"We're not terrorists. We just want information."

"Torture usually leads to the wrong information. Or didn't they teach you that?"

Troy smiled. "You've got guts, I'll give you that. But once these fellows go to work on you, you'll crack anyway and you'll have suffered through it for nothing."

Chang said, "Are you a soldier?"

"I was," Troy said.

"And now you work for money."

Clu said, "Now how did you know that?"

Troy asked, "Have you been warned about us?"

"I know nothing about you," Chang said. "Or what you want."

"I think you do," Troy said. "You remember John Reese, don't you?"

"Who?"

"That's funny. John Reese. He got you and your family out of China. We think he's been to see you lately."

"John who?"

A kick from the side, tipping the chair over. Chang's face hit wet mud. Clu walked over and put a boot on Chang's other cheek.

"The name is John Reese," Clu said. "He killed a man in Washington. Where is he?"

"I don't know what you're talking about."

Troy said, "Mr. Chang, you've already tipped your hand. You seem to know who we are. Maybe you were expecting us. Maybe Reese warned you we might be coming."

Clu shifted the weight of his boot to Chang's neck.

Troy said, "Where is Reese, Mr. Chang?"

"I told you. I don't know who you're talking about."

Clu pressed his boot down.

Chang struggled, but he did not talk.

Troy said, "Hold it. Trent, Matt. Go get his wife, bring her back here."

Two of the men started to go.

"Wait," Chang said.

Clu lifted his boot.

Chang said, "If I tell you what you want, will you promise to leave her out of it?"

Troy said, "If you tell us, yes."

"Your word?" Chang said.

"Yes," Troy said. "You have my word."

"Reese was here, a few days ago. He asked to borrow some money. I gave it to him. He didn't tell me where he was going and I didn't ask. But I think he was going to England."

"How do you know that?'

"Because that's where he used to live. That's where he was the most happy. He wanted to go back."

"I think you're lying."

"What reason would I have to lie to you? John Reese is nothing to me. Years ago, he used me to get information for the CIA. I used him to get out of China. That is the extent of our relationship."

"Yet you loaned him money."

"I wanted nothing more than to see the back of him. I was willing to pay to see him go."

"I still say you're lying. What if I told you I have personal knowledge he is still in this country?"

"Then I'd say he lied to me, too. Torture me all you like, but it won't change what I know."

"Tell me the truth and we'll let you go."

"I have told you the truth. And we both know you're not going to let me go. I've seen your faces."

Troy said nothing, suddenly uncomfortable. This man on the ground seeing him as he was, not as he thought he was.

Chang gestured with his head to Clu and said, "You're going to have this man do it for you."

Troy said, "How do you know that?"

"Because you don't have the courage to do it yourself."

Chang smiled, and Troy pulled a pistol from his coat and shot Chang twice in the head.

TWENTY-THREE

Reese arrived in St. Louis a little after one o'clock in the afternoon and checked into a Holiday Inn near Forest Park. He had stayed the previous night at a cheap motel in Tennessee and slept badly on an uncomfortable bed. He signed the register as Paul Bryan. In the hotel's courtesy fax/Internet room, he checked Senator Preston's Web page again and confirmed that he would be at the fund-raiser at the Chase Park Plaza at six that night. Reese returned to his room and debated taking a nap, then decided against it. He showered and shaved. Then he put on a new suit, brown-and-blue twill. White shirt, a tie, and cordovan shoes. The suit was off the rack from an Atlanta department store. Carrying the briefcase, he would look like a lawyer or a businessman. Inside the case was the disassembled rifle.

It was approximately two o'clock when he drove to the Central West End.

By three, he had secured an apartment on the tenth floor of a building across the street from the Chase Park Plaza.

TWENTY-FOUR

Hastings and Klosterman had to come on duty three hours early because of the fund-raiser. Rhodes and Murph would have to stay on shift late, as well, at least until the fund-raiser wrapped up. There were other police officers there, all of them in uniform. But only a few.

Hastings and Klosterman were at the Chase Park Plaza before the senator and his wife. Hastings conferred with the hotel's chief security officer and the hotel manager. After that, he and Klosterman stood in the lobby and watched a procession of limousines pass through the porte cochere.

It was not a red-carpet celebrity event. Some politicians are attractive, but a good many of them look like the rest of us. Klosterman followed politics more than Hastings and he recognized a few faces. A couple of senators were there, but most of them were members of the House. Representatives Tim Early of Texas, Robert Boudreau of California, Dana Caine of New Hampshire, Paula Enzbrenner of New York, and James Saunders of Illinois. They were all members of Senator Preston's party. They were also all members of the House Homeland Security Committee.

The fund-raiser was sponsored by Cushman and Holt, a global law firm headquartered in St. Louis. Donors attending the dinner had to pay three thousand dollars.

Klosterman said to Hastings, "See, if it's a luncheon, they would have had to pay only two grand."

The senator and Mrs. Preston arrived after their guests. The senator wore a dark suit, not a tuxedo as Hastings thought he might. Mrs. Preston wore a black dress, flattering to her figure but tasteful. Hastings watched them as they walked up the aisle. Cameras flashed and the senator gave one of those politician finger points and a bright smile to a guy in the crowd, as if he was surprised and glad to see the person. It turned out to be someone he had spoken to only an hour earlier.

Hastings looked at the senator and then at Mrs. Preston. He turned his gaze as they walked by.

In the banquet room, Hastings and Klosterman took positions near the back and listened to the senator talk about the War on Terror. He spoke about the dangers of appeasement and Munich and Hitler, Iran and Iraq, pausing at times for applause. The speech was relatively short, about fifteen minutes, and he took a few questions afterward, one of which Hastings knew came from a plant. The senator asked twice if there were any members of the media in the room. The police officers knew there were not and knew the senator knew it, too. It was clever, Hastings thought. Letting the audience know he was confiding in them, making them feel special.

After the question-and-answer session concluded, the banquet attendees divided up into what was called "issues breakout sessions."

Hastings watched the senator work the crowd, moving from table to table, shaking hands and touching shoulders. He was good, Hastings thought. If you didn't know him, you would think he liked people.

Hastings did not loathe politicians as a rule. He attended the

Police Academy with a guy named Steve Fawcett, who left the department ten years later to run for a seat in the state Senate. Fawcett was okay. He fought for better police pay and state pension benefits in the legislature and he did not look down on people. Fawcett told Hastings about the time he shook Bill Clinton's hand and Clinton looked into his eyes and said, "Thanks, man," and made him feel like he was the most important person in the room. "It's the ones who can do that that you gotta watch out for," Fawcett said, though not without some admiration.

Another cop Hastings knew had left the department to become a lobbyist in Jefferson City. Bobby Hahn was his name. Most of his clients belonged to municipal unions—police and firefighters, mainly. He attended every police department Christmas dinner, was always dressed to the nines, and was very difficult not to like. Of course, Bobby Hahn was working for them.

Hastings did not believe that Fawcett and Hahn were bad guys. He wasn't even sure they were attracted to power. Fawcett went into politics because he was bored with police work. And Hahn became a lobbyist because he sensed, correctly, that he would probably be better at working for cops and firefighters than anyone else in Jeff City. To be sure, both men liked the limelight and liked wheeling and dealing. But vain men are not necessarily corrupt men. Moreover, they enjoyed politics.

Neither Fawcett nor Hahn was at this thing, though. This was another level.

Hastings remembered Dan Anthony telling him that Preston might run for president. Now Hastings wondered what it would be like if Preston actually got there. Would he tell his grandchildren that he'd once gotten bawled out by the president? That the president was a jerkoff? That he had a very cute wife?

Hastings watched as Senator Preston stopped at another table and extended his hand to a boyish-looking man. The man wore his hair cut short, almost military style, and he wore a nice blue suit and a red silk tie. Hastings saw the senator's expression change—just. Where it had been jovial and open, now it was concerned and agitated. Hastings did not believe it was feigned, an attempt to show empathy over hearing about the death of a friend or a loved one. The senator seemed very uncomfortable.

Hastings moved forward.

The man talking with the senator did not fit the description of John Reese. He was too young, to begin with. And there was no way he could have gotten into the fund-raiser. Still, he made Hastings uneasy.

Hastings walked over.

When he got there, the senator turned to him and said, "What?" his tone short.

"Just wanted to know if everything is all right," Hastings said.

"It's fine," Senator Preston said. "When we're ready to leave, we'll let you know."

"Yes, sir."

Senator Preston made a sort of shooing gesture to him, and if not for this, Hastings would have left quietly.

Hastings turned to the younger man and extended his hand.

"George Hastings."

"George," the man said, "Kyle Anders. How are you?" His tone was friendly and pleasant. All-American.

"Fine," Hastings said. "Hope you're enjoying our city."

"I am. It's a lovely place. You're a police officer?"

The senator frowned at Hastings.

"Yes," Hastings said. "A detective."

Anders looked briefly at Senator Preston, then back to Hastings. "Well, I'm glad to see the senator's in good hands."

"We try," Hastings said. "It was nice meeting you."

He walked away, and a few moments later, Klosterman walked over to him.

"What was that about?" Klosterman asked.

Hastings said, "He seemed bothered by that guy. I wanted to check it out."

Klosterman looked at Kyle Anders, who was still talking with the senator.

"He doesn't match Reese's description," Klosterman said.

"I know."

Murph was on the roof of the hotel, patrolling the perimeter. With him was a uniformed police officer who was a member of the tactical team. The tact team officer had a rifle slung over his shoulder. His hair was high and tight—a marine's cut—and when there was a trace of daylight, he wore a pair of Oakley sunglasses. Paramilitary, though no one had asked him to be.

Murph used binoculars to look at the ground and the buildings around them. See if any cars got through the blockades, delivery trucks in the area that had not been authorized. To the north, there were no buildings as high as the hotel. To the south, there were two

THE SILENT PLACES 151

apartment buildings. Murph scanned the windows. Left to right, down a row, then right to left.

Murph's two-way squawked and he answered it.

"Go," Murph said.

"Murph," Rhodes said. He was at the hotel entrance, where the car would take Senator Preston away. Rhodes said, "George just buzzed me. The senator will be leaving in five minutes."

"Okay."

Murph repeated the message to the tact team cop and the cop said, "Good. It's getting fucking cold up here."

It was, too. Dark now and the wind blowing. They could hear traffic from Lindell and Kingshighway below—city lights spreading out before them, darkness over Forest Park, which was about a hundred yards away.

Murph took another pan of the apartment buildings with the binoculars. One more sweep and in a few minutes the senator would be in his car and he and Rhodes would be relieved and could go home. He would call his wife on his way home, see if she had saved any dinner for him. . . .

And then he saw it.

An open window in the apartment building across the street.

It probably didn't mean anything. Plenty of people opened their windows. Even on a cold night. Some people couldn't sleep unless it was cold.

But there was no light in the window, no light at all.

Murph held the binoculars on the open window and tried to see beyond the black square. Movement, a person, something.

Nothing.

He called Hastings on the two-way.

"Yeah."

"George, this is Murph. Probably nothing, but I see an open window on the other side of Lindell Boulevard."

Hastings asked, "What building?"

"The Ambassador."

"See anything?"

"No. It's dark. The lights are off."

"What floor?"

"I've counted. Let me recheck. . . . It is the . . . tenth floor . . . the sixth window from my right. . . . From the western side."

"Is the window within range of the front of the hotel?"

"I can't tell from here, but I would presume it is."

"Okay. Stay there, keep an eye on it. I'm going to redirect the senator to a different exit. Over."

Hastings relayed the information to Klosterman.

Hastings said, "Stay with Preston. Get him out the north door— the back alley. I'm going to check things out."

Hastings radioed a patrol officer and met him at the hotel entrance. Together, they walked across the street.

Reese went to the window and looked down at the hotel entrance. There was an awning from the door of the hotel to the semicircular drive. The awning blocked his view. But he remembered what sort of car the senator had arrived in and he knew that activity would buzz once Preston came out. Between the end of the awning and the car, there would be a space of approximately twenty feet. That would be the window. With his infrared scope, he would be able to see the target. However, he would only get one shot before Preston reached his car. Also, he could not stick the rifle out the window and steady it and wait, because there was a chance someone would spot the rifle. He would have to steady the rifle, aim, and hit the target quickly and confidently. Not the easiest of conditions.

But it would be enough.

Reese moved to the window and took another look.

Hastings held the two-way in his hand now and was ready when it squawked.

"Yeah?"

"George, it's Murph. I just saw movement in the window. A form. A man, I think."

"The light still off?"

"Yeah."

"You still got Walters with you?"

"Yeah, he's right here."

Hastings hesitated. He had always been uncomfortable with tact team members. He didn't think they were trigger-happy, per se. But he had known more than one who had been disappointed to leave a hostage situation without getting to shoot a bad guy. Hastings didn't know Walters well. Walters was a young cop, with about three years in the department, and he'd been very happy to get the slot on tact.

Hastings said, "Tell him to put his rifle on the window. *But he is not to shoot unless he receives a direct order from me.* Is that clear?"

"Yes, sir."

———

Hastings showed the desk attendant at the Ambassador his identification even though he had a uniformed cop with him. Quick explanations were given and the desk attendant summoned the night security guard. Hastings hoped he was an off-duty cop, but he wasn't. An older man, unarmed, which was probably a good thing. They walked with the guard to the elevator.

Reese saw the senator's car pull up to the awning. He reached for his rifle, taking it by the stock.

A man approaching the car—

But not the senator.

A black guy. Tall, wearing slacks and a sport coat. Looking confident and in charge. A cop.

Getting into the front seat of the senator's car.

What?

The car's brake lights coming on. And then the car was moving forward, pulling out of the drive. The senator nowhere to be seen.

Shit.

Preston wasn't coming out the front.

"Goddammit," Reese said. "God*damm*it."

It would have to be another time.

He disassembled the rifle and put it back in its case. He put his jacket back on and then his overcoat. Then he left the apartment and moved into the hallway. He walked to the elevator, and when he was halfway there, he heard it ding and saw the light flash on, signaling that it was stopping and someone was about to get off.

TWENTY-FIVE

Shortly after Reese was recruited by the CIA, one of the instructors said to him, "No one doubts you're a good soldier. But that's not going to be good enough for intelligence work. If I've got a choice between having a good soldier and a great salesman, I'll take the great salesman every time." Reese later realized that *salesman* was a kind word. The instructor really meant con man. Persuasion, *acting*. Anyone can shoot a gun. But a real pro can bluff his way out of many situations. The key is to act as if you're in your surroundings. Act as if you belong. And through acting, *become* the other. If you believe you are the other, those around you will believe it, too. The instructor quoted Buchan, saying, " 'A fool tries to look different: a clever man looks the same and *is* different.' "

Normally, that's what Reese would have done. When the elevator dinged, he would have gotten on and persuaded the occupants by his mere presence and body language that he was a tenant, not an intruder. He would even have made polite small talk.

But in a split second, something told him that would not be a good idea.

Perhaps it was the fact that Preston had not left by the front door. The black cop getting into the senator's car, directing it elsewhere . . .

Reese saw the doorway to the stairwell and went through it just as the elevator doors opened.

Hastings was the second one out of the elevator, coming out after the apartment building's security man. The uniformed cop was behind Hastings. Hastings saw and heard the door to the stairwell close. He kept his eye on it as he followed the security guard to the apartment, the security guard removing his passkey from his pocket.

Hastings turned to the uniformed officer and said, "Check the apartment."

Before the patrolman could reply, Hastings went through the stairwell door. The door shut behind him and he peered down the stairs.

He saw no one. He stood still and listened. Heard footsteps.

Hastings moved down the stairs, hurrying now.

Reese heard the steps above. A man, moving quickly. Reese kept moving—not running, but picking up the pace. He thought about stopping at the sixth floor—maybe the pursuer would continue down the stairs—but then that could backfire if the man stopped on that floor, too, Reese being in the middle of a hallway, exposed. Reese did not think the pursuer had seen him. He had not heard the door open until he was on the eighth floor—he had a two-floor head start. He would continue to the bottom, go out the front door, slip into crowds and traffic. Blend in, disappear.

Hopefully, circumstances would prove his evasive action was unnecessary, the pursuer merely a tenant of the building.

Then he heard the voice from above.

"*Hey!* You down there. Stay where you are. I'm a police officer. I want to talk to you."

Reese started running.

Hastings heard the man run. He, too, started running. And now both men were going down the stairs as fast as they dared, Reese keeping the attaché case in one hand, touching and gripping the stairway rail at times to prevent himself from falling, Hastings about two flights behind him and as Hastings turned the corner on a landing, he almost tripped, but he kept his balance and the two-way radio clattered to the ground, but Hastings kept going.

Reese reached the doorway to the lobby. He pushed it open then stopped when he saw a uniformed police officer on the other side of the glass doors. Reese continued down the stairs, only one floor left, and when he got there, he saw an exit door that said EMERGENCY ONLY and he knew that it would trigger the fire alarm, but it was the only way out and he hit it hard and heard the bell ring loudly as he went out into the dark alley.

In the street, the uniformed officer tilted his head, having heard the alarm. He hesitated a moment, then walked into the lobby.

The desk attendant looked at him and said, "That's the fire alarm. Someone must have gone out the back door."

Hastings stopped at the basement door, the alarm *brrrriiinng* piercing his cerebellum. He drew his .38 snubnose. Then he pushed the door open and moved his head out and then back in. He moved his head out again, stepped out, and saw a figure to his right running full tilt. Hastings ran after him.

The man had about eighty yards on him, running with a briefcase in hand. To Hastings, the man was a form in the darkness. Slim, obviously in shape, wearing a suit. Hastings tried to quicken his pace. He had been an athlete in college—a baseball player on scholarship—running laps and sprints at practice, but that was twenty years ago. He had not gotten fat over the years, but he had not set aside time for jogging, either. If he had, maybe he could have closed the distance on this man, maybe even getten close enough to discern his features. But the alley was only as long as the apartment building; it would spill out into Kingshighway Boulevard, a busy street between the Central West End and Forest Park. Hastings could see the man and, beyond that, he could see and hear the heavy traffic on Kingshighway. A man would have to be mad to run out into that traffic.

Reese turned only once to see the man chasing him. A quick glance and he saw someone in a jacket and tie, in his late thirties or early forties, running after him. Reese kept going. If it was a mercenary, a friend of one of the crew he had met up north, the mercenary would just shoot him. Though it would be hard to hit a running target at night. The man on the stairs had said he was a police officer. Probably he was telling the truth. Mercenary or cop, it wasn't good either way.

Reese saw the alley coming to an end, light from Kingshighway illuminating it. That wasn't good. He didn't need traffic or illumination. Reese reached the end and hesitated for only a moment before he rushed out into traffic. A car honked and another one screeched, and then he stopped as another one whipped in front of him. He ran behind it and then he was crossing another three lanes, this time the southbound traffic. He ran around the back of a bus and then almost got nailed by a Cadillac, its driver slamming on the brakes, putting the car in a four-wheel slide, but then Reese was in the third lane and out of the street and into the cover of Forest Park.

Hastings was not as bold as Reese. He reached Kingshighway in time to see his quarry run around the bus and somehow dodge the front of a maroon Cadillac. Hastings let a couple of cars go by and then a couple more and then when he thought it would be something less than suicidal, he ran into the traffic. A truck blew its horn at him, making his heart jump, and he reached the center median and waited again as a stream of vehicles went by. He ran behind them and then was beyond the street.

He was on the edge of Forest Park.

Christ, Forest Park. A rectangle about a mile wide and two miles long. It contained a skating rink and a zoo and other tourist attractions, but it had a hell of a lot of hills and trees, too. Great place for a man to hide until the police helicopter came with its spotlight and thermal sensors. It would take about twenty minutes, minimum, to summon one. Besides, he had dropped his two-way radio in the apartment building.

Hastings moved into the park, walking quickly, taking note of trees and brush—places where an armed man might hide. He moved farther into the park, the light and the sound of traffic receding behind him. He waited for his eyes to adjust to the darkness, and they did. He walked farther in, and if not for the distant sound of traffic and Barnes Hospital looming a couple of blocks away, he could have been in the country.

If he were running from a cop, what would he do?

He would not move north, because doing so would bring him back to Lindell Boulevard. More traffic, perhaps a police cruiser looking for him, shining a spotlight into the park. Indeed, he would probably want to get farther south, but southwest, so as to avoid being seen from Kingshighway.

Hastings moved southwest, running some, trotting, but stopping from time to time to look and maybe hear.

There. Movement maybe a couple of hundred yards away.

Hastings moved forward.

Reese ran through hills and past trees, but then the ground opened up and he feared he was coming upon a flat, open field. The grounds were better kept, the grass lower. A flag . . .

Christ. A golf course.

Stupid. Now there would be no cover. He should have proceeded due west, kept a course where there were trees. Places that would keep him hidden from police helicopters and determined policemen.

He wondered if the guy had been dumb enough to follow him into the park. Most city cops would avoid parks except to arrest homosexuals. Chasing an armed man, the typical police officer would call for assistance and then the park would be swarming with police cars and searchlights, maybe a couple of K-9 units, too, sending a German shepherd his way. Reese saw another hole ahead, a flag sticking out of it. To the left of the putting green, there was a sand bunker. If he could get there, he could cover himself in the sand and maybe that would keep him from being found by a thermal sensor. He could spend the night there if need be.

He ran full out to the sand bunker and jumped into it.

He lay on his stomach. Then he crawled back to the lip and peered over the edge.

In the distance, he saw a man.

Reese opened his attaché case and removed his starlight scope. The scope put distant objects on a light green screen and could magnify the light of a match a million times. Reese put the scope to his left eye and did a left-to-right pan.

There, about two hundred yards away. The cop.

Stupid, Reese thought.

Reese began to assemble the rifle.

Hastings's cell phone rang. He removed it from his coat pocket. "Yeah, Murph," he said quietly.

"George, where the hell are you?"

"I'm in the park. About half a mile in, west of Kingshighway. I'm on the golf course."

"What the fuck, George." Murph was relieved, but pissed off, too. Hastings leaving without telling them where he was.

"Sorry," Hastings said. "I dropped my two-way in the stairwell. I think our man's in the park. Send units in and call a chopper."

"Yes, sir. George, don't—"

"I won't," Hastings said, then clicked off the phone and dropped it in his pocket.

He looked suddenly to his right, his heart jumping. Sound, motion—bipedal, an animal? He relaxed. It was a couple of people on bicycles. Riding through Forest Park at night. Dumbasses.

About twenty seconds later, the first shot came.

Reese assembled the rifle and loaded it. He rammed the bolt home and put a shell in the chamber. Then he steadied the rifle on the lip of the bunker and got the cop in his sights.

The starlight scope gave him the cop's head and shoulders on a light green screen. Now he could discern the man's jacket, his tie over a white or pale blue shirt. He could put one between the eyes or one in the chest. A quick kill. He didn't want to paralyze the man, prolong anyone's suffering.

He put his finger on the trigger, began to squeeze....

Then he hesitated.

Where was he? A park in an American city. The man in the distance an American policeman. He didn't know the man and the man didn't know him. What difference should it make? See? Right there, in the man's right hand, a gun. A revolver. That proved he was a cop. No mercenary would carry a snubnose. A cop, then. Wouldn't the cop kill him if he could?

Reese leaned forward again.

Murmurs, perhaps even a shout, movement behind him. Reese jerked and the rifle spat out a shot. Reese turned and saw two young men on bicycles riding on a path approximately thirty yards behind him. He rammed another cartridge in the chamber and turned the rifle on them.

But saw they were not police officers. Just kids on bikes, going for a night ride. They couldn't see him from the bike path. He heard one of them say, "What the fuck was that?" And even then they remained unaware of him. He was hidden in the bunker. They increased their speed and rode away.

Reese turned back and looked out on the green.

The policeman was down.

TWENTY-SIX

As Klosterman and Rhodes had left the hotel to escort the senator home, Murph was the lead detective on the scene. After he got off the phone with Hastings, he grabbed a patrol officer standing by a police car and said, "Is this your unit?"

"Yeah, Murph. What's up?"

"Let's go."

The patrol officer got behind the wheel of the Chevy Impala, Murph in the passenger seat. Pursuant to Murph's instructions, the patrol officer made a U-turn on Lindell Boulevard and hit the sirens and lights. They slowed at the intersection of Lindell and Kinghighway to avoid a collision, cleared a path, and then roared through.

Went another quarter mile and took a hard, screeching left onto Grand Drive, taking them into the park. They were soon at a fork in the road and Murph yelled, "Left. Go *left*."

Another screech of tires on road and Murph picked up the com and radioed for assistance.

He could not measure the time between the sound of the shot and the instant it hit him. They say you never hear the one that hits you. But he had heard it. He heard it hit *him*. When he would look back on it, he would think he had heard it hit his body before he felt it.

A sort of *thhhp* sound. And then he twisted back and fell. As if he had been shoved suddenly and violently. Hit with a hard object and knocked to the ground.

Now Hastings became aware of what he was seeing.

The sky. Night. Stars.

He was on his back.

He was still holding his gun.

Then he felt the pain. He started to move his left arm and felt the pain in his left shoulder increase. He winced. With his right hand, he reached across his body and touched his left shoulder. It was soft and wet.

Well shit. This is what it's like to be shot.

He put his right hand back on the right side of his body and set the gun on the grass. Then he used his right hand to grab his left wrist and pull it to the right side of his body. Then he got to his knees and picked the .38 back up. He stood and ran.

The second shot peeled out as he reached the knoll and fell behind it.

The knoll was about three feet high at its peak and it was between him and the shooter. There was a pause and then he heard another shot, this one thunking into the knoll and staying there. The shooter telling him he knew where he was hiding.

Hastings started to shiver. He felt nauseous. He looked to his left and then his right and had trouble seeing things in the distance. His vision was blurred. *Christ, no,* he thought. Signs that he was going into shock.

It's just a shot in the shoulder. He'd known cops who'd accidentally shot themselves in the foot. Looked down and said, "Oh no." And then driven themselves to the emergency room. No big deal. Just a flesh wound, as they say on television. Slap a Band-Aid on it and get back to work.

But what they don't say is that a flesh wound can bleed the life out of you in just a few minutes. If the hole's big enough. If you leak enough blood, because you've only got so much of the stuff. And if an artery's been hit, you just as well kiss it all good-bye.

Hastings was aware of the wetness of the wound. But he had not seen a geyser of blood. So he had that going for him.

He had the cover of the knoll. For now, he had it. And maybe he could lean over it and shoot back at the guy.

Yeah . . . with a .38 Smith & Wesson Chief's Special with a two-inch barrel. Good for shooting at someone about twenty yards away, but not much good beyond that. The man coming after him had a rifle. A fucking rifle. Hunting Hastings now in the deadly, silent places.

If he left the knoll, the man would shoot him. If he was still out there. If he had not run away. Or the shooter could make a wide semicircle and creep back and shoot him from the side. He would not be dumb enough to come close enough to the knoll so that Hastings could get a close shot at him.

Hastings retrieved his cell phone, fumbled with the buttons.

Before he could finish dialing, he heard a voice, steady and authoritative. Its confidence chilled him as nothing ever had before.

The voice coming across the field, saying, "You shouldn't have come after me."

Reese stood behind a tree, on the other side of the fairway. The knoll was in view; the cop was not. If the cop came out from behind the knoll to shoot him, he would not know where Reese was and that would be the end of him. Reese steadied his body against the tree, the butt of the rifle in his right shoulder, his finger on the trigger.

He waited for the cop to say something back to him. Maybe beg for his life, say something about a wife and kids.

But he heard nothing.

Reese put his eye to the starlight scope and saw the knoll in the light green screen. Waited to see if the man behind it would stand and try to make a run for it. . . .

A flash of color coming into the screen—

Reese took his eye off the scope, looked across the park. Now he could hear the siren.

A police car, its blue and red lights flashing, coming around a bend in the road. A pause as the car got closer; then he saw two gunfire flashes as the cop fired two shots.

Reese stepped back behind the tree, taking cover.

Then he realized the shots were not directed at him. The cop was doing it to signal the police car. Shooting at the sky, as if to send up a flare.

It was working, the police car skidding and then coming onto the golf course, its spotlight sweeping across the field.

Reese stepped away from the tree and then ran south.

The police car reached the knoll and scrunched to a stop, leaving ruts in the close-cut grass. Murph got out holding the shotgun.

"Stay down," Hastings said. "He's got a rifle."

The patrol officer continued to shine the spotlight across the dark, revealing nothing but trees and ground.

Murph bent over and ran to Hastings, dropped to the ground next to him.

"You hit?" Murph asked.

"Yeah," Hastings said. "Shoulder. Get something pressed down on it, will you? Did you call for backup? I don't want this fucker getting away."

Murph's focus was on the wet patch on the lieutenant's shoulder. Murph had been shot before. Worse than this, he thought, but it's never good being shot. And somehow it was worse when you saw another's wound.

"Murph," Hastings said. "Did you call for backup?"

"Yes, I did. Christ, George." Murph turned and shouted, "Get a fucking ambulance here, you idiot. He's been shot."

The patrol officer hesitated, still manning the spotlight.

And Murph said, "*Never mind that shit.* Get that ambulance now."

"Yes, sir."

"Murph—" Hastings said, his voice gravelly and low.

"Shut up, George. If we don't get the guy today, we'll get him tomorrow. He's not worth your life."

Hastings fell back. He looked up at the sky again. Looking at dark blue night, stars . . .

"Murph?" the patrolman said. "The ambulance is coming. Is he . . ."

"He passed out," Murph said.

Now there were more sirens.

Reese could hear them throughout the park. And he could see

them in the distance. Police cars finding their way in, slipping in like snakes. Reese ran down a hill and crossed a road. As he did, he looked to his left and saw a police car come out of tunnel. It was at least a hundred yards away, maybe even two hundred, and maybe the officers inside wouldn't see him as he moved up the hill on the other side, still carrying the rifle. But then the car approached, its siren piercing, and he could hear its motor, too, and he threw himself flat on the ground. The noise of the oncoming police car increased, then reached a pitch as it passed him and kept going.

Reese stood up and kept going, leaving the rifle on the ground.

TWENTY-SEVEN

They kept him in the hospital overnight. He vaguely remembered waking at six or seven in the morning, the room still dark but a hint of gray at the window, and a nurse came in and gave him a shot of something. He wanted to ask her to tell his daughter he was fine and that he would be home later, but then he fell back asleep. When he next opened his eyes, it was almost noon.

Eileen was standing there, tear stains down her cheeks, her blond hair pulled back in a ponytail.

"Yes," she said, "it's your ex-wife."

Hastings said, "Ohhh. Does this mean I've died and gone to hell?"

Eileen laughed, emotion mixing with it.

"You idiot," she said.

"Sorry. Bad joke."

"No, not that. I meant going after that psycho by yourself. You want to leave my daughter without a father?"

"No. Eileen, don't say things like that. Please."

She was chastened by his words, which was not common for her. "Okay," she said. "I won't."

There was silence between them for a while. Then Hastings said, "How is Amy?"

"She's okay, I think. She's downstairs. The doctor told her you had minor surgery. Just to clean out the wound. Something called an I and D?"

"Irrigation and drainage. Yeah, that's what they told me, too, before they put me down. I guess they were telling the truth, huh?"

"Yeah." Eileen shook her head. "Jesus, George, you scared me."

"Sorry. Who notified you?"

"Joe. God, I haven't spoken to him in years. He's never liked me, has he?"

Hastings did not answer her.

Eileen said, "Anyway, when he called me, I knew something bad had happened. He said up front that you were fine but that you had been shot. Or 'grazed,' he said. Whatever that means."

"It means there's no bullet in me."

"I guess he wanted to contact Amy through me. That's something, isn't it?"

"You *are* her mother."

"Ted's here, too. Downstairs with Amy. He wants to know if there's anything he can do."

Hastings thought about a transgression years past. Well . . . the man was here. Christ, modern family arrangements.

"Tell him thanks," Hastings said. "Really. They told me last night that if the surgery went well, they would release me today. Is that what they told you?"

"Yes."

"Good. Listen, Eileen."

"Yes?"

"I don't want Amy coming in here, seeing me like this. It may be a little much for her."

"She wants to."

"I know. But if I can get out of here in a couple of hours, see you down in the lobby, I think that would be better. For her, I mean."

Eileen looked at her ex-husband and he looked at back at her. For a moment, he persuaded himself that he had fooled her and perhaps himself, too.

"Yeah," Eileen said. "For her."

TWENTY-EIGHT

Eileen agreed to let Hastings drive Amy back to school. Before that, Hastings took her to lunch at Blueberry Hill, where they both ordered cheeseburgers. Hastings didn't have much of an appetite. But he didn't want to worry the girl. He hoped he looked normal, though he winced in pain when he moved his arm to get into the booth. He was thankful the girl did not notice this.

Amy sipped at her soda while Hastings alternated between a cup of coffee and ice water. He felt the coffee go straight to his head, though not in an altogether bad way. The food arrived and she worked on it without engaging with him. Hastings ate a couple of bites and left it alone. The morphine had worn off and now he had entirely lost his appetite.

She kept watching him. But at the same time, she would not make eye contact with him. Like she was fearful he would leave her. The poor child. Hastings told himself to hold on. If he wasn't careful, he'd start bawling in front of her, and that wouldn't do either of them any good.

Hastings said, "Amy, it's not that bad a thing."

She looked up at him and for a moment did not say anything. Then: "But you could have . . ."

"I didn't. It was like an accident."

"You were shot accidentally?"

Hastings smiled, in spite of things. She could be a little smartass, like her mother.

"No, that wasn't accidental. More police officers die in car wrecks than from anything else. It's a very, very rare thing to be shot. Or even be shot at."

"But you *were*."

"Yeah. And now I'm fine."

She continued to watch him, as if she feared he would fly away.

Hastings said, "Amy, look at it this way. The odds of being shot are, like, one in ten thousand. Now it's happened and I'm fine. I've got another ten thousand chances."

"I don't think that's funny."

"Sorry. I'm sorry I frightened you."

She looked away from him. "Why don't you just quit?"

Hastings hesitated, then said, "I don't know."

"That's not an answer," Amy said. "You get mad at me when I say I don't know."

"Do I?"

"All the time. You say, 'Don't say you don't know when you know.'"

"Sorry. Look, I can't explain why I do this. I like doing it, I guess. Maybe I could do something else. Go to law school or"—he almost said *Christ*—"or sell real estate. But I wouldn't be very good at it. I don't think I'd like it."

"You like this?"

"I think so."

Amy said, "Jenny Novacek's dad used to be a policeman. Now he owns a business."

Hastings had met Jenny's dad once while waiting to pick Amy up at school. Novacek had wasted little time telling Hastings that he had been a cop with County PD and left because there was no future for a dude who wanted to make some money. Now he owned a convenience store and gas stop on a well-chosen intersection in Alton and he had a house in Creve Coeur and a summer home on the Lake of the Ozarks. Hastings thought Novacek was a yutz.

Hastings says, "Well, that's good for him."

"Jenny said they got a bigger house and she's going to Country Day next year."

Hastings smiled. "So you want me to make more money?"

"I didn't say that." She looked at him, a bit ashamed now, but hurt, too. She said, "I didn't say that, Daddy. That's not what I meant."

"What did you mean?"

"I just meant it would be nicer. That's all."

"To have nicer things? A better school? I know that."

"I'm not talking about nicer things. I'm not complaining. I'm saying it would be nicer not to have to be scared. Not to have you gone at night. You're not the only one, you know."

Her voice broke at the end and then she was crying. Hastings moved around the booth and sat next to her, taking her in his arms. She wept, and he stopped himself from weeping and held her and told her he was sorry.

After awhile, Amy said, "I'm sorry."

"You've nothing to be sorry for," Hastings said. "I was being a jerk."

"Kinda."

Hastings said, "Maybe it is selfish of me, staying with this. Maybe if I'd known I was going to have a family, I would have chosen something else. But now I'm—now I'm a little too...old...to make changes."

"You're not that old. You just don't want to."

"Maybe that's true, too," Hastings said. "But we don't get to choose who or what we are. Not completely. Your friend's dad, he was probably a businessman who shouldn't have been a cop. But I'm not a businessman. I'd die of boredom if I had to run a convenience store."

"There are other things."

"I know. But this is *my* thing."

She looked at him and he said, "I don't know if I can explain it to you. Even if you were a grown-up, you probably still wouldn't understand it."

"Does Mom understand it?"

"She does, actually. She always has."

"Mom?"

Hastings shook his head. He knew Amy often had trouble respecting Eileen. And he knew that he had had a part in creating this. Now he made his voice firm and said, "You understand things she doesn't. But there are some things she understands that you don't. Okay?"

"...Okay."

"When you get older, you'll choose what you want to do. It won't be my decision or your mother's. It'll be yours. And we'll try to back you as best we can." Hastings leaned back, his shoulders touching the booth. "Sorry, but that's the best I can give you."

They were silent for a while. Then Amy looked at his plate.

"You're not going to eat that?" she said.

"I'm not very hungry," Hastings said.

Amy said, "I'll ask the waitress for a to-go bag. We shouldn't waste it."

TWENTY-NINE

The secretary told Hastings to go on in, and he did. He was somewhat surprised to see Captain Anthony in Deputy Chief Murray's office, too. Captain Anthony stood to greet Hastings, and Fenton Murray was forced to stand also.

They took seats and Murray asked Hastings what had happened.

Hastings gave his side of it and said he had not talked with the guys on his team since he left the hospital, so he couldn't speak for them. He told the story slowly and deliberately, as if he were typing out a report or his words were being recorded.

He finished and Murray said, "Did you get a good look at the man?"

Hastings said, "I can't say that I did. I didn't see him on the stairwell, just heard him. I saw the back of him in the alley, about forty to fifty yards from me. But if I were asked if I believed it was Reese, I would say that I do."

Murray said, "Why?"

"I don't know, exactly. The weapon he used. The way he ran. The position he took in the apartment building."

Murray let silence fill the room. Then he said, "That's it?"

"Well," Hastings said, "no, that's not all of it. It was also the way he spoke to me."

"Spoke to you?" Murray said. "I thought you said you didn't see him?"

"That is what I said. We didn't have a conversation, no. But I heard him. He called out to me."

"What did he say?"

"He said, 'You shouldn't have come after me.'"

"'You shouldn't have come after me.'"

"Yes, sir."

"He said this when?"

"After he shot me."

"Anything else? I mean, did he say anything else?"

"No."

"And these words, they make you think the shooter was John Reese?"

"Yes."

Murray displayed another skeptical frown and said, "The senator thinks you overreacted."

There was silence for a moment, Hastings waiting for some sort of elaboration. He didn't get one.

Hastings said, "Overreacted to what? Getting shot?"

Murray said, "He's not saying you didn't get shot. He's saying it wasn't Reese who shot you. Or shot at you."

"He wasn't there."

"Reese?"

"No, the senator. He wasn't in the park. I was."

Captain Anthony spoke, trying to pacify him, saying, "George—"

Hastings said to Murray, "Who does the senator think it was?"

Murray shrugged. "A junkie. Or a burglar trying to rob the apartment."

Hastings said, "I got shot with a high-powered rifle. At night, from about two hundred yards. Not a Saturday-night special. That was the work of a professional. Not a fu—not a junkie."

"Then how come you're alive?" Murray said.

Hastings could still feel the pain in his shoulder. The physician had told him it would hurt for a few days, the way any severe bruise would. Like getting pounded with a sledgehammer.

In a controlled voice, Hastings said, "I don't know why I'm alive. Maybe I got lucky. Maybe he got distracted. Maybe he was showing mercy."

Murray said, "Mercy? That wouldn't exactly be in character for our suspect, would it?"

"I wouldn't know."

"You seem to know it was him you were chasing."

"I said I believe it was him. I don't know it was." Hastings looked at Anthony, as if to make an appeal to reason. He said, "Look, Preston wasn't there. I was. Why are you giving more weight to what he says?"

Murray raised his hands in some sort of gesture, suggesting Hastings was being overly sensitive. "I just want to get it straight, that's all."

"Are you sure?" Hastings said.

Sensing insolence, Murray leaned forward and said, "What do you mean by that?"

"Nothing," Hastings said. "I guess I'd just like to get it straight, too."

Murray said, "You think Senator Preston has some personal thing with you? A city police officer?" Murray giving him a patronizing smile now.

"I don't think it has anything to do with me," Hastings said. "But, yes, I think he seems to want to discourage people from thinking it was John Reese I pursued."

"And why would he want to do that?"

"I don't know," Hastings said. "For some reason, he doesn't want federal protection. But he wants some sort of protection, and he's been getting it from the local police. In my opinion, he wants to have the protection without seeming to want it. Or have people think he wants it."

Murray said, "Well, that wouldn't say much for him, would it?"

"No, it wouldn't."

This wasn't quite the response Murray had been expecting. He said, "Maybe you're the one who's feeling something personal here."

"Well, I got shot. Wouldn't you take it personally?" Hastings looked at Captain Anthony and then back at the deputy chief. "It could have been my life out there. Or the life of one of my men. No one's asking for a thank-you, but it would be nice not be second-guessed. Or accused of lying."

Murray said, "Preston hasn't called you a liar. He's simply said he thinks you're mistaken. He's entitled to that opinion."

Hastings shook his head. "Not really."

"I see," Murray said. "Maybe it would be better if we removed you from this assignment."

"I'd rather you didn't."

"Excuse me?"

"I said I'd rather you didn't."

Murray said, "Now *I'm* confused. From what I understand, Lieutenant, you didn't want this assignment in the first place."

"That was before."

Murray said, "And now you do want it?"

"I'd prefer to stay on, yes."

Now Captain Anthony spoke. "George," he said. "I don't think you understand. The senator has requested that you be taken off the detail."

Hastings looked at both of the other men in turn. He said, "May I ask why?"

Anthony said, "He told us he doesn't think you're qualified." Anthony raised a hand. "No one here is saying he's right. In fact, I think he's wrong. I think you did well. You, Murph, Rhodes—all of you. But it doesn't matter what I think. It's what he wants. And what he wants, the chief is going to want. Sorry, George, but that's how it is."

Hastings asked, "Who's going to take it over?"

Anthony said, "Me, I suppose. If anyone."

Hastings looked at him for a moment. Then he said, " 'If anyone'? I don't understand."

Anthony said, "Senator Preston's not sure he wants police protection anymore."

THIRTY

The hotel waiter pushed the serving cart into the hotel suite and started to set the table. He held a short glass of an orange-colored liquid and asked, "Carrot juice?"

Clu Rogers said, "That's mine." The waiter set it on the table and Clu added, "It's good for the eyes."

Dexter Troy took a glass of ice water with his lunch. Kyle Anders had a tall glass of milk. The waiter left them and they began their meal.

They were in a suite on the eighteenth floor of a high-class hotel in Clayton. Their balcony overlooked Forest Park.

A few minutes passed and then there was a knock on the door. Clu answered it. Standing there was Senator Alan Preston.

"Alan," Anders said, getting to his feet. He wiped his mouth with a cotton napkin and went over to greet him.

Preston frowned at Anders and said, "I presumed we would be meeting alone."

"Where are my manners? This is Dexter Troy, and that's Clu Rogers. Two of our best employees."

Preston observed and dismissed each man in turn. Anders said, "Can I order you something?"

"No. I'm not hungry. May we speak alone?"

"Of course."

They moved out to the balcony, sliding the glass door behind them. Looking through the glass, Preston could see Clu dipping bread into an egg yolk. Eating breakfast for lunch.

Anders made a gesture to the vast park beneath them. He said, "That's a real jewel you got there. Forest Park. It's not as big as Central Park, but it's bigger than most."

"We like it," Preston said, waiting for Anders to stop playing with him.

Anders said, "You think he's still in there?"

Alan Preston smiled. "Who?"

Anders said, "You know," reproof in his tone.

"Like I told the police," Preston said. "It could have been anyone. A junkie. A burglar."

"Does a junkie know how to use a high-powered rifle? How to hide at night? How to stake out a defense position and shoot a police officer from a couple hundred yards?" Anders smiled. "If he did, maybe I'd recruit him."

"No one saw him. No one got a good look."

"Maybe not," Anders said. "But *we* know, don't we?" Anders looked back out to the park. He said, "He's here in the city. We know it and the policeman knows it. What's his name, again?"

"Hastings."

"The one I met, right?"

"Yeah."

"What do you think of him?"

"Not much. I asked the chief of police to have him taken off the detail."

Anders said, "Why?"

"Because he doesn't know what he's doing."

"Are you sure it isn't the other way around?"

The senator turned to look at him.

Anders said, "Maybe he knows exactly what he's doing and that's why you wanted him taken off."

"He's not a concern. Not anymore."

"Why did he come up to us when we were talking? What was that about?"

"I don't know. Why don't you ask him?"

"Calm down, Alan. I'm on your side. Besides, we both know why you want the police out of it."

"Suppose you tell me what we both know."

"You want the police out of the way so we can eliminate Reese. Now that you've got confirmation that he's here."

"I never said I wanted that. In fact, I never told you to go after him in North Dakota. I had no part in that. That was your decision."

"Was it?" Anders said, and looked hard at the senator.

Preston made his voice firm. "Yes," he said.

"As I remember it," Anders said, "I asked you if there were any impediments to your being elected president. And you told me about John Reese. I don't think you told me everything, but you told me enough to let me know you were worried."

"I never said you should kill him."

"No. You didn't use those words. Men like you never do."

"And what about you, Kyle? A man of honor? The untarnished soldier?"

"I believe in my country. And doing what's necessary to defend it."

"A patriot."

"Excuse me?" Anders said, his face registering anger and offense.

"Forget it," Preston said.

Anders said, "You're worried that you framed a man. Perhaps you think you framed a guilty man. If so, you should know that I think he was guilty, too."

"You don't know what you're talking about. It was years ago."

"Alan, do you think I'd invest all this time and money in you without having your background checked?"

Preston turned to him, taken aback.

"Yes," Anders said, "I've known about it for a long time. Before you told me."

Preston said, "We should have just left him in prison."

"No. Things like that have a way of getting out. Particularly when a man runs for the highest office in the land. The problem needed to be addressed."

"I don't like this. I don't like any of it."

"Alan, the man's a traitor. You did what you thought you needed to do. And the proper sentence for treason is death, not prison. That's what the judge should have done in the first place. Don't you agree?"

Preston wasn't sure. He had put it behind him. Now, though, he wondered if Kyle Anders was quite sane.

"... I don't know," Preston said.

"You know he's guilty. You told me yourself he was."

"He is. But ..."

"If he's guilty of treason, he deserves to die." Anders's gaze at

Preston was steady and assured. "He's here now, here in this city, coming after you. You believe it, don't you?"

"I don't know."

"I do. I think you do, too." Anders turned back to indicate the two mercenaries eating their dinner. "But not to worry. I've got these two and a few more. There will be at least half a dozen men covering your house at all times. And these are professionals. Not a bunch of Keystone metro cops."

Preston gestured to Dexter Troy and Clu Rogers. He said, "You're going to have these guys follow me around?"

"Not exactly," Anders said. "They're not guards. They're hunters." Anders smiled again. "Don't worry, Alan. If Reese is in town, they'll find him."

THIRTY-ONE

Hastings sat at his desk, looking at the bottle of pain pills he had been prescribed. His shoulder hurt and he wanted to part with the pain. But he had never liked taking pills. Even antibiotics kept him awake at night. He wondered if he could just take a couple of Tylenol and get a full night's sleep. He wondered if John Reese would still be in town when he woke up. He wondered if pain medication would affect his thinking, his ability to track Reese. He wondered what it would be like to be back there in the darkness, looking up at the sky, waiting to die. He wondered if he would be able to turn off the memory. He wondered if he would be able to stop feeling scared.

The telephone on his desk rang.

"Hastings."

"George?"

"Carol?"

"Did you—were you shot?"

"Uh, not really. It was more of a graze."

"You were, weren't you? God, why didn't you tell me? I heard about it at the courthouse today. Why didn't you call me?"

"Sorry. I—really, it's not that big a deal."

"Are you okay?"

"I'm fine. Just a little bruising. Like knocking your shoulder into a door."

"You were shot. Why didn't you tell me?"

"I'm sorry. It's just— I'm sorry."

"Is it because we've broken up? You think you can't tell me about a major event like that because we're not seeing each other anymore?"

"I don't know."

"Like I wouldn't care?"

"I never thought that—"

"For God's sake, George. Give me some credit, will you?"

"Sorry."

"Don't do that to me. Okay?"

"Okay."

Silence for a moment. Then Carol said, "Are you all right?"

"I'm fine. Just a little pain in my shoulder."

"Did they get the bullet out?"

"There was no bullet to get out. I told you. It just passed through."

"Well, don't get short with me."

"I'm not. Sorry."

"And quit saying you're sorry. Jesus." Carol said, "George?" a familiar tenderness in her voice.

"Yeah, sweetie?"

"I miss you."

"I miss you, too."

"But we did the right thing, huh?"

"I think we did."

Another silence. Then Hastings said, "Carol?"

"Yes?"

"... Nothing."

Carol said, "Do you want me to come over tonight?"

"Well…" It was exactly what he'd been going to ask her. He leaned back in his chair. "Yeah, I guess so," he said.

"You guess so." He could hear a smile in her voice.

Hastings sighed. "I don't know, Carol. It's a bad idea. You broke up with me for good reasons. I'm lonely and I'm horny and I'm— well, I'm…"

"A little scared, too. Am I right?"

"Yeah, you're right."

"There's nothing to be ashamed of, George. You could have been killed. I cried when I heard about it. Even when I was told you were okay."

"Sorry."

"I told you to stop that."

"I know."

Another silence. Then Carol said, "Will you be home in an hour?"

"…Yes."

"I won't stay the night. Can you understand that?"

"Yes."

"Okay," Carol said, and hung up the phone.

He awoke from an unpleasant dream around three in the morning. The room came into focus and he looked to his right and saw Carol lying naked in a fetal position, her back toward him, her skin pale, her figure beautiful. She was sleeping peacefully beside the covers. She had always been comfortable with her body, comfortable being naked. She swam thirty laps a day, five days a week, and it showed.

Hastings's shoulder throbbed. The Tylenol had worn off. He

quietly climbed out of bed and walked to the kitchen and took two more. He stood in the dark for a moment and then he walked to the large front window of the condominium. An old habit. He looked out the window at the street and saw his car parked below. Still, quiet, no traffic on the street. He looked beyond the street to Francis Park. Nothing going on there. Nothing he could see anyway.

Go back twenty-four hours and change. A man running through another park. A man hunting another man, the hunter becoming the hunted. Shot, wounded, vulnerable. Very vulnerable. A fucking victim.

Had Reese shown mercy? Had he let him live? Or was he stretching out the kill for his own satisfaction? For sport. What if Murph hadn't shown up when he did? Lighting up the park with the police car.

He'd survived the night. And now he had to hide things. Hide his fear from his daughter, his ex-wife, the men on his squad, and, perhaps most importantly, the department brass. He couldn't let them see weakness. He couldn't let them see that he felt . . . ashamed. Ashamed, and he didn't know why.

Carol saw through him. Consequently, she offered herself to him. He needed her and she knew it. Maybe he needed her particularly or maybe he needed just someone for the night. Either way, she wasn't going to ask him which. Maybe she needed to be needed, though that would be a chickenshit way to think about it. She was a good lady.

You shouldn't have come after me.

That was what Reese had said. It haunted him now. What had the man meant by that? That Hastings wasn't in his league? That he was outclassed? A fool? Were they the last words he was to hear before getting the last, fatal shot to the head or the heart?

Or was it just a taunt? An insult to be added to the mercy.

He was out of it now. The deputy chief and Captain Anthony had told him he was relieved of duty, taken off the assignment. Senator Preston had apparently had enough of him. For reasons Hastings could not understand.

He could walk away, be done with it. Senator Preston was a nasty piece of work anyway. The best thing to do with such people was to avoid them. If Preston was intent on being stubborn, leaving himself open to Reese, that was his problem. Walk away. Be glad you're alive. Be glad you have people in your life who care about you.

Hastings thought of Bobby Cain, a cocky young sergeant who had been assigned to his squad when Klosterman was in the hospital with cancer. Hastings had not liked Cain. Cain had a big mouth and he had political connections and a rank that he probably hadn't earned. But to Hastings's surprise, Cain had been a courageous, thoughtful, diligent detective. And when he was killed in the line of duty, Hastings's grief was genuine.

What had he told Cain? What had he told him after they left the prison where the inmate had talked smack to Cain and Cain wanted to tear his head off? Hastings had expressly told Cain not to take the work personally. That a turd was a turd and should not be a concern to any police officer. If the turds got away, they would eventually die or be arrested for something else or otherwise wither away. What difference should it make to a police officer? Life was too short.

Yeah, good advice, Lieutenant. Hastings wondered now if he was any smarter than Cain had been.

He returned to bed and pulled the covers over Carol and within a couple of minutes he was asleep. When he awoke the next morning, she was gone.

THIRTY-TWO

Klosterman set the rifle on Hastings's desk. He said, "They found it in Forest Park, a couple of hundred yards away from where you were shot. No prints. He was wearing gloves or he wiped it clean."

Hastings examined it. A Model 70 Winchester .30-06 Springfield. A scope on top. Hastings thought of himself being sighted through that scope.

Hastings said, "This is a good weapon."

"Not a junkie's weapon," Klosterman said. "You have no doubt it was Reese?"

"None. I wish I had physical evidence, though."

"Okay." Klosterman said, "You think he's still in town?"

"Yeah," Hastings said. "He hasn't got what he wants yet."

"But he knows we're onto him. Why not clear out?"

"Because he's determined. Maybe he's got nothing else."

"I thought we were out of this," Klosterman said.

"We're off the protection detail," Hastings said. "But John Reese is wanted on suspicion of assault with a deadly weapon. A weapon he used on me. So I'm going to find him and I'm going to arrest him. *Before* he leaves town. He's in our jurisdiction now."

"Okay, George. But how are we going to find him?"

"I'm working on it." Hastings sighed. "I guess we won't be getting any help from Preston or his people."

"I don't understand that. Why would he deny that you saw Reese?"

"I don't know. He told us that he'd never wanted our protection, that he was doing it for his wife. Which I never believed. Now he says he doesn't want our protection anymore. And this is *after* we have evidence that someone was after him."

"It doesn't make sense," Klosterman said. "You'd think it would have scared him. I mean, *someone* shot at you."

"With a rifle. Preston's a fucking squirrel. He hasn't played straight with us from the beginning."

"Maybe we should question him. It is a felony investigation now."

"Maybe."

"I don't know," Klosterman said. "Then again, maybe we shouldn't."

"What's your concern?"

"My concern is, maybe the deputy chief would haul you in and ask you what you're doing bothering an upstanding public servant, treating him like a felon. He'd say, 'George, the man hasn't committed a crime. What are you messing with him for?' and you know what else?"

"What?"

"He'll say that you're just trying to rattle Preston's cage because he pissed you off. And now you're taking it personally."

"Would you think that?"

"Not for a minute."

Hastings said nothing.

"... George?"

"Kyle Anders," Hastings said.

"What?"

Hastings said, "That's who Preston was talking to. Let's find out who he is."

"All right, George. But what about Reese?"

Hastings said, "I think he's going to look for another rifle."

THIRTY-THREE

Reese chose the regular targets, the ones with the circular bull's-eyes. The proprietor of the shooting range gave him a headset for ear protection and two boxes of ammunition for the 1911 .45.

The shooting range was outdoors, about five miles outside of the town of Piedmont. It was about an hour-and-a-half drive from St. Louis.

Reese wished he had not driven the Mercury to the shooting range. It was black, and at a distance people might think it was a law-enforcement vehicle. But people might also think he was a militia man, wanting to look tough. Reese had come to the range in dungarees and a flannel shirt and boots. Apart from the car, he blended in.

Reese set up his targets and began shooting.

He had to wait a couple of hours before he found a mark. Two men in their late thirties who came in separate vehicles. They had a lot of handguns but seemed to spend most of their time shooting heavy .44 Magnums, long-barreled hand cannons that sent bullets through the paper-man targets and burrowing into the sand mounds behind. They conversed between shots, sometimes switching their guns. Reese overheard them using the term *law dogs* and making curt remarks about the prospect of having "George Jefferson in the White House." He also heard one of them talking about where to get a decent Austrian army tent.

The one who spoke about the tent was the one Reese followed.

Kolonel Tom Boback parked his Jeep in front of his small house. The house was in an isolated area in the Ozark hills. He carried his bag of guns into the house. On the wall of Kolonel Tom's living room was a Confederate flag. He lived alone.

He'd had a girlfriend once. Her name was Missy and she was a militiawoman and, like him, a free-born White Christian American. He had taken her to northwest Arkansas, konsecrated Klan kountry, for a militia campout last year and she had taken up with Kaptain Jim Casey and sent him home alone. She had told him she was moving on. Left him for someone of lesser rank. After that, Kolonel Tom smashed out the headlights of her car. The new boyfriend did nothing about it. If he had tried, Kolonel Tom would have shot him in the head.

Kolonel Tom had been drawn to the militia movements when he was a teenager. School had been difficult for him. He was awkward-looking and not athletically inclined and he was often picked on. This experience did not make him any more sympathetic to the weak. The kids who tormented him were mostly white, yet their conduct only seemed to increase his hatred for Jews and blacks. He was expelled from high school after he pushed a girl down a flight of stairs and broke her arm. The girl had laughed at him about something he had forgotten. Life was a series of fits and starts after that. For six years, he managed to hold down a fairly well-paying union job at a supermarket. But then a Wal-Mart was built down the street and they closed the supermarket and Tom lost his job. Kolonel Tom attributed this misfortune to the continuing collapse of the U.S. economy as well as to the invasion and colonization of the country by illegal aliens.

Now he put a burrito in the microwave oven. A few minutes later, he ate it in front of the television set and washed it down with Mountain Dew. He watched the news of the senator from Illinois's progress with mixed feelings. The possibility of a coon president disgusted him, to be sure, but it gave him comfort, too, because it was a sign that the end of the nation was at hand and that the ultimate victory would be with him and his brethren so long as they put their faith in their Lord and Savior.

Then he heard the lawn mower.

No. It wasn't a lawn mower. It sounded like an ATV.

His ATV.

Grabbing a shotgun, Kolonel Tom went outside to investigate.

From his porch, he saw his ATV bump and roll across the front yard, no one riding it. Then he felt a gun being pressed against the side of his head.

"Drop the weapon," a voice said.

Kolonel Tom turned swiftly. He saw a gun move in a quick arc. It made contact with his head and he went to the ground.

When Kolonel Tom regained consciousness, his vision was blurred. Then he realized that the intruder had taken his glasses. The Kolonel was very nearsighted. He was also tied up, his hands bound in front of him, looped through and around his belt. When he tugged his hands up, it lifted his belt and his pants hitched. He was on the couch in his living room.

A form before him, vague and nondistinct. A man.

The man said, "Where do you keep the rest of your weapons?"

After a moment, Kolonel Tom said, "Get out of my house, zog."

" 'Zog'?" Reese said. "Oh. You think I'm a cop?"

"A fed. Yeah. Probably ATF."

"Well, you're wrong. You see this? It's your shotgun. If you don't tell me where the rest of your weapons are stored, I'm going to put the muzzle against your knee and pull the trigger. With the load you put in it, you'll lose your leg."

"Now I know you're federal."

Reese moved closer to him and pointed the shotgun at his knee. "You want to find out?"

"I keep the rest of my guns in the cellar," Kolonel Tom said.

"I checked the cellar."

"There's another one in the barn."

"Is it locked?"

"Yeah."

"Come on, then."

Reese got him to his feet and walked him out to the barn. Kolonel Tom unlocked the barn's cellar door, which was almost flush with the ground. Then he flipped on a switch, illuminating the area beneath.

Reese said, "You first."

Kolonel Tom began descending the steps.

Reese poked him in the back with the shotgun, saying, "You try to reach for a weapon, anything, I'll blow a hole right through you."

"I hear you," Kolonel Tom said, his voice hoarse.

Reese took the room in and thought, Bingo. It was about what he'd expected, maybe even a little better.

On the wall was a black-and-white photograph of a World War II Tiger tank, some German soldiers standing around it. Another photo was of Field Marshal Rommel conferring with Hitler. Other assorted trinkets of the Third Reich lay about. There were several weapons on a cafeteria-length table. Rifles, shotguns, a couple of AK-47s, Chinese assault rifles, an ArmaLite with a leather strap, various handguns, an antitank rifle, two Uzi submachine guns, and a Mac-10.

Reese smiled and said, "Planning a war?"

"Yeah, actually," Kolonel Tom said.

Reese couldn't resist it. "Were you in the service?"

"No. Been in combat, though."

"Where?"

"Training exercises. Northwest Arkansas."

"I see."

Reese looked at other rifles hanging on the wall. He said, "Have you got rounds for that Lee-Enfield?"

"Yeah. On the workbench. Over there."

Reese was referring to the SMLE—short, magazine, Lee-Enfield. It had been the standard British infantry firearm in World War II and was probably the best all-around combat bolt-action rifle ever made. It could hold ten cartridges. The Enfield had a leather strap, probably vintage.

Reese took the rifle down and inspected it. It had scope mounts already drilled into it. Sporterized, though the stock was original. Reese shoved a cartridge in the breech, then rammed it home with the bolt action.

Kolonel Tom flinched.

Reese said, "Where's the scope?"

"I traded it last year. For a television."

"What kind of scope was it?"

"A Mauser."

"You should have held on to it," Reese said. "It was worth more than a television." He put a box of rounds in his coat pocket. Then he took a wad of notes from his pants. He counted out a sum and put it on the table.

Reese said, "That's a thousand dollars."

"It's worth more than that."

"It's what you're getting," Reese said. "I'm going to leave you down here. You'll be able to get out, but I wouldn't advise trying it too soon. Now listen to me: I'm giving you money for your rifle and I could have easily killed you. You come after me, I *will* kill you. Trust me, I've done it before."

Kolonel Tom said, "You're a thief. Worse than that, a federal thief. Paying me with taxpayers' money."

"Yeah, whatever. Now you remember what we talked about."

Reese took the man's eyeglasses from his coat pocket and set them on the table. "Here are your glasses."

Then Reese went up the steps, keeping an eye on the nut job. When he got out, he closed the door behind him. Reese looked around the barn to see if there was an object he could place on top of the cellar door. His eyes came to rest on a bale of hay. But he decided it would be too heavy and the nut wouldn't be able to get out at all and he would suffocate amid his Nazi treasures.

Reese backed out of the barn, training the Enfield on the door. If the man came out, he would kill him. He wouldn't wait to see if he was armed. Shoot between the space on his glasses.

He put fifty yards between himself and the barn, then a hundred. Soon he was at his Mercury, which he had parked out of sight of the house. He got in it, started it, and left.

He felt better when he was a few miles down the road. Good enough that he could laugh about Kolonel Tom. He'd known guys like that in boot camp. Hate-filled Gomer Pyles who couldn't adjust to civilian life but needed to identify with something. Some of the recruits in boot camp were already men, their personalities already formed. Some of them were borderline retarded. And then there were a few assorted mental cases, some of whom were salvageable. The military might have been able to save Kolonel Tom, Reese thought. He had known a handful of hard-core racists who, through military training, overcame their prejudices for the sake of becoming good soldiers, who learned to think not so much in terms of black and white but more in terms of military and civilian, enemy and friend. The military was one of the few successful government social programs in that respect.

Reese had been sent to the army by a judge. Once there, he adjusted and he accepted. He made a decision not to look back. A year after finishing boot camp, he volunteered for the army Rangers. He completed the training and attended all the schools, including SERE (survival, evasion, resistance, and escape). Most of the SERE training was done in the mountains of northern Georgia, near Fort Benning. During one of the training exercises, he crossed paths with a particularly vicious marine, who had been assigned the role of enemy pursuer. Reese at that time was a mere corporal, training with two other noncommissioned officers of higher rank and a navy ensign. The ensign fell apart early and Reese took de facto command. The ensign was ultimately caught and beaten by the overly zealous marine. The next day, Reese told the others to move on. He hung back, found a tree that he liked, climbed up it, and waited. Eventually, the marine came along and Reese fell on him.

The marine fought back, treating it like regular combat, and got his arm broken for his trouble. Reese seized his weapon and took his pursuer captive. Reese was later promoted to top sergeant.

In 1983, he parachuted into Grenada with other army Rangers. It was a short-lived military action with few casualties. But Reese distinguished himself in combat. He was approached by the CIA a month later. He was interviewed and tested. They found he had an affinity for learning languages. That he was proficient with small arms, particularly grenades and submachine guns. That he was quiet and modest in appearance. That he was a natural soldier. That he was a loner, with no close friends or long-term girlfriends. That he was intelligent and a natural problem solver. That he was not psychotic but still had a rational, cold-eyed view of human nature. Eventually, they asked him if he would be interested in becoming part of what they called the "intelligence community."

As part of his suitability check, he was interviewed by a series of psychologists to see if he was mentally stable. During one of the interviews, the subject of how he joined the army arose. Reese told the story without emotion.

The psychologist said, "Before the fight with the other boy, had you had some sort of training in self-defense? Martial arts, anything like that?"

"No."

"Then how did you know what to do?"

"I just knew."

"No one taught you?"

Reese said, "I don't think you teach someone to do that."

"Do you think you're a violent man?"

"No."

"Do you feel anger at your father?"

"I don't know my father."

He was recruited and trained. The next ten years saw him in El Salvador, Angola, London, Beirut, Beijing, and Berlin. In time, he spoke French, German, Spanish, and Arabic with a natural ease. He was less adept with Chinese and Japanese, but knew enough to get by. Working with the French intelligence agency, he was instrumental in tracking down the planner of two airline hijackings. Thereafter, the planner was shot and killed outside his hideout in the Lebanese mountains. The planner's associates believed the killing was done with a rifle and the shooter was at least eight hundred yards away.

At this time, Reese was what the intelligence community called a "blue badger"—that is, someone working directly for the CIA.

It was sometime after the hijack planner was killed that Reese informed his superiors he was more interested in gathering intelligence than he was in being an assassin. The CIA chiefs did not interpret this as a sign of weakness, but, rather, as a sign that Reese wanted to be in management, as opposed to labor. They acceded to his wishes and he became active in E&E (escape and evasion) work. During the last few years of the Cold War, Reese was instrumental in bringing burned-out, or "blown," agents out of the Soviet Union or China. Like David Chang, most of the agents understood that they owed their lives to Reese and his team. Some were grateful to him, others not so much.

Reese's last E&E job had been in East Germany. He was trying to sneak a scientist across the border when they were ambushed by Stasi agents. There was a firefight. Reese and his people managed to escape, but not before Reese took a bullet in his back.

The surgery was performed in Frankfurt and he was evacuated to a hospital in London for recuperation. Doctors told him that the bullet had narrowly missed his spine and he was lucky that he would be walking again.

It was in the hospital in London that he met and fell in love with a nurse.

Her name was Sara Jennings. She was fair-skinned and brown-haired and she had a funny-looking, beautiful mouth. She was only a few years younger than Reese (he was in his early thirties then), but she talked to him as if he were an older man, her tone patronizing and warm. "How's our Mr. Reese this morning?"

She seemed to sense that he was depressed by what could be a long, painful recovery. He would walk again, but not without enduring strenuous physical therapy. Sara Jennings also sensed that for all his machismo, he was perhaps lonely and vulnerable.

Reese flirted with her, but soon he saw that she would be no quick, easy seduction. During his second week, she came into his hospital room and caught him watching a British ballroom dance show on television. He was captivated by it.

"Are you enjoying this?"

"I am," Reese said. "We have nothing like this in the States. They do this every week?"

"Yes," she said. "Have you not been in England before?"

"I live here on and off," he said. "But I've never had time to watch your television shows."

"Would you prefer *Dynasty*?"

He was struck by this. This cute English girl referencing American pop culture in her English voice. Teasing him. Taking the piss, as the British say.

"No. I like this better."

Eventually, she took to visiting him in his room before she went home. Sometimes she would sit by his bed with her coat over her uniform, signaling she wouldn't be staying long, guarding herself. They learned small things about each other. She was from Islington and her father had been a soldier who had helped evacuate Dunkirk in a fishing boat when the Germans were coming over the hill. He had returned to France on D-day. She asked Reese if he was a soldier, too.

No, he told her. He was a businessman.

She smiled at him then and he knew that she knew he was lying.

She said, "You were shot."

Reese shrugged and changed the subject.

A few days later, she said, "You are a soldier, aren't you?"

"Sort of," Reese said.

"Have you got a wife, children?"

"No."

"What, then? Just short-term affairs, a sad steady series of trollops?"

Yes, there had been women. Some of them prostitutes. In Berlin and Hamburg and Hong Kong. He was not ashamed of any of it.

Still, he did not discuss this with her. Before he had met her, he had presumed that he preferred the short term. He also presumed that she would tease him again about his bachelorhood.

But what she did was look at him plainly and say, "There's a void in you, isn't there? A sadness."

Reese smiled at her. "I think you're imagining things," he said.

"No."

"And what about you?"

The nurse said, "That's none of your business."

Within a couple of weeks, he became accustomed to tea at four o'clock. She would sit with him while he drank his tea and ate the buttered toast she brought him. She would chat with him about seemingly mundane subjects, which he enjoyed very much. He had never known pleasant domesticity.

He would eventually say to her, "I think the English are the happiest people I know."

"You don't know many English," she said.

"I've worked with some."

"Made any friends?"

He didn't answer her.

And she said, "We're very different. You Americans love success. We wallow in failures. We love our flops."

"Like Eddie Eagle?"

"Exactly," she said. "You're always looking for something better, something more. Have you worked with British soldiers?"

A moment passed. She's smart, Reese thought. He said, "Yes."

"Have you ever heard a British enlisted man apologize for his rank?"

Very smart.

"No," Reese said.

"Do you miss America?"

"...I don't know. Sometimes, I guess. What are we talking about here?"

"We're having tea, that's all."

An agent from the Tokyo station had once told Reese that the perfect setup was to have a Japanese wife, an American salary, an English garden, and a Chinese cook. The worst combination: Japanese garden, Chinese salary, English cook, American wife. Something like that. He had not resided in the United States for any length of time after being recruited by the Agency. Accordingly, the notion of marrying an American woman had not really been an issue. Indeed, he had never given serious thought to marriage at all.

Until he met Sara Jennings. Like Miles Copeland, another American CIA operative, he was falling in love with an Englishwoman. And, in the process, he was becoming an Anglophile. Teatime, soccer, television shows about ballroom dancing, and so forth. He was becoming attached to these things, attached to this culture.

He was an American and he did not suffer from any identity issues. Circumstances had forced him to become a soldier. In time, he came to realize that he was good at soldiering and relieved to be out of what would have been a dead-end life in Texas. No one had forced him to join the Agency. He had been recruited and he saw it as an opportunity to do more interesting work. He still believed he was working for his country.

An attachment to an Englishwoman would complicate his life as well as his career. Perhaps even complicate his identity.

Shortly before his release from the hospital, he made a decision. He would ask the woman to go on a weekend trip with him. If she refused, that would be the end of it. If she agreed, he would take her away for a couple of days and get her out of his system.

He asked and she agreed.

Reese rented a car and together they drove to the English West Country. They stayed in a bed-and-breakfast that did not have an elevator. Climbing the stairs, Reese realized he was still weakened by his injuries and had to stop. Sara took the luggage from his hand and assisted him the rest of the way.

They had dinner at the inn and then got drunk at the local pub. Reese had never had so much fun in a bar before. He joked with Sara and talked with the locals. He had intended to maul her once he got to the room, but once there, he didn't have the strength to try. He fell on the bed with his clothes still on. He remembered seeing her come out of the bathroom in a robe. She climbed in with him and then he was asleep.

The next morning, they made love. Tentatively at first, but then enthusiastically. After, she said, "Better?" And he laughed.

It was at breakfast that she told him she knew what he was up to.

There weren't many other people in the dining room. It was an old-fashioned place, with small tables and black-and-white pictures on the wall of Brits walking amid rubble caused by German planes, the British people unfazed.

There was contemporary music on the radio, coming from the kitchen. Tears for Fears singing "Everybody Wants to Rule the World."

Reese sat with the woman, comfortable being quiet with her.

Sara was looking at her menu when she said, "So when were you planning to do it?"

"Do what?" Reese said.

"Give me the piss-off."

"Excuse me?"

"The brush, as you Americans say. When are you going to say good-bye?" Her soft brown eyes lifted from the menu and rested on him.

"It's okay," she said. "I know."

Reese said, "You don't know anything."

"I know more than you think," she said. "That man who came to see you the other day, he's no businessman."

"He's a friend."

"He's with MI6. If you know him, it's because you work with him. You're a spy, Mr. Reese."

"I was a soldier. Now I'm in business."

"Don't worry," she said. "We're onto that sort of thing at the hospital. We've been vetted, sworn to secrecy, everything."

For a while, Reese said nothing. Then he looked at her with a certain resignation. He said, "Have I lied to you?"

She gave him a minx look. "Small lies," she said. Then her expression softened and she looked sad. "It's okay, though. I'm not sorry, you know."

"Not sorry about what?"

"That I met you. I'm glad, in fact. It was something, wasn't it?"

Reese stared at her for a moment, the word *was* suddenly very painful to him. "What is this?" he said. "A preemptive strike?"

"Sorry?"

"Are you ending this?"

"It's what you want."

"Who says?"

"It what you've been thinking since we left London. I'm not a bloody fool, you know."

"Okay," he said, "maybe it is. But that doesn't mean I can't change my mind."

"And what?" she said. "Drop by for a quick shag every time you're in London. Sorry, I don't fancy that."

"That's not what I had in mind," Reese said.

"What, then?"

Reese thought about it. The biggest decisions he'd ever made, he'd made quickly and without much thought. He looked at a British family at a nearby table: the father pasty-looking and wearing thick glasses, helping his son with his food, the mother looking at a tourist's map, Tears for Fears drifting out of the kitchen. He knew then what he wanted, and knowing gave him a comfort and faith he'd never had before.

"Well," Reese said, "I'd have to seek a transfer to the London station. And do administrative work. I don't think that should be a problem, particularly since I've been injured. It might take a few weeks to get it resolved. Then we could get married."

She did not answer for a moment. Then she said, "You love me, then?"

"You know I do."

Sara said, "Well then, kiss me, you stupid bastard."

They kissed. When they parted, he saw tears in her eyes and he wiped them away.

"Don't cry, Sara. I'm going to make you happy."

"You'd better."

They married a month later.

The Agency was not willing to take Reese completely out of the field. He was too valuable and few agents had his extensive knowledge of the Middle East. It was eventually decided that he could reside in London and report to the London station chief. However, he was strongly encouraged to assist the Beirut station chief as well.

After a year of that, Reese started to consider retiring from the CIA. At that time, he had been married for a year. The marriage was a happy one, happier than he'd thought it would be. When he thought of what he had said to her—"I'm going to make you happy"—he laughed at himself. It was she who had made him happy, had brought him to life. He had gotten the best of the bargain, and she knew it all along. Now they wanted to start a family. Reese discussed it with his station chief. A week later, he was flown to Washington to discuss it with an assistant deputy director.

The assistant deputy director's name was Burl Woods. He was old-school CIA, a cowboy. It was Woods who had recruited Reese to the CIA and had overseen his career since.

Burl Woods asked Reese to become a "green badger"—a contract employee for the CIA. He was told he could make a lot of money.

"Doing what?" Reese asked.

"Selling arms," Woods said. "We would finance you. You'd be in business. It would give you cover, you'd make some money, and we'd get some information."

"I don't know."

"John," Woods said, "come on. What are you going to do? Come back to the States, sell real estate?"

"Maybe."

"Maybe my ass. You haven't lived here in over ten years. What were you when you went in the army, seventeen?"

"Eighteen."

"What, are you going to go back to Texas? That's not who you are anymore. Are you going to tell me you can go back?"

"Maybe."

"You're not going to like civilian life here. You've been spoiled. I know your wife's not going to like it."

"Don't talk about my wife."

"Okay. But am I right in saying you'd rather stay in London?"

"You might be right."

"Then this is ideal. You'd be working with us, not for us. You'll make some money and you'll be helping your country."

"Well, this is awfully nice of you, Burl," Reese said. "But tell me. What have I done to deserve such generosity?"

"You're the best man for this job. You know intelligence. You know Europe. You're good with Arabs. You get along with people. You haven't become paranoid or otherwise fucked up by the work. You can run a business."

"Like Air America, huh?"

"Ah, that was a long time ago. Look, you know how this trade works. We need 'independent' businesses for cover and we need people we can trust to run them."

"You trust me?"

"Sure. I recruited you, didn't I? *I'm* no fuckup."

Reese smiled and Burl Woods smiled back at him.

Burl Woods said, "Just think about it, will you?"

That was how Reese became an arms dealer.

Over the next few years, Reese dealt in weapons and information. During that time, virtually all his contacts with the CIA were made through Burl Woods. Reese provided details and photographs of terrorist activity in Amman, Khartoum, Baghdad, Syria, Qatar, the Balkans, Eastern Europe, and Tehran. Those doing business with him knew he was an American, but they believed that he was a man without country or conscience. To them, he was an affable rogue. A charming mercenary, unburdened by shame. Most of them were aware that he had been a soldier who, they believed, at some point decided to quit being a chump. He seemed to like nice things: cars, homes, girls, boats, and liquor. Sometimes he was known to provide these things, if the order was large enough. He made a lot of money and at one time was rumored to own shares in the top brothel in Hamburg, Germany.

Through his contacts with both the people seeking arms and his old friends in the European intelligence agencies, Reese learned that Europe was becoming a breeding ground for terrorists. He documented this in his written reports to Woods. In one of his reports, he warned that more terrorists were being bred in Hamburg and Barcelona than in Iran or Iraq. He wondered, though, if his reports were being taken seriously. At times, he even missed the relative simplicity of the Cold War.

Meanwhile, he and Sara were having trouble making a baby. Though he was often away from London, their sex life was relatively active and healthy. He made efforts to be home when she was ovulating. But nothing had happened. It upset her. Reese had told her not to worry about it. The doctors had examined them both and found nothing wrong. It would happen in time, Reese told her.

Once in awhile, they still socialized with people in the London intelligence community. It was at a dinner party that Reese found himself in a pissing contest with A. Lloyd Gelmers. Gelmers was still doing intelligence work then, though not very well, by most accounts. It was known that the chief of London station wanted to get rid of him. Gelmers had by then made friends with people in the Clinton administration.

After dinner, Gelmers was flirting with the wife of an attaché and he called out to Reese in an effort to embarrass him.

"Still doing consultation, John?"

Reese said, "Yeah."

Gelmers gave his female friend a smirk and said, "John used to be one of us."

The woman said, "A spy?"

"I was in the army," Reese said.

"Were," Gelmers said. "Now you're living in a town house in London with a pretty British wife. Makes you wonder, doesn't it?"

Reese shrugged.

Gelmers said, "So, John. What do you think about this situation in Yugoslavia?"

"I think it's a mess."

"What should we do?"

"Stay out of it."

"Stay out of it? Shall we just let the Serbs massacre at will?"

Reese was not surprised at Gelmers's hawkishness. The Clinton administration was drumming up support for intervention in the Balkans. Gelmers, who didn't believe in much of anything, wanted a post in the Clinton administration. As usual, he blew with the wind.

Reese said, "There are massacres everywhere, every day."

"You defend Milošević? You defend fascism?"

"Milošević is a Communist, not a fascist. I know your people would rather forget that. Far more people were killed in Rwanda than in Bosnia. About eight hundred thousand more. We didn't get involved then."

"Let me understand you. Are you saying the Clintons are socialists as well as racists?"

"I'm saying it's more convenient for Clinton to call Milošević a fascist than a small-time Communist thug. Which is what he is."

"The Serbs are killing civilians."

"We intervene, we'll be killing civilians."

Gelmers smiled at the girl. He said to Reese, "I had no idea you were such a fan of Serbia."

"I'm not. But I'm no fan of the Albanians or the KLA, either. Their leaders are gangsters, too. The Balkans have a long history of slaughtering each other. It's not something we're going to fix. And we shouldn't try."

"You're a cold man. And a fucking hypocrite."

"All that and more," Reese said. "But not ambitious."

Gelmers glared at Reese for a long time. Reese smiled back at him. Then he walked off to join his wife.

A week after that conversation, Reese sold weapons to a group of Syrians. It was no different from what he had done before. Even so, he advised Burl Woods of his mission before he left London. Woods wished him luck and said he would speak with him when he returned.

A few days after that, Reese was in Belgium for a meeting. He was arrested at the train station. Hours later, he was on a C-140, heading for Washington D.C. An agent on the plane informed him that Burl Woods had died in an auto accident two days earlier.

Reese immediately thought of A. Lloyd Gelmers and how expensive vengeance can be. He thought the worst. You should have walked away from him, Reese thought. How dangerous cowards can be.

Burl was dead. Who would take his side?

For perhaps the first time in his life, Reese felt a rising panic. He said to the agent, "I need to call my wife."

"Fuck you, traitor," the agent said. "You're going to prison."

THIRTY-FOUR

"Escobar."

"Efrain?"

"Yeah."

"George Hastings. How are you?"

"Hey, George. What's up?"

Efrain Escobar was a detective with the county PD. He and Hastings had worked a case together. The Springheel Jim killings. Escobar was a conscientious officer; he had shared leads with Hastings and been respectful, which couldn't be said of all policemen working in rival agencies.

Hastings explained his situation to him, whom they were looking for.

Escobar said, "And you think he's going to get another rifle?"

"Yeah, I do."

"How come? If he's one of these Hinckley types, he can just get close and use a handgun."

"He's not a Hinckley," Hastings said. "I don't think he's insane. And I don't think he wants to get caught, either."

"He escaped from prison?"

"Yeah."

"Why doesn't he just stay hidden?"

"I told you. He wants to kill Preston."

"And you still say he's not crazy?"

"Ah," Hastings said, "how the hell should I know?"

Escobar laughed. "Okay, George. How many people you got working this?"

"Not many. There are politics involved. Reese hasn't committed a homicide in the city. Least not that we're aware of. Also, the senator's denying that Reese is the man I followed. So I'm not in a position to request a dozen detectives."

"Not on an ADW."

"No. Not on an ADW."

"Well," Escobar said, "I suppose I could spare a couple of detectives, ask them to check out a few gun stores outside city limits. If you think it'll help."

"Every little bit helps. Can you have it raised at patrol-shift briefs, too?"

"I think so. Let me type up a draft. I'll e-mail it to you, see if it's okay."

"That'll be great. Listen, Eff, I'll be frank with you. I don't think our man is just going to walk into a local sporting goods store and buy a rifle over the counter. He'll have to present identification, sign a lot of forms, and wait three days, minimum. And he's not going to wait. The senator's going to be in town for only a couple more days."

"And when the senator's gone, your man's gone, too."

"Yeah, that's about the size of it."

"Which would piss you off, I suppose."

"You're right about that, too," Hastings said.

There was silence on the line, Hastings wondering if Escobar was judging him for a lack of professionalism, taking shots from a perp personally.

Then Escobar said, "You were saying something about sporting goods."

"Oh, yeah. I think he's going to be looking for a rifle on the black market."

"Well, that's cool," Escobar said. "It only expands the scope of our search about twenty-fold."

"I know. Sorry I don't have much more than that. But . . . anything you can do."

"We'll do what we can. Listen, George. Don't put too much on this thing, okay? The guy you're looking for, he's just another turd."

"I wish he was," Hastings said. He waited a moment, then asked, "Was there something else?"

A pause on the other end. Then Escobar said, "Yeah. How are you?"

"What do you mean?"

"I mean, you just got shot. You shouldn't be working."

"I'm just a little bruised. It's not a big deal."

"It's a very big deal. At County, you're involved in a shooting, you get forty-eight hours paid leave, mandatory. Even if you're not injured."

"I don't need it."

"You sure? A man gets shot, it does things to him. Makes him scared, gets him thinking of the fragility of life and all that stuff. You need a few days off to work those things out."

"After this is done," Hastings said, his voice tense. "You going to help me or not?"

"Don't get mad."

"I'm not mad."

"All I'm saying is, it's okay to feel like that. You wouldn't be human if you didn't. And, George, it's not going to go away just because you concentrate on work. That might make it worse, actually."

Hastings said, "I respect what you're saying, Eff. But it's going to have to wait for a while. Okay?"

"Okay, George. I'll be in touch."

THIRTY-FIVE

The lady behind the desk asked if he would be staying through the Thanksgiving weekend. Reese thought it would be suspicious to say he wasn't. So he said he was.

The lady said that was good and was surprised when he paid for the room in cash. She said, "You don't have to do that. You can pay when you check out."

Reese said, "I prefer to do it this way."

"Okay," the lady said, a little uncertainty in her tone. She took the money and said, "I'll show you to your room."

The woman's name was Molly Mangan and she was the owner and manager of the Chestnut Inn Bed and Breakfast, located in Webster Groves, Missouri. She was forty-one years old, divorced, and the mother of a fifteen-year-old boy. The boy's name was Connor. His bedroom was on the third floor.

The house was a large Colonial that had been built in the 1920s. It had been owned by a prominent attorney who had ten children. He died in the 1970s and the house passed through a succession of owners, the most recent being Jeff and Molly Mangan, who bought it in 2003. Jeff and Molly had been college sweethearts at Santa Clara University. They married two months after college graduation and Jeff began a career in Silicon Valley. Jeff made a lot of money in the silicon-chip business and by his late thirties was ready for a change in career and lifestyle. He and Molly and their son decided to move to the Midwest and open up a bed-and-breakfast. They were attracted to the St. Louis area because of the trees. They preferred the landscapes to the brown-and-yellow hues of California. They grew to like the St. Louis seasons as well, even the stifling humid summers. The bed-and-breakfast turned out to be harder work than they had seen on *Newhart*. For the first two years, they did not make a profit. Jeff was philosophical about this, saying they had the money now, so what was the point of going back to Silicon Valley and being miserable? Things would pick up. And things did pick up. The next year, they broke even. That same year, Jeff died of a heart attack.

It happened while he was working in the garden. Molly heard him call out her name, and by the time she got to him, he was gone. He had never smoked and had been of normal weight. He was from a long line of men with bad hearts. He died at thirty-nine.

Molly decided to stay in St. Louis. She had no close relations in California and she feared that Jeff's family would attempt to take too much control in bringing up her son. She stayed and ran the business and she kept her grief to herself. She did not date or even entertain the idea of becoming involved with another man. Jeff had been the only one. The only one she had ever been to bed with, the only one she had ever loved.

She did not wear much makeup and her clothes were not flashy. Her figure was buxom, though not plump, and some people thought she looked like she worked in a bank. She thought of herself as plain.

Now she said to the guest, "This is your room. As I said before, there's no television. But there's one in the sunroom downstairs and we have DVDs and videotapes. Breakfast will be served in the dining room at eight o'clock. Tomorrow will be French toast and sausage. Thursday is Thanksgiving and there will be just a continental breakfast, if that's okay."

"That'll be fine," Reese said.

"Sorry, but we don't expect many guests for breakfast on Thanksgiving. The other guests are here to visit family for the holidays. Do you have family in St. Louis?"

"No," Reese said. "Just passing through."

"Is it your first time here?"

"Yes."

Molly Mangan was not worldly. But she could pick up social cues, and now she thought the man did not want to chat.

She said, "Well, we won't be serving dinner this evening. But you're about twenty minutes' drive from some lovely restaurants in the city and I'll be glad to recommend one if you like. There are coffee and refreshments in the parlor and some magazines and books. Oh, one more thing: This is a nonsmoking inn and we don't allow smoking anywhere on the property. I'm sorry if that's a problem."

"It's not."

"Well then, I'll leave you to your room. I hope you have a pleasant stay, Mr. Bryan."

"Thank you, Ms.—"

"Mrs. Mangan," she said. "You can call me Molly."

Reese watched her briefly as she walked down the hall. He closed the door before she reached the stairs. He felt guilty looking at her backside. Okay, she had a good figure, even though she did nothing to show it off. But she was a nice lady, treated him decently.

Guileless and inexperienced. A mousy nerd. Probably got straight *A*'s in school. But she didn't know what he was. She was the sort that probably thought the best of people. She made him feel sad, for some reason. He told himself to forget about it.

Reese locked the door and drew the shades. He began unloading his bags. From a golf bag, he removed the Lee-Enfield rifle. For the next thirty minutes, he went over it, cleaning it, examining it, breaking it down and putting it back together. He had fired an Enfield before, but never at a human target. He liked the weapon and he liked its sight. But he still wanted a scope for it. He had done a quick scan in the neo-Nazi's basement but hadn't seen anything he liked. He would need to find a scope, bring it back here, and mount it on the rifle. The Nazi had already put in the drill mounts, but Reese couldn't tell yet if they would line up well with a scope and remain true. He would have to see when he got the scope. If it worked out, it would take at least an hour to secure it properly. He could do the work here so long as he didn't need to do any additional drilling.

He had no reason to believe the police knew his identity as Paul Bryan. Still, he thought it was best not to stay in one place too long. Especially after taking a shot at a cop. That's why he'd checked out of the Hampton Inn. Too commercial, too open. Better to be in a bed-and-breakfast.

Reese thought of the cop now. The man who had come after him in the park. Coming alone at first, armed only with a pistol. Dumb. Reese wanted to believe the cop was in over his head. But instinct told him not to count the policeman out. The way the cop had kept his cool and not panicked, the shots he had fired into the air to let the other cops know where he was . . . Probably the cop was stupid

and unsuited to chasing soldiers and should stick to busting intoxi-
cated wife-beaters and street-corner drug dealers. But to believe that
was to violate the cardinal rule of never underestimating your
enemy. The cop was doing his job, protecting Senator Shitpoke Liar,
but if the cop got in his way, Reese would not hesitate to put him
down, too.

THIRTY-SIX

Klosterman came in to Hastings's office with a file on Kyle Anders and Ghosthawk. They talked for a while.

Klosterman said, "He's basically the Howard Hughes of contract security work."

Hastings said, "You mean mercenaries."

"He doesn't like the word *mercenaries*," Klosterman said. "In fact, if you work for his company, you're not supposed to call yourself that. He's a funny guy."

"He didn't seem funny when I met him."

"I mean funny—unusual. Since the Iraq War, Anders has made tons of money. He's got contracts in Iraq, Afghanistan, some in Central America. These contracts, they're worth millions and millions of dollars. You know, when I looked him up and saw Ghosthawk, I remembered the name. We got a couple of cops working there."

"Really?"

"Not anyone in homicide, but, yeah, a few patrol officers quit the department and took jobs as bodyguards there. But it's not like you can just get hired there. You have to go to this training facility he's got in Tennessee and audition, so to speak. They don't take too many cops, though. They might take one for every fifteen ex-military guys. You know what they call cops?"

"What?"

"Zipperheads."

"I don't get it."

"I don't, either. I can see why a young patrol cop would be interested in doing it, though. You get like a hundred thousand a year, minimum, for being over there, and it's tax-free. And apparently it's not like the work is that hard, either. You're basically a guard. Escorting dignitaries, protecting contractors, and so forth."

"Sure," Hastings said, "but you're in a war zone. Car bombs, ambushes."

"Yeah, there's that," Klosterman said. "But these young cops, they want action, a rush. You remember how it was."

"Yeah, I remember. I don't miss it, though."

"Besides," Klosterman said, "they get to see the world." Klosterman smiled, being sarcastic.

"They get to see Iraq and Afghanistan," Hastings said. "And that ain't much."

"You never considered the military?"

"Never. I guess I was never that curious. You?"

"Ah, I thought about it when I was younger. But I was going with Anne and I didn't want to leave her. Howard was in the navy; they paid for his college. He told me he joined because *he* wanted to see the world and he didn't have any money for college."

"He told me he wasn't that crazy about it," Hastings said.

"Yeah, he told me that, too. He saw more of Norfolk, Virginia, than anyplace else and he said it sucked. They slated him for aircraft mechanics and he thought he'd die of boredom. So he got out when his tour was up. Good thing, I guess. But you know Howard's real serious about that serving your country stuff, even if it's just for a while. He thinks we should still have the draft. I kind of agree with him, too."

Hastings did not, but he kept that thought to himself. He said, "So I guess Mr. Anders is something of a war profiteer."

Klosterman said, "Yeah, you could put it that way. If you want to be cynical about it."

Hastings smiled. "How would you put it?"

"I don't know," Klosterman said. "He's just a businessman, probably no worse than most."

"Yeah, I guess," Hastings said. "Do you think Senator Preston has a role in awarding these government contracts?"

"It's possible. Do you want me to look into it?"

"Yeah."

Murph appeared in the doorway.

"What's up?" Hastings said.

Murph said, "How you feeling?"

"I'm fine."

"Should you be at work?"

"Doctor said it was okay," Hastings said. Which was a lie, and they both knew it. But he didn't want to have this conversation again. Hastings said, "You got something for me?"

Murph said, "You wanted an update on Preston's appearances. I've got it."

"Any changes?"

"Yeah," Murph said. "He's speaking before the Veterans of Foreign Wars the day after Thanksgiving."

"Oh God. Where?"

"The Soldier's Memorial. It'll be outside."

THIRTY-SEVEN

Reese was having a cup of coffee in the dining room, reading the *St. Louis Post-Dispatch*. That was how he found out Senator Preston would be giving a speech downtown. It made him think. The speech had not been posted on the senator's Web site. Why would he do that? Why would he take such a risk? Preston was not a courageous man. He had to know. Why would he put himself in the open?

Giving a speech to veterans, no less. Reese snorted to himself. Preston had never been in the service. Men like him didn't do that.

During his time in prison, Reese had kept tabs on Preston's career. Had read about him being elected to the U.S. Senate, read about his avid support of the war in Iraq. It never changes, Reese thought.

Now he heard a commotion coming from the other room. Reese ignored it for a little while, but it didn't stop. Reese walked out of the dining room and into the lobby. The newspaper was folded in his hand.

In the lobby, a tall, well-dressed man was standing at the front desk. Behind the desk was the proprietor's teenage son. The tall man was holding a couple of papers in his hand. His tone was ugly and threatening. Reese imagined he was around forty. A bully who had probably not been in a physical fight since he was twelve.

The boy was saying, "I'm sorry. But the policy is to put faxes in your box."

"This arrived over five hours ago. You should have contacted me *immediately*."

The boy said, "I understand, but—"

"What is the matter with this place? Can't you do something as simple as that? Or is that something beyond your intelligence?"

Reese moved closer to the desk. He said, "Excuse me."

The tall man stopped and looked over.

Reese said, "Is there a problem?"

"It's none of your concern," the man said.

"It's all right," the boy said.

Reese continued to stare at the man. He said, "If you have a complaint, why don't you discuss it with the manager? He's just a kid."

"I'm a guest here and I'm discussing an issue with an employee. Why don't you mind your own business?"

"Or would you like to discuss it with me?" Reese said, and stepped just a little closer to the man.

Reese had sized the tall man up correctly. Unsurprisingly, the man stepped back a bit. The man said, "What?"

Reese did not answer him. He just stood there for a moment. Then he leaned against the desk, as if he would stand there as long as he liked. The whole time, he continued looking passively at the tall man. The man moved back another step, his fear showing now. Reese continued looking at his face and said nothing. The man looked at Reese and then at the boy. Then the he made some sort of sigh that was supposed to register impatience and insult but didn't, trying to save face. The tall man walked away.

Reese opened up his newspaper and began to read it.

The boy said, "Thank you."

Reese said, "Forget it. Who was that guy?"

"He's a guest here. He's a lawyer."

"I'm not surprised."

"He got a fax from his office. I guess he wanted us to tell him as soon as it got here."

"Yeah, I heard."

Reese waited for the boy to call the lawyer a name or otherwise cuss him. But the boy didn't. He just returned to work. For some reason, this affected Reese.

Reese said, "What's your name, son?"

"Connor."

"You're Mrs. Mangan's son?"

"Yes."

"How old are you?"

"Fifteen."

"You handled that guy pretty well."

"I didn't do anything. He'd've kept yelling at me if you hadn't come along."

"That's all he would have done. He's a bully. If he comes back and gives you any more trouble, give me a call."

"I can handle it," the boy said, his tone defensive.

Reese smiled. "Okay," he said, and moved away.

A couple of hours later, Reese was working on the rifle when he heard the knock on his door. He knew who it was, but he called out "Who is it?" anyway.

"Mrs. Mangan."

"Just a minute," Reese said, and stored the gun under the bed. He answered the door.

Molly said, "Connor told me what happened. Is it true?"

"I don't know what he told you," Reese replied.

"He said that the guest from Lexington was being rude to him and that you ran him off."

"I didn't run him off. I just made him see that he was ... being unpleasant. It was not a big deal."

"It was to Connor. He was very impressed by it."

Reese made a sort of shrug. He was self-conscious. He said, "Would you like to come in?"

The woman looked at him, a startled expression in her eyes.

Reese said, "I don't mean—I didn't mean any—"

"I know," the woman said. "I know you didn't. No, thank you. I guess I was hesitating because I wanted to tell you something else. Connor asked me to apologize to you."

"For what?"

"He thinks he may have been rude to you after you helped him. He feels bad about it. He was embarrassed and he, well, he didn't know what to say."

"He handled himself very well. You've got a good kid there."

Mrs. Mangan smiled. "Yes, I think so. Do you have children, Mr. Bryan?"

"No. We— No."

There was a silence between them, the woman hesitating.

Reese said, "Well."

"Well," Molly said. "Good night, Mr. Bryan."

"You can call me Paul."

"Good night, Paul."

She looked at him in a way that was terribly unself-conscious, and it struck Reese that she was actually very pretty. She smiled at him again and turned and walked down the hall.

THIRTY-EIGHT

Hastings was stopped at the subdivision containing Preston's house. There were four black Chevy Suburbans that he could see. A man in black jeans and a black turtleneck held a hand up in front of his Jaguar. Another man, also dressed in black, came to the car window as Hastings rolled it down.

Hastings took him in. Tall and hard-looking. No security contractor here. This was a mercenary.

Clu Rogers said, "What do you want?"

Hastings showed him his identification and gave his name. He said, "I'd like to speak to the senator."

Clu said, "You're not on the list."

"What list?"

"The list of approved guests." Clu pointed back down the hill. "So beat it."

"It's police business," Hastings said. "You interfering?"

"I'm doing my job. You gonna arrest me?"

"If need be," Hastings said.

They looked at each other impassively for a few moments, both of them armed and trying to hide their anger.

Clu said, "You want to try that, you better come back with more men."

Hastings smiled at him. "Are you a tough guy?"

"Yeah."

"Then what are we arguing about?" Hastings said.

It confused the man for a moment. Then he regained himself. Clu said, "Listen, I'm going to—"

"Hey!"

Clu Rogers turned around to face Sylvia Preston.

She was in her overcoat, putting her icy glare on him.

"Mrs. Preston," Clu said.

"What are you doing?" she said.

"Ma'am," Clu said, "he was trying to barge in here."

"It didn't look like that to me. Now get out of the way."

"Ma'am, he doesn't have an appointment."

"This is my home and nobody is going to tell me who comes and goes. Now step aside."

Clu looked at the other bodyguard, trying to save some face; then he stepped back and Hastings drove past him and parked the car. When he got out of it, Mrs. Preston was walking up to him.

She said, "I saw you from the window."

"Thanks," Hastings said. "Sorry about that. I guess I should have called first."

"No, I'm sorry," Sylvia Preston said. "About them. And about something else, too."

"What?"

"We can talk about it later. Do you mind if I ask what you want to see my husband about?"

"I don't mind. I'd like to talk to him about the speech he's going to give before the VFW."

Sylvia said, "You don't want him to do it."

"No, I don't."

"Come on," she said, touching him on the arm, leading him into the house.

Preston was alone in his study and on the telephone when Sylvia escorted Hastings in. Preston was dressed casually, slacks and a sweater. He saw Hastings, made a point of not acknowledging him, and continued talking on the phone. Hastings heard him say, "Well, he's finished anyway.... Yeah, down by eleven points, and there's no way he's going to catch up...." Then he laughed at something and bid the caller a warm good-bye.

Preston said, "Mr. Hastings, I was informed you were no longer on this case."

"That's right," Hastings said.

"Then what can I do for you?"

Hastings said, "I'm conducting an investigation."

Silence as the men looked at each other. Then Preston said, "On who?"

"John Reese."

The senator took his eyes off the policeman and put them on his wife. "Sylvia," he said. "Would you excuse us?"

Sylvia Preston looked at her husband, then at Hastings. Hastings nodded at her, a gesture of gratitude, and she left the room.

When she was gone, Preston said, "I have a golf game in a half hour. I would appreciate it if you would come to the point."

"You're going to play golf?" Hastings said. "Where?"

"Not that I need to tell you, but a private club in Chesterfield. I doubt you're familiar with it."

"Senator, there is a man in town who wants to kill you. And you're golfing, making speeches outdoors. You're exposing yourself to unnecessary risk. Why?"

"*You* say there's a man."

"No, you said it. You specifically asked the chief for police protection because you thought John Reese would come after you. It turns out you were right."

"My wife—"

"Please don't put this on your wife. It would not have been done if you hadn't wanted it done."

The senator gave Hastings one of his authoritative glares. "Are you questioning my integrity, Lieutenant?"

"Senator, I'm sure you have your reasons for doing what you're doing. But I'm trying to find a man who's threatening to kill you. For reasons I cannot comprehend, you seem unwilling to help me."

"Let me ask you something," Preston said. "Just what is it you saw that night? Did you actually see the man who shot at you?"

"No. Not up close."

"Well, I have seen him up close. I prosecuted him and put him behind bars, where he belongs. I spent the better part of a year building that case. And now you, who knows nothing about him, you come into my home and deign to tell me about him. When you didn't even see him."

"The man who shot me was no junkie. He used a high-powered rifle. We have it. Do you want to see it? Will that make you believe it was him?"

"I'm not interested, Lieutenant."

"Sir, he's interested in you. And he's not going away."

"Just what is it you propose I do? Stay here the rest of my life? Give up public service? I can't do that."

"No one's asking you to. Just lie low for a few days. I'll bring him in. I'll see he goes back to prison."

Preston shook his head. "This is not a homicide, Lieutenant. It's not your jurisdiction."

"The city of St. Louis *is* my jurisdiction. And John Reese is wanted for assault with a deadly weapon."

"Well," Preston said, "good luck with that. Now if you'll excuse me."

Burning at the senator's patronizing tone, Hastings turned and walked out of the room. *Fuck it,* he thought. Fucking senator talking down to him, using his prosecutor's voice. *Let me ask you something?* Jerkoff. Hastings told himself to write a report when he got back to the station, summarizing this conversation. At least his ass would be covered when the senator got shot playing the back nine. *This officer tried to warn the senator that he would be killed by John Reese and the senator told this officer to go pound sand up his ass. Respectfully submitted, Lt. Hastings.*

Sylvia Preston caught up to him in the driveway.

"Lieutenant," she said. "Is that it?"

Hastings stopped and took her in. She was a very pretty woman, too good-looking to be married to such an asshole.

"Yeah," Hastings said, "we're finished."

Sylvia said, "I don't understand."

"I don't, either. Mrs. Preston, a few days ago, you told me your husband was afraid. Is that still true?"

"... I don't know."

"What has he told you?"

"He's been . . . keeping his own counsel the last couple of days. I wish he would tell me more."

Hastings looked at her, saw that she was frightened. Maybe unhappy, too.

Now she said, "Was it John Reese out there in the park?"

"Yeah, I'm pretty sure."

"Why? Why is he so intent on . . ."

"I don't know. Does your husband?"

"Maybe. He won't tell me."

"Ask him," Hastings said.

Sylvia Preston's face contorted. "And then what? Report back to you?"

"It would be for his benefit."

"Are you sure?"

Hastings said, "Are you going to second-guess me, too?"

"No," she said. "It's not like that. You're asking me to—to do things behind his back."

"Mrs. Preston, I want to catch John Reese, and your husband seems not to want to help me. Or himself. Maybe you know why."

"I don't know why. Really, I don't. I do know he doesn't like you."

Hastings smiled, a bit flattered by this. "No, he doesn't."

Sylvia said, "My husband has a big ego, Lieutenant. It's helped get him where he is. You've got quite an ego yourself. Though you're a little better at hiding it. A little."

"Perhaps there's something in what you say," Hastings said. "But I'm not interested in competing with him."

"I wasn't suggesting—"

"I know you weren't. I wasn't, either."

The senator's wife was blushing. She turned away and Hastings said, "Mrs. Preston."

"Yes?"

"If he's in trouble, you should tell me."

She didn't answer him.

Hastings handed her a business card. He said, "It's got my cell number on there. If there's something you want to talk about, call me."

She took the card without looking at him. Then Hastings turned to walk to his car.

"Lieutenant."

Hastings stopped and turned. "Yes?"

"He never thanked you, did he?"

"For what?"

"You know. For chasing that man and getting shot. He never thanked you for it."

"No. But . . . that's all right."

"*I'm* thanking you." Sylvia Preston looked at Hastings now. "He is my husband and the father of my daughter."

"I know that," Hastings said, aware now that she was a woman, too, not just a senator's wife. A flesh-and-blood woman with the same marital troubles and fears as any other woman, unresolved by money and power and access. Hastings looked at her eyes and said, "Will you think about what I've asked you, please?"

"I'll try."

THIRTY-NINE

The boy got up from his table when Reese came into the dining room. He asked Reese if he could get him anything.

"No, thanks," Reese said. "I'll get it." He walked to the coffee stand and poured himself a cup. "Sit down," Reese said. "I'm okay."

The boy sat down and picked up a paperback book. Reese looked at it.

Reese said, "You reading *Lord of the Flies*?"

"Yeah. It's for school. I have to do a book report on it next week."

"You like it?"

"It's okay. Have you read it?"

"A long time ago," Reese said. "When I was your age, we had to read *Huckleberry Finn* for school."

"They recommend that," Connor said. "I mean, it's on a list of recommended books. But they don't assign it at school. I guess it's controversial because it's got the *n* word."

"That's right; it does," Reese said. "But I don't think that's what the book's about."

"I know," the boy said. "Yeah, Huck calls Jim that, because everyone said that back then. But he treats Jim as an equal when no one else really does. And that's the point. It's like the teachers don't think we're smart enough to figure those things out."

Reese smiled. "Maybe *they* haven't figured it out. You like school?"

"It's okay. I kind of want to get out, though. Move on."

"Have you thought about what you'd like to do?"

"My mom wants me to study mechanical engineering. I like working on motorcycles, you know, things. But . . . I don't know yet."

"You have time to sort it out."

Reese sipped his coffee. A few moments passed and the boy said, "A friend of mine, he's got an old car, a Datsun 510? You know what I'm talking about?"

"Not really."

"It's over thirty years old. Kind of boxy? It's got a stick shift. Really cool-looking car. It's got some rust and it needs a new engine, but me and my friend, we're going to buy it this summer and fix it up. Rebuild it. It'll only cost four hundred dollars. I mean two hundred each. That's not too much, right?"

"Probably not. But it sounds like a lot of work."

The boy saw no downside. He only looked forward to things. He said, "When we're finished, it's going to be great."

"I'm sure it will," Reese said. He was trying to remember if he'd ever had a conversation like this with a kid. He didn't think he had.

The boy said, "Did you like school? When you were young, I mean."

When you were young. Of course the boy would consider him old. Reese said, "Not so much. I wasn't much of a student. I guess I was kind of anxious to move on, too."

The boy gave a teenager's shrug, awkward and noncommittal. He said he had to get back to work and left Reese alone.

Reese said, "Let me see that one."

The man behind the counter said, "The Simmons?"

"Yeah."

"You've got a good eye, friend. This one's on sale, three twenty-nine ninety-nine. Me, I think it's as good as the Leupold for a lot less money."

Reese was in Diamond Jim's Gun Emporium. It was in North St. Louis County. The owner was in his fifties and his name was not Jim, but Greg Ashlock. He had kept the name of the business intact when he bought it six years ago.

Reese examined the scope for a while. He nodded and said, "Okay."

The owner wrapped up the scope and rang up the bill. Reese paid in cash and walked out the door.

It was late evening. Cold and darkness falling. Reese's car was parked diagonally in front of the small gun store. He got into the Mercury and backed out.

Looking in his rearview mirror, he saw a police car.

It was unmarked, no lights on top. A white Chevy Impala. But Reese knew it was a police car almost instantly. Now he saw two plainclothesmen in the front seat. Detectives.

The Impala pulled into another diagonal space. Parked there.

Softly, Reese pressed the accelerator. The Mercury started moving ahead. A couple of seconds later, he looked in the rearview mirror again. The detectives were going into the gun store.

Shit.

Reese kept going. The worst thing to do now would be to hammer it. All he had done was buy a scope. He had not bought a rifle. He had no rational reason to race away, no reason to panic. He was a normal man, a citizen. A hunter.

The county PD detectives had visited five other gun shops in North County before they got to his one. They were tired and hungry and they wanted to go home. Escobar had assigned them the detail, so they figured there had to be a reason.

They showed their IDs and asked the proprietor a series of what had become boring questions. Had he sold any high-powered rifles today or yesterday? And if so, to whom? Could they see his list?

The owner said no, it had been slow since deer-hunting season had ended a few weeks ago. In fact, the only thing he had sold since lunch was a rifle scope, and that guy had just left. In fact, just now. He saw him through the window, the fellow driving the black Mercury....

"You probably saw him yourself when you pulled in," the owner said.

One of the detectives asked, "What did this man look like?"

"About fifty. Well built, though. Looks like he takes care of himself."

The detectives exchanged glances.

One of them said, "Could be our man."

And the other said, "We got nothing else to do."

They caught up to the black Mercury about a mile away. It was stuck in traffic, sitting behind a line of other cars waiting for a light to turn green. The detectives were two car lengths back. The light turned green, traffic moved forward, and the detectives slipped the white Impala behind the Mercury and hit the switch that activated the red and blue lights that were built into the grille of the car.

The Mercury rolled along for a few yards, then shifted over a lane and then over to the shoulder. It stopped. The Impala rolled up behind it and the detectives stepped out. They walked toward the Mercury, and when they were almost to the trunk, the Mercury sped away.

"Shit," one of the detectives said.

They both ran back to the Impala.

Reese didn't floor the accelerator. He just pushed it hard enough to put some distance between him and the detectives' car and get out in traffic. He got the Mercury to a yellow light, and floored it, and made it through before it turned red. Moments later, he flicked his eyes to the windshield and smiled when he saw the white Impala stuck behind a couple of vehicles, the lights in the grille flashing as if they were angry.

Reese drove faster, cutting in and out of traffic, doing what he could to escape the sight of the two plainclothes officers. They had seen his car and likely recorded his license tag. So he would have to ditch the car soon. The thing to do was to get to a shopping mall or movie theater, someplace with a lot of other cars and a lot of people, hide it among other vehicles, and simply walk away. Grab another car or hail a taxi or catch a bus. Above all don't get caught in a long-ass

O. J. Simpson chase with twenty police cars and a helicopter with a camera putting the whole thing on television.

It was good advice he was giving himself and he would have taken it, but a squad car drove past him, going in the opposite direction. And Reese looked in his side mirror and saw the damn thing turn around, flick on its flashers and sirens, and come straight after him.

Reese pressed the accelerator down hard. The engine made a sort of *whumpf* sound as the transmission went to a lower gear and the car leaped forward. The Mercury crossed three lanes of traffic, cutting off other cars, causing them to skid and slide, and Reese accelerated up the entrance ramp to Interstate 170, going south.

The squad car joined him on the interstate, soon tailed by another. Two chasing him now, the detectives' Impala not far behind. Reese sped up—80, 90, 100, 105. . . . He kept control of the car and kept his eyes on the road, disciplining himself not to panic and concern himself with what was in the rearview mirror.

He saw another squad car off to his right, coming up an entrance ramp, its lights flashing, and he realized it was on a course to sideswipe him when the ramp joined the highway. Coming, coming . . . Reese kept an eye on it, and then it got close enough that Reese could see the forms of two men in the front seat, the one in the passenger seat holding a shotgun. Reese lifted his foot off the accelerator, then touched the brake. The police car swerved in front of him rather than making contact with his side. Reese pressed the accelerator down and went around the passenger side of the police car. The driver of the police car realized Reese's intention at the last moment and swung the squad car back to the right as Reese attempted to pass it. The sides of the cars made contact, metal against metal, sparks flying in the night, and then the Mercury was past, the police car fishtailing behind.

Hastings and Klosterman were in Hastings's office eating their dinner. On top of the desk were take-out paper bags stained with french fry grease. They were going over a report when a cell phone rang.

"Hastings."

"George, it's Escobar. I think we may have your man in a pursuit."

"Where?"

"He's going south on One seventy in a late-model black Mercury Marauder."

"Now?"

"Yeah, now. They spotted him coming out of a gun shop in North County."

"How do you know it's him?"

"We don't know for sure. George, he ran. You interested or not?"

"I'm interested. We'll head out that way now, west on I-Sixty-four. Call me in five minutes, give me an update."

"Sure."

They took the felony car assigned to Klosterman—a blue Impala. Hastings paying attention to the police radio, Klosterman pushing the car through interstate traffic, cars pulling to the right as they saw the flashing red and blue lights. Klosterman kept his attention on the road; Hastings listened to the excited, frightened voices of the police officers involved in a high-speed pursuit. Hastings resisted the urge to join the buzz on the radio. It would just cause confusion.

Klosterman said, "I thought this guy was smart."

"What do you mean?" Hastings said.

"Getting caught in an auto pursuit like this. Nobody ever gets away."

"He ain't nobody."

More radio buzz. They were posting squad cars at interstate off-ramps, setting up blockades. If the runner tried to leave the interstate, he would be boxed in. State police cars were joining the pursuit and assisting in the roadblocks, wanting a piece of the action, the rush.

Klosterman slipped the Chevy past an eighteen-wheel semi, the police lights reflecting off the white slab side of the trailer.

Klosterman said, "One seventy dead-ends on I-Sixty-four. I say he'll go west on Sixty-four, away from the city."

"No," Hastings said. "The ground's too open. He'll go east, into the city. Look for a place to hide."

More radio buzz. Suspect exiting 170 at Clayton Road. Roadblock ready.

"They've got him," Klosterman said.

Reese brought the Mercury down to seventy after he peeled off the interstate. He saw the police cars at the bottom of the hill after he had already committed himself. He lifted his foot off the accelerator. Sixty-five, sixty. The police cars came into distinct form. Men behind the cars, some of them leveling shotguns across the roofs. Reese saw an opening at the right side of the blockade, let the car drift a bit, then punched it.

A fusillade. Shots booming, cracking out, the first of them going nowhere, but then some connecting. The windshield was hit, making a spiderweb pattern on the glass. Reese lowered his head, keeping it high enough so he could see over the dash. He kept control of the car as cops figured out what he was up to and started running away from the farthest car.

The Mercury smacked the rear end of the last police car and pushed through. Reese spun it around, hammered the accelerator down, and headed east under the interstate overpass, gunfire thacking the back window, hitting the back of the car. None of the shots hit him, but then he heard and felt a sound in the rear and the car began to fishtail.

They had punctured a tire. Reese turned the steering wheel to his right, trying to correct it, but it went too far, and then the car was sliding into the guardrail, all control lost as the car twisted around, doing a near 180 before screeching to a halt altogether.

Steam coming out of the hood. A busted radiator. Or a thrown rod.

Police cars approaching him now, lights flashing, sirens blaring.

Reese got out of the Mercury and ran to the guardrail. On the other side was a steep slope, a dark wooded area. Reese climbed over the guardrail and jumped.

He didn't land right, losing his footing and feeling a horrible twist in his ankle as he stumbled and fell and rolled down the hill. He grunted out in pain involuntarily and then cried out as he felt his head hit a hard object. The sirens were closer now, hurting his ears, and then he heard tires screech to a halt.

He was on his back in the dark. His eyes adjusted to the darkness surrounding him. Looking up the slope, he could see shapes gathering at the top, the cops apprehensive about coming down the steep slope after him. Reese looked to his right and saw a wooden fence. He got to his feet, wincing when he put weight on his left ankle. But he moved to the fence, jumped up and grabbed the top, and pulled himself over.

FORTY

Hastings stood near the smashed-up Mercury, seemingly pinned against the guardrail, about a dozen police cruisers around him. Efrain Escobar showed up about five minutes after Hastings and Klosterman.

Escobar pointed down the slope and said, "He jumped down there, what, maybe five minutes ago?"

Hastings said, "And you can't find him?"

"You want to go down that slope?" Escobar asked. "In the dark? Man, that's something you *rappel* down."

"Christ."

"There's a residential neighborhood at the bottom. I worry he's in one of those houses. We've got patrol officers going through there. We'll find him."

"That's if he's still in the neighborhood," Hastings said. "Shit. Hanley Road is right over there."

"What, you think he hitched a ride?"

"No, I think he stole a car. Either way, I think he's gone. *Fuck.*"

"Sorry, George. We did the best we could."

Hastings regarded his friend. A cop he liked and respected. "I know," Hastings said. "I'm sorry. Anyone injured?"

"No, I don't think so. He totaled a state patrol car."

"Well, preserve his car, will you? I want to see if his prints are on it."

"George, it's being done."

Hastings made another apologetic gesture. "Sorry," he said. "I got people thinking I'm chasing a ghost."

"He's real enough," Escobar said.

Hastings moved away from the slope. Walked toward Klosterman and then saw a black SUV on the other side of the road. A familiar face behind the wheel. Another man next to him.

The man who had stopped him at the Preston house.

Hastings called out to him.

"Hey. *Hey!*"

Clu Rogers looked at him briefly. Then he put the SUV in gear and drove away.

Klosterman said, "Who was that?"

"Preston's goons," Hastings said.

"The mercenaries? What the hell were they doing here?"

Hastings said, "I'd like to know."

FORTY-ONE

Two miles away from the wreck, Reese looked at himself in the rearview mirror of the car he had stolen. The left half of his face was streaked with blood. He felt for the wound and found a gash in his head above the hairline. The blood had dried now and matted his hair. He believed the bleeding had stopped. He could not tell in this light if he would need stitches.

He had stolen a Mazda station wagon with a manual transmission. He did not like having to shift, did not like having to expend the energy. He knew he was weak, feeling dizzy and even a little faint. Also, he had to use his left foot to depress the clutch. The pressure made him wince every time he had to shift. He had twisted his ankle. Even in the dark, he could see that it had swollen to the size of a grapefruit. He wished he had stolen a vehicle with an automatic transmission. He wished he had gone to a different store to buy a scope. He wished he could see the road clearly.

With painful effort, he managed to drive back to the bed-and-breakfast.

He was relieved that Mrs. Mangan was not at the front desk. One of her employees, a younger lady, was there, and she barely acknowledged Reese as he hurried by her, turning his head so that she would not see the wounds.

He climbed the stairs, putting more of his weight on the banister than he did on his left foot. Still, it was excruciating, a pain sharper than he had hoped. He reached his room and managed to get the door unlocked.

"Hi."

Reese turned to see who it was. It was the boy, Connor. He had just come out of the bathroom.

"Evening," Reese said, catching the boy's look of concern before he rushed into the room and closed the door behind him.

Reese removed the scope from his coat pocket and put it on the nightstand. At least he managed to keep that, he thought. Maybe it would make the night's debacle worth it. Though he doubted it.

He sat on the bed and removed his boots. First the right, then the left. The left one did not come off easily. He sucked in a cry as he pulled it off. Then he examined the wound.

It was bad. His ankle and foot were swollen and tender to the touch. Slowly, he placed his foot on the ground and put a little weight on it. He winced again. It wasn't just the ankle. He had probably broken a metatarsal bone in his foot, too.

His room did not come with its own toilet, but it did have a stand-up sink and mirror. Reese hobbled over to it and examined his face in the mirror.

Christ. He looked like a ghoul. He had probably frightened the poor kid half to death.

Reese washed the dried blood off his face and forehead. When it was as clean as he could make it, he examined the wound on his scalp. It was tender to the touch. In the army, they would probably have put in a couple of stitches. Maybe he would do it himself if he had the materials.

Shit, he thought. Forget it. First things first.

He thought again of the boy in the hallway. What would the boy say to his mother? *Hey, remember that guy who was nice to me? He looks like he got run over by a truck.*

He would have to think of a reason for his injuries. A twisted ankle, a busted foot, a cut on his scalp—all could have been caused by falling down stairs. No one else involved. Yes, that was it. Stairs.

First he would need to get cleaned up. Take a bath. Soak the leg in a hot tub, then wrap the ankle in ice. But which to do first . . .

In the mirror, his image blurred. He grabbed the sides of the sink and steadied himself. He moved to the bed and then fell on it. Then he passed out.

FORTY-TWO

The next day, it rained. It was a cold, soft November rain, the sort that does not come down in sheets, but comes on and off all day. It reduced visibility, slowed traffic, and drove the transients off the streets and into the shelters.

It was also Thanksgiving Day. Most people did not have to work. Consequently, the owner of a Mazda station wagon in Clayton did not venture out of her house until almost noon. That was when she realized her car had been stolen and reported it to the police.

Hastings *was* working. Amy was spending the day with Eileen and Ted and Ted's relatives. He had been invited but had declined. Probably he would have declined even if he didn't have to find John Reese. Spending the day with his ex-wife's husband and his family would have been out of Hastings's comfort zone.

Hastings was sitting at his desk downtown, reviewing the government's file on Reese. The U.S. attorney's office hadn't given him much, but he had gotten a copy of the prison file. In the file was an exchange of letters between Reese's attorney and the prison warden—an argument about letting Reese out to attend his wife's funeral. The request had been denied, Reese being deemed too great a security risk. The warden wrote that while he was aware of the tragic circumstances of Sara Reese's long-term battle with cancer, he could not fully sympathize with a man like John Reese, who had demonstrated such callous disregard for the lives of others. The warden reiterated that at no time had Reese expressed remorse for his actions or acknowledged his crimes. The warden finished the letter by saying that a man like John Reese could not be trusted not to use funeral leave as an attempt to escape.

There was also a letter to the warden from Reese, a personal handwritten note. In the note, Reese said he would be willing to say anything the warden wanted if the warden would allow him to attend Sara's funeral. (He used his wife's name.) There was no indication that the letter had been answered.

Cold, Hastings thought. But wasn't the warden right? Hadn't Reese created his own plight?

Hastings's cell phone rang.

"Hastings."

"Lieutenant?"

"Yeah."

"This is Deputy Cudahy, county PD. Eff Escobar gave me your number."

"Oh, good. What's up?"

"We got a report of a stolen vehicle about three blocks from where the suspect crashed his car."

"Yeah?"

"Yeah. It's a red Mazda station wagon, late model. This is the tag number."

Hastings wrote it down. He said, "He's probably ditched it by now."

"Probably. You think it was him?"

"Any other cars stolen in that neighborhood?"

"Not last night."

"Then it's him. No coincidence here."

"Okay. Well, it's in the system."

"Thanks." The phone on the desk rang. "Sergeant? I got another call here."

"Okay. I'll call you if I got anything else."

"Thanks. Bye."

Hastings picked up the other phone.

"Yeah."

"George?"

It was Jack Diedrickson from the technical investigation lab.

"Yeah," Hastings said.

"We lifted prints from the steering wheel and we got a pretty good partial from the knob on the radio. And we ran it through AFIS. John Reese was driving the car."

"Really?"

"Yeah, it's him."

"You're sure?"

"Yeah, I'm sure," Diedrickson said. "Do you mind if I go home now? My wife's supposed to have dinner at two."

"No, I don't mind. Listen, Jack. I'm very grateful that you came in for this—"

"Yeah, yeah. Look, I gave you the preliminary just now. Do you have to have a formal report today?"

"No. But shoot me an e-mail confirming what you just told me, before you go. Okay?"

"All right, George. You'll have it in about two minutes. Happy Thanksgiving."

"Yeah, you, too."

Hastings hung up the phone.

Jesus, it was him. It was John Reese. Here in St. Louis. He had told himself that he had known it all along. The man behind the wheel of the smashed car, the man in the apartment building across the street from the Chase Park Plaza, the man running down the alley, the man aiming a rifle at him. The voice in the darkness. *You shouldn't have come after me.*

Now it was confirmed.

And Hastings was glad.

He knew a decent person should feel ashamed of this. Who should feel relieved that such a man was near? Was still in town? That a senator's life was still in danger? Was he that intent on proving Senator Preston wrong? *I told you. . . .*

But George Hastings knew who he was and what he was. He knew that this was something beyond the senator. He knew he wanted to hunt this man. Catch him, bring him in.

Reese was proving to be smart, but in some ways not as smart as an animal. Why would Reese stay? Why would he risk his freedom and his safety to go after a man who wasn't worth pissing on?

Senator Preston was no statesman. Okay, he was thinking about running for president. But so were a lot of politicians. Preston was no Great Man. Nor was he an American Hitler, ready to wreak havoc on the world. Why not leave him alone? Who was it that said vengeance is for suckers?

What was in John Reese's head?

Alan Preston had put John Reese in prison. Okay. That was a bad thing. But it was what prosecutors did. Often they were threatened by criminals they had prosecuted. Rarely did the criminals actually attempt to carry out the threat. It was mostly jailhouse posturing. *He's gonna pay. . . .* Loser talk.

And what was John Reese? Was he just another loser? Another perp? A criminal who simply had the benefit of military training?

Like most cops, Hastings tended to think of criminals as losers. It was the sort of classifying that had always angered Carol. "They're people, George," she would say. Yeah, they were people. People who were losers. He felt some pity and on some matters—for instance, drug-law penalties—his viewpoints could outliberal most liberals. His thoughts on assassins and the like generally tracked with the experience of most law-enforcement officers. Most assassins targeting public figures were indeed losers. Troubled misfits with very little going for them. Jobless, poor, small, and ignored. Taking a gun and going after a famous man made them big. Gave them fame. Made them important.

But John Reese did not fit into this category. He *had* been important. He had accomplished a great deal. An army Ranger, a CIA operative, a successful businessman. It was Reese who had thrown it all away by selling out his country.

Wasn't it?

It occurred to Hastings, not for the first time, that he didn't know everything he needed to know. Preston had closed up on him. No, actually, Preston had never been open with him in the first place.

What he'd like to do was get John Reese in his office and talk to him. Ask him, "What is your problem? Why are you wasting your life on this? What is this about?" Maybe Reese would give him some straight answers. Preston certainly wasn't.

Hastings looked out the window at downtown St. Louis. The streets were mostly empty. People with better lives than his were home with their families on Thanksgiving. Those streets would move again tomorrow. Even though Friday was also a holiday. People coming downtown to shop.

Veterans coming downtown to watch Senator Preston give a speech at the Soldier's Memorial. Maybe see him get shot. Maybe his goons would be there to watch it happen, too.

"Oh shit," Hastings said.

FORTY-THREE

Clu Rogers walked up to the window of the Jaguar and said, "You again? I guess you don't listen, do you?"

Hastings was back at Senator Preston's house. The perimeter was still guarded. Black Chevy Suburbans, men in dark clothing, hiding their weapons.

Hastings said, "They make you stand out in the rain, huh? Lousy way to spend Thanksgiving."

"Why don't you stand out here with me?"

Hastings said, "You got a hard-on or something?"

"Hey—"

Hastings said, "Listen to me, shithead. I saw you last night. On Clayton Road, by Reese's car. We could have talked then. How come you left?"

"You didn't see me."

"I did. I called out to you and I know you heard me. Why did you take off?"

"I don't have explain myself to you, Lieutenant."

"What were you doing there? That was police business. What the fuck were *you* doing there?"

"What I was doing was—"

"Clu!"

Clu turned around. Dexter Troy walked up. Hastings saw the man direct an angry look at Rogers. A look that said, What the fuck is the matter with you?

Troy said to Clu, "Go back to the house."

Clu gave Hastings another look, intending it to be meaningful. Then he walked away.

Dexter Troy reminded Hastings of a young Arnold Palmer. Natural athletic build, confident and sure of himself.

Troy said, "You'll have to pardon Clu. He can be a little too diligent at times."

"He strikes me as a man who likes his work," Hastings said.

"I'm Dexter Troy, chief of security for Ghosthawk. I'm sorry, but we're all a little on edge."

"Forget it," Hastings said.

Troy said, "The senator's having Thanksgiving dinner with his family. Is there something I can do for you?"

"Actually, it wasn't really the senator I wanted to speak to."

Dexter Troy regarded the policeman.

"Who did you want to speak to?"

"Kyle Anders."

Troy seemed to sense trouble. He said, "What do you want with him?"

"I'd like to tell *him.*"

"Well," Troy said, "he flew to Tennessee this morning to have dinner with his own family."

"When do you expect him back?"

"I don't know. Again, I'm in charge here. Perhaps I can help you."

"Perhaps," Hastings said.

Troy said, "You can park over there."

Hastings put the Jaguar next to a black Cadillac in the driveway.

He walked with Troy to the garage, where the door was open. They stood in shelter, the rain outside coming down.

"So," Troy said, "are you investigating Ghosthawk now?" There was a thin smile on his face. Like the notion was ridiculous.

Hastings said, "John Reese is in town. It's been confirmed. We found his prints on the car the police were pursuing."

Troy lifted his head, unable to hide his reaction to the news.

Hastings said, "But you already knew that, didn't you?"

Troy said, "I don't follow you."

"Yeah?" Hastings said. "I think you've been doing just that. I saw your man at the site of the wreck last night. That's what I was asking him about. How did he know to be there?"

"How should I know?"

"You just told me you're in charge. Don't tell me you don't know."

"We have police radios, Lieutenant. We monitor radio traffic. So what? We're here to protect the senator. Are you trying to tell me where I can and can't do my job?"

"Your job is to protect Preston. Preston was nowhere near that scene last night."

"So?"

"So you and your people had no business being there."

"We go where we want."

"No, sir. You don't go where you want. If you interfere with police business, you're committing a crime."

"No one's interfering with your little problems. And if you think you have cause to arrest me or any of my men, go ahead and do it."

"I would if I could."

"Why? Lieutenant, I'm trying to be reasonable here. We're after the same thing."

"No, we're not. I'm trying to find Reese and bring him in. You guys want to kill him."

Dexter Troy looked off into the rain. "You have no proof of that," he said.

"Mr. Troy, I've got no beef with you or your boss. You want to be bodyguards, it's fine by me. But if you expand into assassination, contract killing, I swear to God I'll arrest all of you for conspiracy to commit murder, the senator included."

"You're a city cop, nothing more," Troy said. "And you've got no proof."

Hastings said, "You tell Anders what we talked about. If I know him, he's going to make sure he's not in town while it happens. And if shit comes down, he'll probably try to hang it on you."

"We're done talking."

"Tell him," Hastings said. "Tell him I'm onto him. And remember one more thing: I may hesitate to shoot you. John Reese won't."

Troy watched Hastings walk away, waited for him to go to his car. But then Hastings turned at the corner and went to the front door of the house.

"Hey!" Troy said. But it was too late.

FORTY-FOUR

Preston found Hastings waiting for him in the living room.

Preston said, "Mr. Hastings, have you no family of your own?"

"I have a daughter," Hastings said. "She's with her mother today."

"I have a daughter, too. I'd like to spend the holidays with her and my wife."

"I'll come to the point. John Reese is in the city. His fingerprints were found on an automobile that was involved in a high-speed chase last night." Hastings looked Preston in the eye. "I presumed you already knew that."

"You presume incorrectly. If it was John Reese, why didn't Chief Grassino telephone me himself?"

"We just got the confirmation an hour ago. We found a shotgun in the trunk of the car. No rifle."

"So?"

"So, I presume he's got a rifle. Another one. He purchased a scope at a gun store in North County last night. That's how we found him."

"I see."

"If you want to telephone the chief for confirmation yourself, you can call him now."

"You don't think I trust you at all, do you?"

"I don't know what you think, sir. Listen, you cannot give that speech tomorrow."

"Why not? Because he's loose?"

"He's here. The man is *here*. You brought him *here*. There was a high-speed pursuit last night. Luckily, no one got hurt. Do you understand what I'm saying?"

"Are you blaming me?"

"In part, yes. You haven't been straight with us since the beginning."

"Don't accuse me of bad faith. You're not in a position—"

"You knew it was Reese who shot at me in the park and yet you denied it. Why? Why did you do that?"

"I didn't know."

"Yes, you did. And we know why, don't we? Don't we?"

"I don't know what you're talking about."

"Yes, you do. You don't want Reese captured. You want him killed. That's why you called the cops off."

"That's slander, Lieutenant. Chief Grassino will hear about it."

"Tell him what you like," Hastings said. "But he's going to figure out you've lied to him, too."

The senator seemed to give him an appraising look. He said, "You seem to think so little of me, Lieutenant. It's a wonder you don't want me killed yourself."

"That's the last thing I want. Cancel the speech. Please."

"You've stated your case," the senator said. "Now get out."

Hastings took another look at Preston, seeing a man trying to hide his fear, then seeing the senator's expression change as he looked past Hastings.

Hastings turned and saw Sylvia Preston in the doorway.

He wondered how long she had been there, how much she had heard.

Preston said, "He was just leaving."

Hastings looked at Sylvia. He nodded to her and walked out of the other door.

When he was gone, Sylvia said, "Alan, what's wrong?"

"Nothing's wrong. He's out of line."

"He's trying to help us. He's a good man."

Preston snorted. "A good man," he said. "And I'm not?"

"I didn't say that. I think you try to do what's right. You do try, don't you?" She almost sounded like she was trying to persuade herself.

Preston said, "I take care of my family. And my country. I try my best to do that."

"Alan," she said. "Are you trying to have John Reese killed?"

"Oh, for Christ's sake. Do I have to explain myself to you, too?"

"I want you to answer me."

"John Reese is a terrorist and a traitor. He's a threat to me and to you and to Emily. The world would be a better place without him."

"You're talking like a lawyer now," Sylvia said. "Please answer my question."

"Would you rather *I* be killed?"

"Oh . . . Alan."

"Maybe you would. If I'm such a disappointment to you."

"Alan, stop. You're being manipulative."

"Maybe you believe the detective over me. Maybe that's what it's come to."

"Stop it. I want you to tell me."

"No, Sylvia. I am not trying to have John Reese killed." He gave her a look she had not seen before. "Okay?" he said. His cynicism was ugly enough to be forceful.

"Alan, I don't even know what to say to you anymore. You didn't even try. You didn't even try to persuade me. It's like you just said the words so they'd be on the record."

"I told you what you wanted to hear. Isn't that enough?"

"Alan—"

"Don't you see, Sylvia? Don't you see? It has to be done. It's not even my decision anymore."

"I don't understand."

He laughed bitterly. "You don't, do you? Look around you. This house, the vacations, all the nice things we have. You don't think we got that on a senator's salary, do you?"

"... Alan?"

"Oh, stop. You know. You've always known."

"Have you been taking money from Kyle Anders?"

"It's business," Preston said. "It's the way things are done. Grease. Don't look at me like that. The contracts would probably have gone to Ghosthawk anyway. I just helped it along."

"But the committee, the investigation . . ."

"Right. You chose to believe it. I don't remember hearing you complain when we got the new house or the other things. You're part of it, too, Sylvia. As much as me."

She walked out of the room, crying.

"As much as me," the senator said again.

When she was gone, he told himself she didn't want to understand.

Good man. A cop, no less. That was what Reese's lawyer had said about Reese. "Your Honor, this is a good man who loves his country." But John Reese was a rat and a killer. It didn't matter whether or not the CIA had disowned him.

There's generally little profit in a politician's self-examination or honest introspection. For most of them, it is better to see themselves as they wish to be seen rather than as they are. Alan Preston was not unusual in this respect. Still, there were times he looked at himself and wondered when it was that he began hating people. Sometimes he believed it had started with John Reese. Well into Reese's trial, the general counsel at the CIA had come to Preston and confessed that the CIA's previous affidavit was "perhaps wrong." Preston was furious. The general counsel saying, well, perhaps Reese had been working with the CIA, just as he claimed. Perhaps. Preston had said, "But you don't know for sure."

"We don't know for sure either way," the general counsel said. "Not absolutely."

We don't know for sure either way. Not absolutely. Christ. Preston had thought of what the judge's reaction would be if he found out the CIA's affidavit was false. He would dismiss the case. He might even sanction Preston for prosecutorial misconduct. John Reese would go free and go back to being a millionaire mercenary. And Alan Preston would be humiliated and disgraced, his career derailed.

He had made the decision quickly and without much thought. And in deciding to suppress the CIA's damaging admission, Alan Preston had told himself that John Reese was trash anyway. He later persuaded the jury and the judge of the same thing and they helped him get John Reese a lifetime sentence.

Since then, he had hated John Reese. And he had learned to hate other men, too. Men like Kyle Anders and, now, George Hastings. Men who reminded him of what he was.

FORTY-FIVE

Hastings was almost back at the police station when he got the call from Chief Grassino. The chief said he had gotten a report on Hastings from Senator Preston. Hastings said he imagined the chief had. Grassino said, "George, you better take this seriously." Hastings said he was, of course. A minute later, Hastings agreed to meet the chief at the chief's home.

Chief Mark Grassino had been hired from Atlanta, where he had been assistant chief. He was about fifteen years older than Hastings. He was tall, thin, and dark-haired. Italian-American in his looks, his voice that of a southerner. He did not shake Hastings's hand at the door. Nor did he introduce Hastings to his wife and children, who were in the living room watching the Cowboys-Packers game.

Grassino led him into a small den and shut the door behind him.

Grassino said, "George, you seem to be upsetting people."

"The wrong people?" Hastings said.

"Don't give me that. I back my officers. When they're right."

"I am right. And I didn't say anything to Preston I wouldn't say in front of you."

"He says you barged into his home, accused him of corruption."

"I didn't make an appointment, no. But—I did need to speak to him about John Reese."

"To warn him that John Reese was in St. Louis?"

"Yes, sir."

"Did it occur to you that that there were other ways you could have done that? You could have telephoned him. You could have telephoned me. And I would have let him know."

"Am I being ordered to treat him differently than I would any other suspect?"

"Suspect? George, you're a homicide detective. Do you suspect Senator Preston of committing murder?"

"In a sense, yes."

"You'd better explain that to me."

"Sir, I think Senator Preston has a very close relationship with Kyle Anders, the owner and CEO of Ghosthawk. Basically, they're hired guns, mercenaries. I think Preston wants them to kill John Reese."

"The man's life has been threatened. He has the right to secure bodyguards."

"They're not just bodyguards."

"What proof do you have of this?"

Hastings told him about seeing Clu Rogers at the scene of John Reese's wrecked automobile. He also told him about his conversation with Dexter Troy, Ghosthawk's chief of security.

Grassino said, "That's it?"

"Yeah, that's it."

The chief of police sighed. "George, that's nothing. You arrest him with that, the district attorney will laugh at you."

"I wasn't trying to arrest him," Hastings said. "I was trying to warn him and Anders not to try to kill Reese."

"It's not your place to warn him."

"I think it is."

The chief regarded Hastings. "Okay, then we have a disagreement. But you're under my command. And I'm giving you a direct order not to harass Senator Preston."

"I understand."

"Don't say you understand, like I'm cutting Preston a break or something, because that's not how it is."

"I didn't mean it that way."

"You did mean it that way and I don't need that shit. Not from you." Grassino exhaled and seemed to let some of his anger out. Then he said, "Let me be clear about something: I'm not going to allow some fucking politician to run this department."

"Then why order me to leave him alone?"

"Because he'll come after you, George. If he doesn't do it through me, he'll do it through someone else."

"Did he request my termination?"

"Yeah," Grassino said, surprising Hastings with his candor. He had thought the chief would use weasel words. Grassino said, "What did you expect? From a man like that."

"What did you tell him?"

"I told him you were one of the best homicide detectives we have and that I had no doubt you were acting in good faith. I told him if he had a formal complaint, he could submit it to the administration, using the standard policy procedures, and that an internal investigation might be conducted to see if his complaint was valid. He was unpleasantly surprised to learn cops have due-process rights, too."

"Thanks."

"Don't thank me, because it's not over yet. You want to go after someone like Alan Preston, get your fucking ducks in a row. Make *sure,* George. Don't go up against him with suppositions and theories. Don't give him that opportunity."

"I won't," Hastings said. He felt now that he had misjudged Grassino, a man he didn't know well. Hastings said, "Out of curiosity, just what did he say when you told him to submit a complaint through administration?"

"He said he had expected better from me."

"Okay," Hastings said, avoiding eye contact with the chief. "Well, what about Reese?"

"What about him?"

"He's still at large. Is Preston still going to give his speech downtown?"

"Yes. I tried to talk him out of it, but he wouldn't listen. He's intent on doing it, for some reason."

Hastings said, "Maybe he wants to draw Reese out. Offer himself as bait."

"Maybe," Grassino said. "But as I said before, keep your theories to yourself. At least for now. I've alerted Charlie Day to get the tactical unit ready. They'll be covering the rooftops. Uniforms on the street. Call Charlie today, coordinate with him. There'll be a briefing downtown tonight at twenty-one hundred. I'll expect you there."

FORTY-SIX

The night had been bad. Marked by fever, sleeplessness mixed with exhaustion. Reese was unable to sleep well, but he was too weak to get out of bed and do something about it. He had no medicines. No pain relievers, nothing to break the fever. At times, he sensed that there were people in the room with him—ghosts—but he had sense enough to know that these were hallucinations caused by traumatic delirium. The sort of thing that often followed injury or shock. He hoped it wasn't shock.

He was almost relieved when he saw gray morning light come through the window. He had feared the night would never end. In time, he lifted his arm to look at his watch, and even that was an effort. Lifting his fucking arm. It was Thursday.

Thursday. The next day. Had the spirits done it all in one night?

But it was morning and the spirits were gone. The fever and the scared, helpless feeling of being sick and unattended remained. He could smell his own perspiration and dried blood. Maybe something more.

Thursday. Thanksgiving Day. His first holiday out of prison in thirteen years. A free man's holiday. Free but not free.

He realized he was still in his clothes. He had not found the strength to undress. He lifted the left cuff of his pants to examine his foot and ankle. The swelling had not gone down. If anything, the pain had increased. Red, throbbing pain. An abscess had formed. Reese hopped over to his bag and retrieved a knife. With the knife, he lanced the abscess. Pus drained out. He cleansed the wound with water from the sink. He knew this would not be enough to get rid of the infection. He would need Betadine or even a bottle of alcohol. He had neither.

He opened the door and looked out in the hallway. He saw no one. He wondered who, apart from himself, would spend Thanksgiving Day at a bed-and-breakfast. He limped down to the bathroom to clean himself. In the bathtub, he fought the urge to vomit. He would have done it, except he didn't want to refill the tub. He feared there would be no more hot water. He closed his eyes, and when he opened them, the water was cold and he realized he had fallen asleep. Or fainted. He didn't know which.

He got back to his room and changed into a fresh pair of shorts and jeans and an undershirt. Then he persuaded himself not to get back in bed. He had work to do and not much time. He started to work on fitting the scope to the rifle. He had at least kept the scope.

He heard the rain coming down outside. It made him feel better. It was always easier to hide in the rain.

He finished fitting the scope about an hour later. Then he put the rifle and attached scope underneath the bed. That done, he found that he was thirsty and hungry. He put a sweater over his undershirt and moved to the door. He would have a light breakfast and then come back to the room and rest. He felt he had earned it.

There was a moment at the top of the stairs when he felt a wave of nausea and he had to grab the banister and steady himself. It passed and slowly he made his way down. Near the bottom of the steps, the wave returned, bigger this time, and he felt shards of pain shooting up his leg. Then things went black and he fell.

FORTY-SEVEN

Coolness. Comfort. Yes, comfort.

Reese opened his eyes and saw the woman above him. She lifted the cold compress off his forehead.

Reese took in his surroundings, realized he was in a bed but not in his room.

The Mangan woman was sitting on the bed next to him. She was wearing a black turtleneck sweater and a black skirt. It's better than her previous outfit, Reese thought. Not as dowdy.

She said, "How are you?"

"I don't know," Reese said. "What happened?"

"I was in the dining room and I heard a crash. You seem to have fallen down the stairs."

Christ, Reese thought. Fell down the stairs. The story he was going to tell if asked. How was that for irony?

"Yeah, I guess I did," Reese said. "You didn't call anyone, did you?"

"Like who?"

"An ambulance. Nine one one."

"No. Do you want me to?"

"No."

"I can if you want."

"No, don't. I'll be fine. If you'll just let me get back to my room." He started to rise but felt another wave. The woman gently pushed him back.

"You're burning up," she said.

"I'm not . . . I'm not comfortable here, ma'am. This is your room, your bed. You have guests."

"No one knows you're here. And I'm not worried about—I'm not worried."

"Where is the boy?"

"He's in Rolla."

"What's he doing there? Is he with his father?"

"No," the woman said. "His father—my husband—died a few years ago."

"I'm sorry."

Molly Mangan shook her head. She had never sought pity. She said, "It's okay. Connor went with a friend of his from school. They have a big holiday celebration there. Family, a big dinner, football in the yard. He'll enjoy himself there more than he would here."

"I see."

The woman looked at Reese for a moment, then seemed to become aware of herself and got off the bed.

Standing, she said, "You need medicine. Can I get you some aspirin?"

"Yes, thank you," Reese said. "Do you have—do you have any antibiotics?"

"I think so. Connor had his wisdom teeth removed last month. I think we still have some Augmentin. Would that be all right?"

"Yes."

"I'll get it."

She returned with the medicine and a glass of water. After he took the medicine, she put the compress back on his head.

"You have a fever," Molly said.

Reese said, "It'll break. Listen, I can't stay here. If you'll help me up, I'll return to my room."

"Your room's upstairs. I don't think you can get back up there with that foot."

"I can."

"Please stay here," she said. "I don't want you falling again. Please stay. At least for a while."

Reese said, "I don't want you doing this." He didn't know what else to say.

Molly Mangan said, "I know."

Then she left the room.

Reese looked at the door after it closed and thought there was nothing to stop him from getting up and walking out himself. But his fever was still burning and he told himself he would leave in five minutes.

Three minutes later, he was asleep.

When he awoke, it was darker in the room. He checked his watch and saw that it was late afternoon. Outside, the rain was still coming down. The sheets beneath him felt clean and cool. He wiggled his toes and realized the woman had taken off his shoes and socks. She had removed his sweater, too. He was still in jeans and an undershirt.

Reese moved his legs to the side of the bed, then sat up. He looked at his ankle. The woman had taped it and cleaned it with alcohol. Reese put some weight on it and winced again. It still hurt.

The door opened and the woman came in. She was carrying a

tray. On the tray were a teapot, two small cups, and some finger sandwiches.

Molly said, "Oh, you're up. How are you feeling?"

"I'm feeling better, thanks."

"I brought you some food. Do you like tea?"

"I happen to love tea."

"I hoped you would," Molly said, setting the tray on the nightstand. "If we were in England, this would be teatime. Have you been to England?"

"Yes. I lived there for a while, actually."

"Oh?" She seemed surprised by this.

Reese said, "It was a long time ago."

"Did you work in the oil business? Sorry if I'm prying."

"You're not. No, I didn't work in the oil business. Why did you think that?"

"My father worked in oil. He worked for British Petroleum. We were Americans living in England."

"You lived in England?"

"For a few years. From the age of five to thirteen."

"Was your father an executive?"

"No, an engineer. He was one of the pioneers on the liquefied natural gas project. I'm sorry. I'm sure that would bore you."

"No, it wouldn't. Tell me about it."

"Well, he helped build that and he was on the ship that first transported liquefied natural gas across the ocean. From Lake Charles, Louisiana, to Dover, I think. That was before I was born."

"That's terrific."

"You think so? I never understood it all myself."

"It's quite an achievement. It's good to leave something like that behind."

"You think so?"

"Yes. Did you like living in England?"

"Sort of. My mother and father put me in a British school, though there's a school there for children of Americans. I guess he thought the experience would broaden us."

"Did it?"

"Well, if you want to call cold classrooms and bad food a broadening experience."

Reese laughed. He said, "I liked it there. But I wasn't a child."

Molly said, "What I remember was the vacations we used to take there. They're called 'holidays' there."

"Right."

"We would load up the car with a picnic basket and drive to the seashore. Go out to the beach and put the blanket down, and you could just see that it was about to rain. And then it *would* rain. And we'd have to pack everything up and get back in the car. We'd eat our sandwiches in the car. That's what I remember about those trips. It was either raining or it was about to rain."

"Right," Reese said again, smiling at the memory. "I guess if you're born there, you get used to it. You don't know anything else. You left, though, when you were thirteen?"

"Yes. We moved to California. A bit of a culture shock. My father missed England, but the rest of us were glad to be back in the States. The American kids made fun of my English accent." She looked at him, suddenly aware of herself talking. "Sorry."

"What?"

"I'm prattling."

"No, you're not. I like it. You still have a trace of an accent."

"Do I?"

"A trace, yes."

Molly poured the tea in the cups. She handed a cup to Reese. Reese sipped it and thought it was very good. Then he took a bite of one of the sandwiches. Egg salad, and that was good, too.

"Thank you," he said.

"Do you like it?"

"Yes, it's very good tea. But I meant thank you for helping me."

Molly said, "You're a guest here."

"I know, but I won't be staying long."

"I know that, too," Molly said, taking his meaning.

They were both quiet for a few moments, having their tea, each feeling something for the other but avoiding direct looks.

Reese said, "Do you have other family, apart from your son?"

"My father died a couple of years ago. My mother and brother live in California. We got along okay, but we're not that close."

"Don't you want to go back? To California, I mean."

"No, we like it better here. Connor has friends—we've put down roots here."

"And you have this business."

"Yes. It keeps me occupied."

Reese felt pity for the woman again. But she didn't seem to feel any for herself. He admired her for it. He said, "Do you think you'd like to get married again?"

"I don't think so," Molly said. "If I had a husband, he would have to fit in here. And then there's Connor. It's a lot to ask of a man." .

"No, it isn't."

The woman blushed and briefly turned her face away. She said, "Are you married, Mr. Bryan?"

"No." Reese hesitated. Then thought, Why lie to her? Why lie to someone like her? He said, "I was. She died, too. Cancer."

"Oh, I'm so sorry."

"It's all right."

"And you never had children?"

"No. We meant to, but . . ." He shrugged.

"I am sorry. But a man like you, there's still time for that. You could meet a young lady and have a baby with her."

"It's a little late for that."

"No, it isn't. And you're a natural with kids. The way you handled Connor. It was very nice."

"Oh," Reese said, embarrassed. "That was fleeting."

"It wasn't fleeting. He likes you, you know. He says you're 'cool.'"

"He's a good kid. You've done well with him."

"No. I've been lucky."

Reese looked at her. A plain woman at first, but not plain. In fact, very attractive. Pretty, really. He said, "You lost your husband and you're alone on a holiday. And you say you're lucky."

Her voice tight, Molly Mangan said, "I was talking about my son. But it all depends on how you look at things."

"You did love your husband, didn't you?"

"Very much. Did you love your wife?'

"Yes, but . . ."

"I guess I just don't see the point, that's all. I don't see the point in being mad about things."

She stood up and went over to get the tray. She avoided eye contact with him. Reese could see that she was struggling to hide her hurt. He felt a shame he didn't think was in him and placed a hand on her arm.

"I'm sorry," Reese said.

She shook her head slightly, still not looking at him.

And Reese stood in the presence of the lady. He said, "I'm sorry, Molly. I'm not used to—I haven't been with people for a while. I'm sorry."

Then, without thinking about it, he kissed her on the cheek. She turned and looked at him, her face registering apprehension. Not of him, but of herself. Reese was about to step back, when she leaned toward him and kissed him on the mouth. Her mouth opened and Reese felt his heart jump, as if he were a teenager. "Hey," he said. And she dropped the tray on the floor.

"Hey," Reese said again.

And now the woman apologized, seeming ashamed and self-conscious in that moment, and Reese stepped forward and put his arms around her to comfort her. He said, "It's all right." He didn't know what else to say.

He pulled her close in the embrace and kissed her on the cheek again. She relaxed in his arms and he heard her say, "I've—I've never done this before."

"What?"

"I mean, not since my husband. He was . . . It's only been . . ."

"It's okay," Reese said. "I'll go."

"Don't go."

"Are you sure?"

"Yes," she said. "I'm sure." Then she kissed him again.

Some things you don't forget. He had not been with a woman in over thirteen years, the last one being his wife. Under normal circumstances, he would have worried about whether or not he would be able to do it. Before Sara died, he had allowed himself to fantasize about making love to her again. In his mind, the truth surfaced and he was released from prison. But even in the fantasy, he was nervous about the first time with Sara. Would prison make him impotent? Sexually damaged? It's not good for a man to be alone. To be without a woman. After Sara died, he stopped fantasizing about another time with her. It seemed wrong somehow. Instead, he thought of the times they had had.

Molly Mangan looked better naked than she did clothed. She looked good. Her body was full and natural and she was an uninhibited lover. She thrust her hips back and forth underneath him, and when he came, she moaned softly. He stayed on top of her and asked her if he was hurting her, his weight on top of her. She shook her head and whispered "No," smiling warmly. And he asked her if she was all right and she said she was fine. The second time, she got on top of him.

Later, they lay in bed, and Reese realized he didn't want to leave. He had been with a lot of women before he was married, and typically when it was done, he wanted to go. He had expected to feel self-conscious around this woman he had pitied, this woman he had mistaken for a frump. He wondered if prison had screwed him up. Had made him consider a life with a woman he barely knew, filling in for the woman's husband, the boy's father. People who should have been strangers to him. That he was lonely, he knew. But he had to be out of his mind to consider a long-term arrangement with this woman and her son. He had told her he would be leaving soon and she had said, "I know that, too." He had not misled her.

She lay nestled against him, her back to his front, his arm around her stomach. She turned to him.

"You were hurt before," she said, "weren't you? Before you fell down the stairs."

"... Yes."

She said, "Can you tell me what happened?"

"It's better if you don't know."

"Whatever it is, I don't care."

"But you should. You should care."

"Why?"

"Because you have a son. And you don't need someone like me in your life."

"Maybe I do need you. Maybe you need someone like me."

"Don't say that."

"What?"

"Don't say 'someone like me.' You're not just a warm body I found. You're a good lady."

She almost laughed at his seriousness. She said, "I mean something to you?"

"You know what I meant."

"I'm not even sure what to call you. Paul?"

"Call me John."

"John?"

"Maybe I'll explain it to you sometime."

"John." She said, "Are you in trouble?"

"Kind of."

"Well, whatever it is, it can't be that bad."

"Why not?"

"Because you're a good man."

"I'm not a good man."

"Seducing a lonely woman," Molly said. "Is that how you see this?"

"I don't know."

"Well, don't. You didn't seduce me. I may not be the most experienced woman, but I'm not stupid, either."

"I know you're not."

"I know what I'm doing. And I'm not sorry, either."

Reese said nothing, looked up at the ceiling.

Molly said, "I didn't plan this. It happened, and I think it's good that it happened. We can't plan everything, can we?"

"No."

"But sometimes it can be good, too, the unplanned."

"Maybe. I don't know."

"I said before that I knew you weren't going to stay. And I wasn't lying to you when I said it. But I want you to think about staying. Because this might be something. Will you think about it?"

"I have thought about it," Reese said. "Am thinking about it. But I'm fifty years old. It may be too late for me to . . ."

"It's not too late," Molly said. "We'll have no more talk of it now. Will you stay with me through the night?"

"Yes."

FORTY-EIGHT

Charlie Day used his pen to point out on the schematic where tact team officers would be placed. He said there would be uniformed officers working the streets and some plainclothesmen. Hastings would be one of the latter. There would be patrols of the Soldier's Memorial and surrounding areas throughout the night in case John Reese tried to set up early.

Also present at the briefing were Ronnie Wulf, Chief Grassino, Howard Rhodes, Tim Murphy, Joe Klosterman, and Capt. Dan Anthony. There were also officers from the county PD who had offered to assist.

Charlie Day took questions, and when those were addressed, he added, "Remember, this man is not a minor leaguer. He was a sniper for the military as well as an intelligence agent. He is extremely dangerous. If you see him, do not try to take him alone unless absolutely necessary. George? Do you have anything to add?"

"No, Charlie," Hastings said.

"Chief?"

"No."

"Then I guess we're adjourned."

As the meeting broke up, Hastings approached Captain Anthony.

"Dan?"

"Yes, George."

"Can I speak to you privately?" Hastings feigned a submissive tone. Anthony would think he wanted a favor.

When they were alone, Hastings said in a different voice, "Did you tell Dexter Troy where Reese was the other night?"

Dan Anthony's face tightened. "What?" he said, his tone tense. "Where do you get—"

Hastings said, "Did you?"

"Who the hell do you think you are, asking me that?"

"Did you, Dan?"

"George, I'm on your side."

"I know that. But I want you to answer my question."

"I don't think I care to."

"Look, Dan, I don't much care if you did. If you did, it may have been innocent."

"Innocent? What makes you think I told them?"

"I asked Troy about it myself. I asked him how his men knew where Reese had wrecked his car. He said something about hearing it on a police radio. Now that's possible, but it's not likely. It's just not likely they picked up something that specific on a police radio or scanner."

"You think I told them."

Hastings sighed. "I'm sorry, Dan, but I do. I don't know who else it could have been."

Then fear was in Anthony's eyes. In a tone just above a whisper, he said, "Who else have you told about this?"

And that confirmed it for Hastings. He was actually disappointed to learn he had been right. He had never disliked Anthony.

"I haven't told anyone," Hastings said. "But I'm not going to lie for you if I'm asked. Do you understand me?"

"George, I didn't think it was wrong. I didn't."

"I believe you. But you can't help these guys anymore. I don't care how nice they are to you."

"They're not bad guys, George."

"Well, I think they might be. In fact, I think they're planning to kill John Reese. Don't ask me why I think that or if I have proof of it. Just trust me. Now there's a line between protecting Senator Preston and straightforward contract killing. So as a friend, I'm telling you, don't get close to these people. Whatever they've offered you, it's not worth it."

"It's not like that. I swear—"

"You don't have to prove anything to me."

"George, I—"

Klosterman walked up to them.

Hastings said, "I'll see you tomorrow, Dan."

Klosterman waited until Dan Anthony left. Then he said, "You asked if there was any sort of connection between Anders and the senator."

"Yeah."

Klosterman said, "I might have something."

It was around eleven o'clock when Hastings got home. He turned on the television and watched the ESPN tally of the day's football games, all of which he had missed. He watched a highlight of a Manning pass caught in the end zone. Then he went to his bedroom closet and took down his Winchester model 52 rifle.

He loaded it in the living room, in front of the television set. While he did that, he remembered Dan Anthony's pained expression as Anthony tried to explain himself, but Hastings had cut him off, saying he'd see him tomorrow. Hastings hadn't wanted to look at Anthony at that moment. He wondered if he would have felt better about it if Anthony hadn't been ashamed. Hadn't shown a human weakness. Sometimes it was easier to deal with the Alan Prestons of the world who didn't seem to feel ashamed about anything.

The hell with it. Dan Anthony was not his problem. Not now. He pushed him out of his mind and concentrated on the rifle.

FORTY-NINE

At 2:45 in the morning, John Reese climbed out of Molly Mangan's bed and got dressed. He looked at Molly for a moment. She really was beautiful. He had wanted her and she had wanted him. But lust fades and is replaced by commitment and tenderness. Things he had not expected to feel again. He did not feel he had betrayed Sara. In a way, he wondered if he had done something for her. If Sara were here—here in some ethereal way—he could ask her what he should do and Sara would say, *Stay.* But he would not ask her and he knew it.

He had not slept well through the night. Whether this was due to having slept a lot during the day or anxiety, he did not know. He did know that for a few short, sweet hours he had entertained the idea of marrying Molly Mangan and beginning a new life with her and her son. But as the night wore on, he knew this was not possible. It was too late for him, as he had tried to tell her. And they deserved something better.

He had given her his first name: John. He had told her because he didn't want to lie to her about his name. But he had lied to her all the same by keeping silent about his past, about who he was. Today, she would find out who he was. Whether he was dead or alive, she would know. Probably it would be on the evening news. Then she would know who she had shared her bed with and she would be stuck with the memory. She would, justifiably, feel betrayed. Reese knew this and it sickened him. He had done this to her. And it made him feel worse to know that he would have probably done it anyway, because he had needed her so badly. Probably more than she needed him. He thought all that time in prison had made him stronger. But he was wrong. This sin was his alone, not Preston's.

He held his breath as he left her room. His ankle was still in pain. He found that he could not avoid limping.

Five minutes later, he left the house.

He parked the Mazda about a mile and a half from the target. He checked his watch and saw it was about ten minutes after three. The sun would rise at 7:06 A.M. He would have liked more time, but he should have enough. He looked around the neighborhood. He didn't see anyone. Houses and cars, but everyone was asleep. He applied black, green, and brown grease-paint to his face and hands. Then he got out of the car, taking the long-stemmed dark green tote bag with him. He slung the bag over his back. This would be his departure point.

He had bought the tote bag at a hardware store. It was intended to store a folded-up summer chair. Now it contained the Enfield rifle.

Under cover of darkness, he slipped from the car into some trees. Then he climbed down into a gully. The gully was bordered by trees and brush and it snaked through the neighborhood that straddled the border between Clayton and the city limits of St. Louis. It would take him within three hundred yards of Senator Preston's house. It's better than being in a field, he thought. In tall grass, you had to slow every movement. You had to move by inches. It could take an hour to cover fifteen yards. There had been a job in South America that required him to go through grass. He'd had to lie still, not even breathe, as men on foot conducted their morning patrols.

But he'd had two good feet then. Now he had a bum leg and the pain was increasing. At one point, he put the bad foot wrong on a stone and it twisted it even further. He swallowed his cry as the pain shot up his leg and into his eyes. He stopped and allowed himself a few hard breaths. He squeezed his eyes shut, and when he opened them, tears came and rolled down his cheeks.

He kept moving. And as he moved, he thought of Preston coming out of his house, walking to his car. He would have that space of time, that opportunity. Plenty of time. Plenty. He thought of Molly Mangan and then pushed her out of his mind and thought of Sara, the other woman he had let down. The woman who had died alone while he was in prison for a crime he had not committed. Some people just have to die, Reese thought.

Yes, die. But my, the water was cold, even though it was only around his ankles. Now he started to shiver and he had to stop again.

Christ. The fever was returning. He thought he had broken it back at Molly's, but it had come back. He had not given himself sufficient time to heal. Any lance corporal would have told him he had to let his body heal. You ain't a kid anymore, son. You're an old man.

But it had to be done. There would be no more opportunities. And if he survived it, he could heal his body later. He couldn't allow this injustice to pass. He could not resist the sordid, empty promise of vengeance.

At 4:18, he came out of the gully. From then on, he crawled. And though it hurt his knees, he was relieved, because there was no longer any weight pressing down on his ankle. He believed now he would make it.

Approximately 270 yards from the Preston house, Reese took his field glasses from his coat pocket. He examined the front door and the semicircle driveway. He repositioned himself to the west. Then he dug a shallow ditch for himself and covered it with leaves and brush. He set his rifle on a wet mound of dirt, finding a point where the dirt would no longer give. Then he removed a washcloth from his coat. He folded the washcloth and put it between the muzzle of the rifle and the dirt. This would prevent dirt from spitting up when he made a shot and decrease the chance of his being seen.

Reese checked his watch. It was 4:40 A.M.

Now he would wait.

At 6:45, he heard voices. Then he heard footsteps. He withdrew his rifle into his cover and held it close to his chest. He would not risk making the noise required to close the hole. The only way it would be seen was if someone crouched right down in front of it. He made his body still and then he stopped breathing.

The voices drew closer.

Men. Two of them. Talking.

Chops, he thought. You don't talk on a foot patrol. Not if you're looking for an assassin. You can't sneak up on anyone if you're making noise. Amateurs not using the weapon of silence.

The voices stopped and now the two men were near him. Reese continued to hold his breath.

He heard the flick of a cigarette lighter. A Zippo.

A man said, "The per diem in Afghanistan is good. But the duty is shit now. Used to be a good pull. Now it's even more dangerous than Iraq."

The other man said, "The best duty is Qatar. They got some good discos and the food is outstanding."

Reese felt the stock of the rifle, then the muzzle. The muzzle was bare and dry.

Christ! He had left the washcloth out on the mound of dirt.

If they saw it, they would examine it. And then they would find him. He could kill one and maybe the other, but there was no silencer on the rifle and he would be blown. It's still dark, he thought. They won't see it if it's still dark.

Another pull on the cigarette.

Then: "Well, at least it's stopped raining."

"Let's go," the other said.

They left and Reese waited another thirty seconds before he let himself breathe. Slowly at first, then taking bigger gulps of air.

Reese let ten minutes pass. Then he took the rifle from his side and poked it, inch by inch, back out on the mound. The washcloth was still there. He put the rifle back in its place.

The sun came up a few minutes later. Forty minutes after that, Reese brought his shoulders and head farther out of his pile. His entire body ached and his fever was still with him. He knew he should be patient, but he had been on his belly for hours and it was getting to him. He wanted the senator to come out of his house. He wanted it to be done. He was ready.

At 8:10, the front door opened. A man came out in a dark suit and an overcoat. Not the senator. The senator's legislative assistant.

No. Not an assistant. A bodyguard. Probably another ex–Navy SEAL. He would be checking the vehicles.

Which meant the senator would be coming out.

Reese leaned forward, his finger over the trigger.

"Reese!"

Reese froze.

The voice was coming from his right.

A man positioned behind a tree, a Winchester rifle aimed at him.

"Take your finger off that trigger," Hastings said. "You won't make it."

Reese thought, I might. Then he swung the rifle at the voice and fired.

FIFTY

The shot hit the tree and Hastings flinched and stepped back, taking cover behind the tree. Then he stepped back out and saw Reese running, limping, but running for cover. Hastings raised the Winchester, aimed for Reese's leg, and pulled the trigger.

The shot boomed out and Reese flipped in the air. Hastings pulled the bolt back to put another shell in the breech, but now Reese had scrambled behind a tree.

Now they both had cover.

Birds flew away in the damp chilly air. A couple of moments passed by.

"Shit," Reese said, loudly enough for Hastings to hear. "How did you find me?"

"Your scope," Hastings said. "It reflected sunlight."

"Goddammit. I forgot to shield that. Dumbass mistake."

"It happens," Hastings said.

"You working for Anders?"

"No. St. Louis police."

A pause. Then: "Are you the one who followed me into the park?"

"Yeah."

"Hell. Do you know I could have killed you back there?"

"No."

"I could have, but I hesitated. If I'd thought you were working for Anders, I wouldn't have hesitated."

"You didn't hesitate just now."

"Well, I didn't know you were a cop."

"You do now. Why don't you throw down the rifle and come out with your hands on your head."

"I'm afraid I can't do that."

"It's over, Reese."

"Don't tell me it's over," he shouted. "Do you have any idea what that piece of shit did to me? What he's doing to other soldiers?"

"What do you mean, 'other soldiers'?"

"His relationship with Anders. Don't you understand? Anders is getting rich off those contracts, and Preston is, too. By supporting an unnecessary war. Men are dying for that. Men with families."

"That's not my concern."

"It isn't? Just who the hell are you working for?"

"I told you. I'm a cop. Besides, this isn't about soldiers in Iraq. You just want revenge."

"Well, wouldn't you? Preston knew I was innocent. The CIA told him I was, but he went ahead and put me in jail anyway. He *lied*. To him, I was nothing. A step in his career."

"Look," Hastings said, "if it's any consolation, I believe you. But you can't kill him. You do that, you're nothing but a murderer."

"He tried to have me killed. How do you think I got out of prison? He sent men there to bring me out and kill me."

"What?"

"You heard me. God, don't you know anything? He's using you, too."

"That's my problem," Hastings said. "But I cannot let you kill him."

"You'd protect him?"

"It's not about him," Hastings said. "Listen to me, John. I know about your wife. I know she died while you were in. Do you think she'd want this?"

"You don't know anything about her, so just shut your mouth."

"I'm sorry for your loss. I'm sorry for the injustice. But you can't kill him. Not in cold blood. Not in my town."

Hastings heard quick steps behind him. He turned just in time to see Clu Rogers hit him in the face with the butt of a machine gun. Hastings went down. Not unconscious, but stunned. He reached for his rifle on the ground, but Clu stepped on it.

Clu pointed the machine gun at Hastings.

"You're not supposed to be here," Clu said, a nasty smile on his face. He raised the gun and said, "We'll put this on Reese, huh?"

The crack of a shot, and before Hastings could cry out, he saw Clu stop. A hole now in Clu's forehead. Clu fell back. One shot, one kill.

Reese rammed another shell in the chamber and turned on Dexter Troy, who was back and to his left. Reese raised the rifle as Troy fired the M16 at him. Shots exchanged, but Reese taking three to Troy's one. Both men went to the ground.

Troy was on his back. He had been shot through the stomach, the shot going out the back. Slowly, he sat up and reached for the M16, and Reese shot him again, this time through the heart.

Hastings ran over, the Winchester in his hands. He pointed it at Troy and said, "Stay where you are! You hear me! You go for that rifle, I'll kill you!"

The shouts were for nothing. Dexter Troy was dead.

Hastings picked up Reese's Enfield and flung it away. Then he turned Reese over. Reese was shot to pieces, his chest and neck open and bloody.

Reese was grinning at him. He said, "You never know who your friends are, huh?"

"Shit," Hastings said, overwhelmed by the sight of it, the man red and busted apart. "Why did you do that?"

"He hadn't earned the right to kill you," Reese said.

"John. You shouldn't have come back here."

"I had to," Reese said. "Now look at me." He gasped out something like a laugh. "What folly. I guess I'm going now."

"What are you talking about, 'going'?"

"You know," Reese said. Then he died.

FIFTY-ONE

Hastings was leaning against the back of one of the police cars parked by the Preston house. Chief Grassino broke away from a group of police officers and federal agents and walked up to him. The chief was holding two cups of coffee. He held one of them out to Hastings.

Hastings took it and thanked him. Grassino leaned up against the car next to him.

Grassino said, "Where were you hiding?"

Hastings said, "I was on third floor of the house across the street. The place we were when we did our stakeout."

Hastings held a cloth over a cut above his eye. The skin had been slashed open by the butt of Clu Rogers's machine gun.

Chief Grassino said, "You had permission from the owners?"

"Yes."

"What about Preston? Did he know you were there?"

"No. His wife did, though."

"You asked his wife?"

"Yes. She said it was okay."

"How long were you there?"

"Since about midnight," Hastings said.

The chief said, "The senator's not happy about this."

"I don't care." Hastings lowered the cloth and looked at the chief.

"Well," the chief said, "I do. It seems pretty clear to me you saved his life. But I wouldn't wait around for a thank-you if I were you."

"I don't plan to."

"How did you know, George? How did you know Reese would come here? That he wouldn't try the assassination downtown?"

"I didn't know for sure," Hastings said. "But I suspected it. A Hinckley, a glory seeker, would have done it at the Soldier's Memorial. Try to make a name for himself. But Reese wasn't after glory. He just wanted to kill Preston. This was the smart move."

"And you say he saved your life?"

"He did. I don't know why."

Martin Keough was striding toward them.

"Oh, here we go," Hastings said.

Keough stood in front of him and said, "You're finished."

"Pardon me?" Hastings said.

"You heard me," Keough said. "Your career is over."

"Why is that?"

"To begin with, who the hell gave you permission to be here? Huh? You were not authorized. We've got two men dead."

"I didn't kill them. Reese did. And I'm glad he did."

Keough leaned in. "What?"

Chief Grassino started to speak, and Hastings raised a hand to stop him. Hastings said, "I said I'm glad he did. One of them was going to kill me. Probably the other one, too. Reese saved my life."

"I say you're lying."

"I don't care what you say. I don't work for you."

Keough turned to Grassino. "What do *you* say?"

Grassino said, "I say it's a police matter, and if you're half as smart as you seem to think you are, you'll move on."

"Excuse me?"

"By the way," Grassino said, "where do you get the idea that you get to determine what is or is not authorized by the police department? You got some special police badge in your pocket? Because if you do, I don't remember deputizing you."

Keough took it in. Then he snorted out one of his shitty little laughs and said, "I see. You're going to protect your own, huh?"

"Whatever I do, it'll be my decision. Not Preston's and certainly not yours. Savvy?"

Keough looked at Hastings, then at the chief, and then at Hastings again.

"You'll regret this," Keough said.

Grassino gave him an up-and-down appraising look, then smiled and said, "I doubt it. Go on." The chief waved his hand as if he were shooing off a child. "Go," he said. And Keough went.

Hastings said, "You know, Chief, you've got quite a way with words. You ever think of running for public office?"

"Don't fuck with me, George. Not now."

FIFTY-TWO

The boy behind the desk was polite and he handled the guests professionally. He gave them directions to the St. Louis Zoo and told them to have a nice trip. They thanked him and left, impressed with his maturity and attitude. The boy made an entry into a computer behind the desk and then looked up at the man with a bandage over his eyebrow.

"Yes, sir?"

"My name is Lieutenant Hastings. I believe Mrs. Mangan is expecting me."

The boy's expression changed.

"Yes," Connor Mangan said. "She's my mother. I'll get her. If you like, you can wait in the dining room. There's coffee in there."

Molly Mangan wore a blue winter dress, which Hastings thought flattered her. She sat with him at a table in the corner of the dining room. She asked if he preferred tea or coffee. Hastings told her he preferred coffee and what he had was good.

Molly said, "You didn't have to come see me. I guess I should thank you."

"I had the time," Hastings said.

"I called after I saw it in the paper," Molly said. "I saw his picture and I knew it was him. He had told me his name was John. He had told me that he'd lived in England."

"He told you the truth."

"He didn't tell me everything."

"Maybe he told you all he thought he could."

"He was kind and I want you to know he didn't try to trick me. Or—"

Hastings imagined what had happened between them. He told himself it was none of his business.

Molly said, "But I didn't know. I didn't know why he came here."

"I believe you. You have no obligation to explain yourself. Not to me or anyone else. I understand he registered here under a false name."

"But he told me his real name."

"Yeah," Hastings said. "He did."

"Where is he now?"

"They buried him in a pauper's grave. It's standard procedure when the person has no funds. Or family."

"Couldn't they have buried him next to his wife?"

"No one claimed him. I'm sorry, ma'am, but that's how it is."

A man and woman came into the dining room. The woman took a seat and crossed her legs. The man went to the long table and poured two cups of coffee and put cream in one of them.

Molly said, "I wanted to ask you something."

"Okay."

"Do you think he would have killed Senator Preston if he could have? If he had had the chance?"

Hastings had no doubt that he would have. But now he said, "I don't know. He never got the chance."

The Mangan woman lowered her head.

Hastings said, "Mrs. Mangan, I want you to know two things.

One, he saved my life when he didn't have to. The second thing is, he was innocent of the original charge. He wasn't lying when he said he was wrongly convicted."

"He could have stayed here," Molly said. "He could have left it alone. I guess he just didn't want to. It's all just such a waste."

Hastings sighed and said, "Yes, it is."

Molly looked directly at him. "Would you have killed him? To save Preston? Would you have done that?"

"That would have been up to Reese. But if it had come to it, yes, I would have."

"Even though you knew the senator deserved it. You'd have done that."

"We can't allow vengeance killing. Deserving has nothing to do with it."

"Some business you're in," she said.

Hastings had intended to tell her not to feel bad about getting involved with Reese. Not to feel dirty or guilty. But now he saw she didn't need that sort of comfort. She was angry at him now. She had to be angry at somebody. It would pass, though. He believed it would pass.

The next day, Rhodes came into Hastings's office and said, "Senator Preston's on television."

Hastings went into the homicide squad room and joined the group of detectives watching a CNN broadcast. It was Preston thanking Dexter Troy and Clu Rogers for sacrificing their lives for him.

American flags were in the background and somewhere else the logo of Ghosthawk, Incorporated. Preston was eulogizing the "heroes" who "gave their lives" selflessly, protecting him from an American terrorist.

Groans in the homicide squad room. Murph saying, "Have you ever heard such shit? He was about to kill a cop."

"Fucking disgraceful," Rhodes said.

Preston kept talking. Klosterman said, "I don't think he's finished."

"... In a time of cynicism and despair, we can take some comfort in the bravery of these men. They are the personification of courage. They represent what is best about America ..."

"Oh, God," Murph said, "this guy is unbelievable."

"... Their sacrifice has moved me to remember that America is a country that deserves better. They deserved better. We need leadership that is worthy of such Americans. Leaders who do not fear the dark of night. Leaders who do not run from terrorists. Leaders who do not negotiate with evil but, rather, face evil and say, 'We will defeat you!' Leaders who do not treat the enemy the same way we treat a shoplifter but, rather, who believe in the old-fashioned idea of treating the enemy as the enemy. Leaders who know that when we are pushed, then, gentlemen, we will take the fight to them."

"Oh no," Klosterman said, seeing what was coming.

"... This is what our country needs. This is what men like this deserve...."

"He wouldn't," Klosterman said.

"Yeah," Hastings said, "he would."

"We will not be intimidated!"

"He's nuts," Klosterman said.

Hastings said, "No, he's quite sane."

"And so it is with great deliberation and careful consideration that I announce that I will be filing a Statement of Candidacy for the presidential nomination. God bless these men. God bless all of you. And God bless America."

FIFTY-THREE

Martin Keough told Preston he shouldn't see the cop. He said the cop was just a loser, a misfit who was obsessing about him. He said the cop was being backed by his chickenshit, loser chief now.

"Don't worry," Preston said, "I can handle him." Senator Preston was feeling a lot better about things these days. In a way, he looked forward to having a final discussion with the cop.

Keough escorted the cop into the senator's office. Preston dismissed Keough with a look.

Then Preston said, "Well, Lieutenant. It seems like you just can't get enough of me. Sit down."

Hastings took a seat. The senator sat behind his desk.

Senator Preston said, "It seems like we both won, doesn't it?"

"How is that?" Hastings asked.

"You caught Reese and I stayed alive. That's quite a feather in your cap, isn't it?"

Hastings said, "I would have preferred to take him alive."

"Sure. But he didn't give us much choice, did he?"

Hastings took particular offense at the word *us*. "Maybe not," he said. "You know, your Mr. Rogers tried to kill me."

"That's not a very nice thing to say about a soldier of the U.S. armed forces."

"Ex-soldier. He died a mercenary and a murderer."

"Well, who's to say what happened out there?" Preston gave him a steady, knowing look. "Reese? He's dead. And so is Mr. Troy. All that's left is you."

"Right."

"And it's a rather moot point now, isn't it? Say you were telling the truth, what would you do? Bring attempted murder charges against a dead man?"

"No, not much point in that."

"Of course not. In fact, I don't see what you have to complain about."

"No, I suppose you wouldn't."

The senator took his meaning. He leaned forward and said, "Okay, let's cut the crap. You believe Reese was telling the truth, don't you? That I did put an innocent man in prison. Why don't you just say it?"

"Okay. I'll say it. You knew Reese was innocent and you went ahead and prosecuted him anyway. You knowingly put an innocent man in prison."

"Now why would I have done that? I didn't even know him."

"Not knowing him probably made it easier." Hastings shrugged. "You wanted to win a trial. You won. And now you're running for president."

The senator smiled. "Well, good luck proving I framed him. You've got no witnesses, no proof. John Reese is dead. And you've got nothing."

"Yeah," Hastings said, "you got away with it. And I guess I helped you do it."

"I guess you did."

"But," Hastings said, "there is that house in Chesterfield."

Silence in the room. Hastings kept a steady gaze on Preston. And he took satisfaction in seeing a slight twitch in Preston's face.

"... House?" Preston put a confused expression on.

"Yes. The house on Walker Place. You sold it four years ago to Kyle Anders. The records show he paid you one million one for it. Which is kind of funny, as its fair market value was about six hundred thousand."

Preston said, "Interesting. Go on."

"Then, seven months later, Anders sold it for five hundred and ninety thousand. That was about a five-hundred-thousand-dollar profit for you."

Preston looked bored. "I see," he said. "And why would Mr. Anders have done that?"

"It was an investment. But Anders got it back, though, didn't he? All those contracts you steered to his company. About a billion dollars' worth. I'd say he got a very good return."

"Wow," Preston said. "That's quite a case you got there, Lieutenant. Should I turn myself into you? Or wait for the FBI to show up? Let them arrest me."

Hastings frowned.

Preston laughed. Then he said, "Do you really believe you're the first one to throw that accusation at me? Do you? Don't you know anything?"

Preston leaned forward and said, "Lieutenant, you are ... amusing, I'll give you that. This, er, payoff scandal you raise, it's already been investigated by the U.S. Attorney's Office in Washington. As well as the Senate Ethics Committee. Two years ago. I was cleared."

Hastings said nothing.

Preston said, "Oh, didn't know that, did you? Well, I'm not surprised. I suppose you don't know much of what's going on outside of this town. No proof of criminal intent, they said. Good-faith offer, et cetera, et cetera. Not only was I cleared; *nobody cared*. Oh, reporters wrote about it, but it was strictly relegated to the back pages. It's just not interesting enough."

Hastings said nothing, his disappointment registering, Preston enjoying it.

Hastings said, "I'll bet there were other payoffs."

"Bet all you like. You aren't going to be able to prove anything. You won't *find* anything. You want to try to bring down big bad Alan Preston, go ahead. Other people have tried and they were a hell of a lot smarter and more powerful than you. And they had resources and connections you couldn't dream of. Still, if you're determined, go ahead."

Hastings thought about saying that maybe he would. But it would sound weak, because it was.

Preston said, "Yeah, that's what I thought."

Preston stood up. He said, "In a few months, you'll forget about this. You'll want to, trust me."

Hastings felt the need to say it. "John Reese was innocent."

"Who's John Reese?"

FIFTY-FOUR

After the cop left, Preston told Keough to get Jeff Crittenden on the phone. Preston asked, "Do you think he saw the speech?"

Keough said, "I'm sure he has. It's all over the networks."

"See," Preston said, "it wasn't a formal announcement. I just said I would be filing the statement. When we do the formal, we'll pick a more regal place."

"Yes, sir. But I don't see how it could be any better than it was then. Just brilliant, sir. Brilliant."

Preston said, "Did you see that cop when he walked out of here? Man, I can't tell you how much I enjoyed that. I still know how to have fun."

"Sir, the man is an absolute nothing. You've forgotten more about the game than he'll ever know."

Preston walked out of the office and down the hall to the kitchen. He was humming to himself. The tune was "The Sunny Side of the Street." "Grab your coat and get your hat . . ." He got a bottled water from the refrigerator and started back to the office. He saw Sylvia standing on the stairs.

In her hand she held a suitcase.

Preston said, "What are you doing?"

"I'm going to my sister's in Chicago."

"What? What are you talking about?"

"I'm going to my sister's in Chicago."

"I don't understand. When were you going to tell me?"

"I am telling you."

"Going there for a few days? . . . What?"

"For a while," Sylvia said. "We'll sort out the details later."

Preston looked at his wife for a long time. The *details*? A realization was dawning on him now. She wouldn't . . .

He said, "I don't . . . Sylvia, are you leaving me?"

"Yes."

"What? You're joking."

"No, Alan. I'm not joking."

"Look, you're mad. I understand. I didn't tell you what I was going to say in that speech. I'm sorry. But that was not a formal announcement. See, I was just testing the—"

"Oh, Alan, don't bother. I'm not mad at you for making that speech. In fact, I wasn't even really surprised. Which is rather sad, if you think about it."

"Sylvia—"

"But what's sadder is, I know what you did to that man years ago. You let an innocent man go to jail. And I was willing to overlook that. I was willing to stay with you even though you'd done that. Maybe that makes me a good, loyal wife; maybe it makes me a whore. I don't know. But . . . now you're running for president. And that means I have to talk about you. I have to go on television and campaign for you and tell people why you're such a great man and a great husband and a great father and why you'd make a great president. And Alan, I just don't think I have it in me to do that. Even if I wanted to do it, I don't think I could. I don't have that sort of ambition. I can't keep up with you."

She walked past him and to the door.

Preston said, "Wait a minute, Sylvia. *Sylvia.* Don't do this. Let's talk about this."

"You had your chance to talk to me about it before."

"All *right*. I'm sorry I didn't okay it with you first. Okay? I'm sorry. Now we'll talk about it."

"It's too late."

"*Sylvia.* Don't do this to me. Sylvia. Don't you realize what you're doing?"

She kept going and he said what was truly on his mind.

"Don't you understand? *I can't possibly be a viable candidate if my wife is divorcing me.*"

Sylvia Preston opened the front door and looked back at him.

"Ah," she said. "The real concern." She sighed and let that sink in, giving him a long look of tired contempt he'd probably never seen before. Not from her. "Good-bye Alan. I'd like to wish you good luck with the campaign, but somehow I can't."

FIFTY-FIVE

In the Jaguar, his cell phone rang. A number he didn't recognize. The chief telling him he'd just received another interesting call from Preston? Or maybe Keough calling him to say, nice try, loser. Oh hell. Just answer it.

"Hastings."

"George? This is Eileen."

"Eileen? What number are you calling from?"

"Oh, I'm at pay phone at a goddamn convenience store. I got a flat tire about two blocks from here and I left my cell phone in the car."

"Don't you have triple A?"

"What?"

"You know, an auto club."

"What's that?"

"Never mind. Where's your husband?"

"He's on his way. Listen, I'm supposed to take Amy to basketball practice tonight, but—"

"Oh. I'll take care of it."

"Call me after you pick her up, okay?"

"I will, Eileen." Hastings laughed.

"What's so funny?"

"I don't know," Hastings said. "Maybe I'll tell you about it later."